IT WAS [illegible]
DOWNHILL TOO FAST

Wolfe knew it was time for a resolution. He could see the cornered gunman's finger turning white from its pressure against the trigger of the little submachine gun.

In a clear, crisp voice, Wolfe said one word.

"Enough!"

The effect was electric. Harold Howe's face snapped toward him, the features contorted by fury, the lips drawn back from the teeth. As his head turned, the MAC turned, too. Wolfe was aware of a flash at the muzzle of the submachine gun, but his primary visual focus was on his front sight as he calmly, smoothly pressed the trigger.

Also available in this series:
SPEEDBALL
DEATHRIDE

CODE ZERO

OPERATION BARBARY COAST

D. A. HODGMAN

A GOLD EAGLE BOOK FROM
WORLDWIDE
TORONTO • NEW YORK • LONDON
AMSTERDAM • PARIS • SYDNEY • HAMBURG
STOCKHOLM • ATHENS • TOKYO • MILAN
MADRID • WARSAW • BUDAPEST • AUCKLAND

First edition November 1992

ISBN 0-373-63406-4

Special thanks and acknowledgment to
D. A. Hodgman for his contribution to this work.

OPERATION BARBARY COAST

Printed in U.S.A.

OPERATION BARBARY COAST

1

Early March was colder than usual in the wooded mountains of eastern Washington State, and Bob Passeretti was glad the heater in the Jeep Wagoneer worked well. For the first time that night, he was also glad he was the pointman working alone on the cocaine buy-bust.

He shifted in his seat, checking the position of his Ruger P-89 9 mm automatic. He carried it in the front of his pants on the left, butt forward, only at times like this when he was stuck for long periods behind the wheel of a vehicle. For that situation, it was the easiest position from which to quickly access the 16-shot handgun. Normally he kept it on his right hip. But it was a big gun and, especially when the seat belt was on, it was awkward to reach for his hip when he was sitting down.

The DEA—Drug Enforcement Administration—had recently approved the Ruger pistol. He had drawn this one from the armory at the Seattle office because he thought it would fit in well with his cover. He had long since given up trying to pretend that he wasn't carrying a gun when he was undercover. Passeretti had discovered that often, during a drug buy, he was the only one who wasn't visibly armed, and it made him stand out. The Ruger fit in with the kind of good ol' cracker boys he was going to meet tonight in an attempt to purchase fifty thousand dollars' worth of flake cocaine. An inexpensive gun, built like a three-quarter-ton Chevy truck, and just as reliable and all-American.

He checked his wire, the hidden microphone, one more time. "Hey," he said aloud in the lonely silence, "you guys still there?" He turned on his Motorola Securenet walkie-talkie to wait for the answer.

It came in a moment. "Yeah, bro, but we won't be for long if we can't turn on the car and warm up like you, you fat white SOB. By the way, you're coming in fine."

THE NIGHT FOREST was a godforsaken place.

At least, it seemed godforsaken to Ichiro Komeito and Dan Warren. Japanese-American and African-American respectively, they were also city boys. Dan had grown up in Boston's Roxbury district, and Ichi, in Los Angeles. They were comfortable in the concrete jungles. One of the things they hated about working for the DEA was that occasionally the drug labs or even simple buys like tonight's took them out into the uncharted boondocks. Ichi had made a point of putting a compass in his hip pocket and a Mini Maglite flashlight in each shirt pocket. Dan just had a huge Maglite with six D-size batteries on the floor, and he kept the Litton night-vision binoculars under his hand.

"I thought you guys worked with computers in comfortable offices, and didn't have to spend nights in the boondocks on some dirty mission," Dan said with a grin.

Ichiro chuckled. "Whoever told you that was away from Centac for a while. That was in the old days, under Dennis Dale. We were the Untouchables of the DEA, a bunch of lawyers and accountants who put the international cases together with spread sheets and kicked their asses in court rather than on the street. That shit's been over for a long time, partner! From the stats I heard in refresher training, DEA is getting into more shoot-outs per agent than any other federal law-enforcement agency, and Centac is getting into more than any other DEA branch."

"Hey, Ichi, I could take a shoot-out," Dan said plaintively. "If nothing else, it'd warm me up. But look where we are, man. This place looks like the ads for iced vodka in *Playboy*. If they needed to send us to Siberia, they could have been open about it. Man, there ain't even a 7-Eleven in fifty miles of here where we could get some coffee."

His partner smiled. "Just as well. It's a diuretic. I don't like this any better than you. Anyway, we have to keep the engine off, and the coffee would only steam up the windshield and screw up our visibility."

Dan's grin split the darkness. "Now, there's a cogent point for agent survival," he noted acidly. "The hot coffee might steam up the windshield, fuck up our visibility. Now, never mind there's only the three of us alone up here without even Sergeant Preston and his sled dog, Yukon King, to help us out. Never mind we've got no idea who's coming in with the dude that's meeting Bobby, and never mind we've got no backup for our own selves."

Ichi wasn't smiling anymore. "Dan," he said softly, "I agree with you, believe me. This is one of the prices of being Centac instead of DEA. If this was a regular DEA op, we'd have backup coming out of our ears. But more and more the past few years, the director has been keeping our things separate. I thought when DEA expanded, Centac would expand to more than a hundred. If anything, it's been just the opposite. It's like we're closing in on ourselves."

"I don't like it," said Dan. "We're supposed to be the elite of DEA, so what are we doing making a crummy fifty-K buy?"

Ichi shrugged. "Boss wants to find out what happened to Eddie Melchior, I guess. We were following Eddie, ready to step on the biggest flake distribution center in the Northwest, and bang—Eddie deals with these guys and he disappears. Bobby was able to get in with them, arrange for an initial feel-each-other-out buy... Hey, give it time. Let's see where it leads."

"Leads to an early grave, if you ask me," grumbled Dan Warren.

"Not to worry," said Ichi. "Who in his right mind would try to rip us off for a lousy fifty thousand when they know we're ready to deal half a million in a couple of days?"

"Shit," said Agent Warren. "I'm not talking about getting ripped off. I'm talking about freezing my ass to death!"

THORVALD VAN HOUTEN kept clenching and unclenching his hands on the wheel of the Plymouth Voyager minivan. The dashboard instrument lights cast an eerie green glow on his face. Tiny shadows spread from the craters of his acne-pocked skin. Over the forehead the light ended with a shock of hair that was so blond it was almost white.

Next to him, Danny Queen blew his nose, hoping he wouldn't get snot in his beard and mustache again. This setup made him nervous. The big blond guy who sat next to him, the huge muscles straining as he kneaded the steering wheel, made him nervous. Going all day without a drink *especially* made him nervous, but it was what Will demanded, and Will's word was law. He felt his sinuses clogging. He desperately needed a drink.

Behind him a tall, gauntly thin man with spectacles and a long, scraggly black beard sat nearly motionless. In his lap was an Ingram MAC-10 .45-caliber submachine gun. It looked like an overgrown, squared-off pistol. A leather thong hung down from its truncated barrel, for the shooter's forward hand to grasp. A long magazine extended from the butt. The tall man gently stroked the gun, almost absentmindedly, like an old man petting a cat. For Walter "the Armorer" Leonard, the comparison would have been apt. His guns were his pets. They were the only things he loved in this world. His guns, and Will, and the Team.

On his left sat Harold Howe. A big man, sandy haired and clean shaven, he was thirty but looked forty-five. Prison had been hard on him. Before that, his daddy had been harder. Harold had bought beer for the other kids before he dropped out of high school because at age sixteen he could pass for twenty-one.

"Thor," Harold said nervously, "I ain't too fuckin' sure about this. Don't you think it's a little early for the takedown? Why do you think Will wants us to do this guy when he's only got fifty thou with him? Fucker wants to do a big shit deal, why don't we wait till we got the big money?"

Van Houten's muscles tightened, but his face didn't change. His body, not his eyes or his mouth, reflected his moods. "Because," he said, forcing himself to be patient, "Will says this is the way it's going to be."

"Hey, hey, I know. That's cool! All I meant," Harold said plaintively, "was why does he say do it this way? I ain't questioning, Thor. I just wanna learn. I wanna be able to figure things out for myself when I'm a squad leader, so I don't have to bother you and Will with it, man."

Van Houten paused to gather his calm before he answered. "Very well. First, we don't really need the money. The takeoff on Eddie Melchior left us nice and fat. But Will says, 'Don't wait till you're hungry to start gathering food.' This idiot is here, and his money is good.

"Second, you all need the practice. We are a combat cadre. Without combat, we get rusty and soft. Third, if he can get half a million dollars to buy cocaine, he can get half a million dollars to keep us from cutting his balls off.

"Which is very damn fortunate and convenient for us," the muscular blond man finished, "because we don't have any fucking cocaine to sell him."

The gaunt man in the backseat broke in. "We're getting close," he said. "Might be a good idea to touch base with the second squad one more time before we make the hit. And I think, as team armorer, we all ought to check our weapons one more time."

J. J. QUEEN, Danny's brother, huddled in the back of the big Dodge Power Wagon with the king cab. No booze, no brother, not even Will there to guide them. Rhino was in charge of the squad, and J.J. lived in terror of him. He fondled his Taurus .357 Magnum revolver and wondered if he'd have the guts to shoot the man whose bulky shoulders and close-cropped bullet head was only inches in front of him. He didn't think so. Even with Rhino's back turned toward him, he didn't dare trust the .357 Magnum bullet to penetrate the base of the big man's skull. Rhino was the most frightening human being he'd ever known.

The driver, Jack Murphy, wasn't that scared of Rhino. He knew why the big man with the thick spectacles was called that. Nearsighted and short-tempered, he would charge and kill without provocation. He was also, like his namesake, stupid. Jack always sucked up to Rhino, complimenting him on his strength and courage. He knew Rhino wanted to keep him around to keep the compliments coming. Still, whenever he was near Rhino, Jack found the Springfield .45 automatic in his belt a comforting thing to have.

The big man in the right front seat shifted. Born with the name James Fields, Rhino was proud of his nickname. He had long since come to accept his ugliness and his bulk and the fact that he wasn't an intellectual. He hated people who were good-looking and slim and intellectual and had made the blessed discovery very early in his life that he had the power to hurt them. That hurting had grown more pleasurable over the years. A bully as a child, Rhino at twenty-nine was a certifiable monster. The only times he had ever felt as though he belonged in his society had been when he was in reform school, when he was in prison and now, as a member of the Team.

He worshiped his leader. Will was the only man who had ever given him power without being forced to, the only man who had ever readily admitted Rhino's strength and ability without being hit over the head first. The only other person on earth he cared about was the Armorer. He and the gaunt man had developed a symbiotic relationship, like the birds in the veld that picked insects from the tough hide of his namesake. The birds got fed, and the real rhinoceros got its itch scratched. The Armorer fed vicariously on Rhino's strength and support, and in turn, he gave Rhino the guns that allowed him to increase his power, to extend his will beyond the reach of his huge, crushing fists.

The Armorer had built the rifle that Rhino was cradling between his knees. It was an M-1 Garand of World War II vintage, fine-tuned and accurized by the Team's cadaverous gunsmith. It mounted a big infrared telescope sight. In Rhino's lap were the lightweight goggles that complemented the scope, allowing him to see in the dark. Not as well as with a passive night-vision device, the kind of equipment he lusted for, but Will would provide that soon, Rhino knew. Will had promised.

The portable walkie-talkie on the front seat crackled alive. "T to R," the message came curtly. Rhino picked up the handset and thumbed the microphone key.

"Yeah," he answered bluntly.

"We're three minutes out," Thor's voice said through the receiver. "What about you?"

"About the same," Rhino grunted back. "Slow down, let us go through a couple minutes ahead so's I can scope it out 'fore you get in."

"CAR COMING," Agent Ichiro Komeito told his partner.

"No sweat," answered Agent Dan Warren. "Ain't our guy. He isn't even slowing down."

The car swept past, a big black Dodge Power Wagon. "See," Warren said triumphantly. His partner shrugged. Neither man had bothered to pick up the Litton night-vision binoculars on the seat, which had cost the Agency several thousand dollars. The black truck hummed off into the night.

RHINO'S VOICE exploded over the portable walkie-talkie in the confines of the minivan. "R to T," he barked. "We got trouble, man. Wagoneer's sittin' there all right. So's a couple guys in a Blazer, up the little loggin' road behind where the fucker's parked."

The anger was visible in Thor's face for a change, the pale nordic skin turning red under the clump of platinum hair. "Shit! See any guns?"

"Nah," answered Rhino, "but ya know they gotta have 'em."

"Okay," said Thor grimly. "Team, condition red. We'll go in just like we planned. R, you and your guys be ready. We ain't gonna change nothin'. But if those motherfuckers in the Blazer give us any shit, they go home to their dope-suckin' mamas in bags."

THREE MINUTES LATER Bob Passeretti saw the first faint glow down the road that told him a car was coming. He glanced at his watch in the dark. The green LED readout told him 7:30 on the dot. Well, Eddie's associates were punctual, at least. As the glow turned into the glare of a car pulling into the roadside turnaround area where he was parked, Agent Passeretti said into the body microphone, "Be ready, guys. It's going down."

The agent's big four-wheel-drive truck was parked heading north, on the south side of the little access road that had come off Highway 395. Thor pulled the minivan in with his own left front door level with the grille of the Wagoneer, his headlights pointing up the logging road where he knew the Blazer still had to be. He couldn't see anything. The steep upward angle of the mountain logging road kept the Blazer out of sight of the headlights. Thor grinned inside, but his face remained impassive as he flexed his muscles. Oh, these bastards were good! They'd even plotted out the light angles on the road.

Only the parking lights of the Jeep were on. In the amber glow Passeretti could see the shapes of three men still in the minivan. No weapons were visible. He didn't know that Danny Queen in the right front seat, facing him, was holding a Stevens 12-gauge pump shotgun, sawed off in front of the slide handle and behind the pistol grip. It was loaded with one-ounce rifled slugs that would blast through the closed door of the minivan, the windshield of the Wagoneer and through any human being, with more than enough power to exit from the back of the vehicle.

In the backseat Harold Howe leaned way back. The man beside him had a submachine gun that fired so fast the shots would sound like canvas ripping, and Harold was directly in the line of fire. He noticed, though, that the Armorer was hunched forward, so he would clear Harold if he opened up with the submachine gun. Harold clutched nervously at his guns. One was the custom 14-shot .45 automatic the Armorer had built for him, his personal gun that Will had told him never to take on an operation. He knew he shouldn't, but for Harold it was like an icon. The other one, stuffed into the opposite side of his belt, was a World War II vintage German Walther P-38.

In the Wagoneer, Bob Passeretti's right hand rested close to the butt of his own 9 mm. But in the amber lights, backlit by the glare of the minivan's high beams, he could see that Thor had just the black nylon bag in his hand. It was a fanny pack, the kind all the joggers used. Smart, thought Passeretti, who hadn't seen that before. It was a handy way to carry dope, and you could sling it over your shoulder as you ran, if you had to.

The blond man with the acne-pitted face and the chiseled muscles did not appear to be armed. He had pulled his van into a T-bone position vis-à-vis Passeretti's vehicle. That wasn't consistent with a setup. He'd brought the stuff, that was all, and just felt more comfortable having a few of his buddies along in case the new customer got hinky on this lonely back road. Well, that was to be expected.

Thor was at the window now. He extended his hand, and Bob reached through the window he'd opened a moment before and shook. The power in the man's hand was amazing, but Bob tried not to wince. He was beginning to relax. This was going to go smoothly.

"Hey, bro," said Bob. "Right on time."

"Gotta be," Thor answered smoothly. "Punctuality's a part of doing business."

"Got my goods?" Bob asked.

"You bet," purred Thor. "You got my money?"

Bob picked up a large padded mailing bag from the front seat and handed it out the window. Thor took it with his left hand as, with his right, he handed the black fanny pack through the window. He didn't bother to open the envelope or count the money. He just watched as Bob unzipped the nylon bag. Thor's right hand slowly went behind his back.

UP THE HILL, Dan Warren watched through the Litton night-vision binoculars. It turned the darkness below into green daylight. The headlights off to the side created a whiteout on the left of Dan's field of view, but he could clearly see what was happening.

"He's made the exchange," Dan whispered tensely to his partner. "The blond guy's got the money envelope. I don't—Shit! Watch it! I think he's going for a gun!"

They were perhaps forty paces up the trail, off slightly to the side, hidden by the brush. Both men burst out the car doors as the silver-colored pistol snaked out of Thorvald Van Houten's hip pocket and into his right hand, and swung up toward the undercover agent.

Dan Warren held the heavy Littons up to his eyes with his left hand as his right clawed under his down vest and the space blanket that now hung half on, half off his shoulder. In a moment the SIG P-226 was out in his hand. He began to scream, "DEA! Don't move!"

But he didn't make it.

There was a bright flare to his right, and a sledgehammer impact as something smashed into his hand and into his face at the same time. Suddenly he couldn't see and his eyes hurt terribly, and around him the thunder of powerful gunfire enveloped him like a cocoon.

RHINO LUMBERED heavily through the woods, working to the flank of the car that was hidden on the logging road. He knew he couldn't move quietly. Fortunately the men inside the cold car kept their windows rolled all the way up until the glare of the other Team car's headlights had shown through the trees, and then they rolled them down. But it was too late for them to hear him, because Rhino was already in place.

The big man dropped into an Indian squat, his feet flat on the ground and his knees deeply flexed. He rested on his haunches, no tension at all on the hamstrings, his massive weight supported by his heavy bone structure as he rested his elbows just slightly forward of his knees. In the hellish red glow of the goggles and the infrared scope, Rhino could see a black man and an Oriental in the car. The former seemed to be holding night-vision equipment of some sort, but he was aiming it down the road at the cars, not at Rhino.

The big man knew he had it knocked. Jack Murphy was on his left flank with a shotgun, and J. J. Queen was on his right with a .357 Magnum. He didn't think J.J. had the substance of a fart in the wind, but Jack seemed cool, and besides, Rhino himself had the situation well in hand. His cross hairs rested just where the black man's jaw met his neck.

And suddenly the black man jumped. He scrambled to get out of the car. Rhino saw an automatic come out from under his down vest.

He didn't even stop to think about it. He fired. The kick of the .30/06 cartridge made the muzzle jump, and the muzzle-flash blotted out the infrared scope's image enough so that he couldn't see the bullet hit. But when he got the man back on target, he could see the night-vision device gone, and the black man clawing at his face.

Rhino tried to aim carefully as he fired one more shot into the black man, and then he swung the gun on the other man, who was taking cover on the far side of the car.

THE BLASTS of Rhino's M-1 shattered the night. Bob Passeretti dropped the black nylon bag. He started to go for the Ruger automatic in his belt when he felt something hard and cold press roughly against his ear and he heard Thor's voice, no longer velvety smooth.

"Don't fuckin' twitch, sucker!"

He realized instantly what was happening. There were more shots on the hill, and he heard the passenger side door of the van in front of him slide open. He turned his eyes to his left. Thor stood grinning, holding a stainless-steel Walther PPK automatic against his head.

Passeretti had been trained by the best. His reflex was instantaneous. He ducked aside, grabbing for the small pistol with both hands.

Thor pulled the trigger, but it was too late. Passeretti had twisted his head out of the way. The muzzle blast of the .380 automatic next to his head ruptured his eardrum, stunning him like a hammerfist, but he held on grimly, clutching the gun with his left hand and the blond man's hand with his right.

His vision tunneled in on the gun. He could see that his antagonist was still pulling the trigger, but the gun did not go off. Bob realized that his hand was so tight on the little gun when it fired the first time that the slide could not cycle. The pistol was jammed.

Now, you bastard, Passeretti thought, it's my turn. He let go with his right hand and grabbed his own Ruger, pulling the trigger as soon as the big automatic came in line with his opponent. There was a bright orange flash, though his deafened ears could not hear the shot, and he saw the big man twist away.

Glass shattered around him. Something stung his face. The man in the window was gone. He threw himself down onto the seat, trying to get under the swarm of bullets that tore through the windshield.

HIGH ON THE HILL, Ichi Komeito had rolled out of the car and into the bushes on his left when the deafening roar of the high-powered rifle had split the night. A Remington 870 12-gauge shotgun and a Colt 9 mm submachine gun lay on the back seat. He couldn't reach either. Reflexively he drew his 9 mm pistol, a SIG-Sauer identical to his partner's.

He was on the left of the Blazer. The muzzle-flashes were to the right. He leveled his pistol at the orange flares on the far right, lining up the three glowing green dots of the weapon's nightsights, bracketing the area as he fired again and again. Even though his ears were ringing, he could hear the whacking sounds of bullets hitting trees, and then the dull thud of one striking flesh. There was a gurgling sound in the darkness. No more muzzle-flashes came from the right, but on the other side of the car, his partner was crying out to him. "Ichi! Help me, man! I'm hit! I can't fuckin' see!"

Rolling deeper into the bushes, shivering with something more than the cold, Ichiro Komeito aimed at a muzzle-flash and pulled the trigger. Nothing happened. He had fired all sixteen shots already. He pressed the magazine release button with his thumb as he ripped a fresh magazine from the leather pouch on his hip, shoved it into the butt of the pistol to replace the empty clip he'd just ejected and pressed the release button. The clacking sound of the gun closing drew another of the unbelievably loud rifle blasts, and he could feel the bullet hum past his head like a hornet.

THE HORROR of the metal and glass in his eyes, the terror of the darkness, was worse than the pain by far. Dan Warren could still hear, though. It was as if the instant he'd lost his sight, there had been a compensatory increase in his ability to hear.

On his left, his ears told him, his partner was reloading. On the right, there was a man breathing raggedly with a bubbling sound. Good—Ichi had got one of the bastards. But also on the right was the roar of the rifle fire.

They'd blinded him. God damn them. In his mind's eye, the only eye he had left, Dan Warren pictured himself as an old blind beggar man. The rage swelled in him, red and deadly.

He let out a bloodcurdling scream and charged toward the gunfire, pointing his pistol at the sound and jerking the trigger.

Something unbelievably powerful smashed into his chest. There was time for him to think that it felt cold instead of hot. Still, he fired toward the sound, driving himself forward. His foot caught on a root and he pitched onto his face, but even from the ground he fired, again and again, as the bullets thudded into him. Something hot this time tore into his left side. He ignored it.

His gun wouldn't shoot anymore. He ejected the empty magazine by feel, the way he'd been trained, as he grabbed the fresh one from his belt and shoved it in. He had just thumbed the slide release to complete the reload when the final impact took him, smashing into his head with a shock devoid of pain.

In an instant his darkness became permanent.

WHEN THE SHOOTING STARTED, Harold Howe ducked back and fired one shot from inside the van. In the enclosed space, it reverberated like the blast of a hand grenade. The 9 mm bullet from his P-38 punched through the side of the van and into the windshield.

The shock of the blast stunned him so much that he dropped the gun. The big Walther landed on the floor behind the driver's seat. Suddenly Harold realized he was alone in the van, and everyone else was outside, shooting.

Oh, God, no. He'd fucked up! Only now did he remember Thor saying, "If I get shot, just shoot through the car and kill the fucker. But if not, as soon as I make my move, I want you out and covering me. Danny, you're in the front seat, come around the front. Armorer, you're right rear, buttonhook right around the back end of the van and come up on the other side. Harold, whatever looks best by the time you get out. You'll be the last one out of the car."

His ears hurting and ringing, Harold started to clamber out of the van. He could hear the ripping sound of the Armorer's MAC-10, and the *chong-chong-chong* of the heavy bullets slamming into a car's sheet metal. From the front came the deep boom of Danny's shotgun, and someone was firing a pistol.

He fell as he was getting out of the van. Scrambling to his feet, he realized that the P-38 Will had given him was still inside the vehicle. He snatched at his personal gun, the .45 the Armorer had crafted with the special frame and magazine that held fourteen shots instead of the usual eight. He ran toward the rear of the car.

The Armorer was there. His gun was empty, and the gaunt man had drawn back behind the van to reload. He screamed to Harold, "Get him! Get him! Thor must be hit, he ain't shooting back!"

Suddenly Harold Howe saw his chance. The two heavy hitters on his team down—the Armorer out of ammo for the next second or two, and something wrong with Thor—and Harold with a loaded gun in his hand. He would live in the Team's songs and stories, the courageous Aryan warrior who had rescued the flag from the faltering hands of the old champions.

Harold Howe lunged from around the back of the minivan, the big .45 extended at the end of his arm, a cry of triumph on his lips.

The bullet from Bob Passeretti's gun slammed into his right arm, entering the bicep and exiting the tricep. The arm went numb. He saw his custom-made pistol arc in the air, gone from his nerveless hand. It was the last thing he remembered before he fainted.

BOB PASSERETTI'S Wagoneer formed the long part of a T, crossed at the top by the minivan. He had popped up and aimed out the right window toward the rear of the van in time to see the man with the .45 emerge. He had lined up the sights as best he could in the dimness and fired two fast shots. He thought the second one missed, but at the first he'd seen the man with the pistol jerk violently, seen the gun fly slowly into the air as the man toppled back and sprawled on the ground.

He was sure he had shot the first one, the contact man. That meant two down, two to go with this crew. Shooting was still ranging up the hill, fast and furious: the high hard crack of a Magnum, the staccato rattle of fast-firing 9 mm weapons, and interspersed with those, the awesome crash of a high-powered semiautomatic rifle.

The right side seemed clear. He shoved the door open, popping the lock and the latch with his left hand. There seemed to be nothing behind him. He had forgotten he could no longer hear with his left ear. He started to unsling himself from the car, peering intently into the darkness with dazed eyes.

HEART POUNDING, tongue stuck to the roof of his dry mouth, Danny Queen cautiously peeked around the left front of the van. He couldn't see Thor anywhere. But shots had come from the right side of the Jeep, pointing toward the other end of the van. The other end was just fine with him; it meant Danny was safe.

He saw the outline of the man with the pistol getting out the right front door of the Jeep. Opening the door had turned the inside dome light on, and in the glow Danny could see blood coming out of the man's left ear, and more blood on his face. The ugly big automatic in his right hand was pointing toward the back of the van, where Danny's friends were, and his back was to Danny.

Swallowing hard, Danny stood and shoved the sawed-off shotgun toward the back of the man, who was less than twenty feet away. Then he was firing, and he pumped the gun and fired again as fast as he could.

One of the .12-gauge rifled slugs caught Bob Passeretti behind the left ear. It punched a hole three quarters of an inch in diameter in the skull wall, and roared through the center of his brain at 1400 feet per second. By the time it exited, it had flattened out like a lead washer and torn away the agent's right cheekbone and right eye in its passing.

Agent Robert Passeretti was dead before his body thudded to the dirt at the roadside, but the spectral man who called himself the Armorer had appeared out of the darkness and loomed over him with a freshly reloaded MAC-10 in his hands, and held the trigger back. The bullets tore into the corpse with buzz saw fury, spraying blood and bits of flesh and cloth, but the agent was beyond feeling them.

ICHI KOMEITO was reaching to his side with his left hand for leverage to push himself to his feet when he saw one more flash and felt the crushing blow to his right hand. The next thing he knew he was on his back. His eyes were adjusting to the darkness.

He saw that the hand was mangled, and most sickening of all, he could smell raw meat. The high-powered rifle bullet had smashed into the pistol where the trigger met the high-strength aluminum frame and ricocheted into the hand, traversing it lengthwise and shattering the wrist. The pain was unspeakable.

Gritting his teeth, he stoically grabbed the pistol with his good left hand as he rolled away from where he'd been. The movement came just in time. Another great bloom of fire sundered the darkness, and a geyser of dirt spewed upward where his head had been as a 180-grain bullet traveling 2500 feet per second smashed into the earth instead.

But something was wrong. The pistol didn't feel right in his left hand. It wasn't just the slickness of the blood. Then he realized that the trigger had been broken away from the frame by the powerful rifle bullet. Ichi Komeito's gun had been destroyed.

He felt a rage he had never known before. The rage to kill that the samurai long before him must have heard singing in their veins. But he knew also that at least two men with guns were left out there in front of him, and God knew how many more down below, and he had nothing left to fight with.

Ignoring the agony of the shattered bones and frayed nerve endings, he lurched to his feet and dived for the bushes, rolling down the hill, the gunfire echoing behind him. He would live, he swore to himself.

He would live to kill these sons of bitches.

THE GUNFIRE HAD STOPPED more than a minute ago. Thorvald Van Houten strode out of the brush by the side of the road and joined Danny Queen and the Armorer and an ashen-faced Harold Howe, who was tightly clutching his upper right arm, a thin trickle of blood oozing through his fingers.

The Armorer stood with a third magazine loaded into his MAC-10. He had already picked up the empty ones and shoved them into the hip pockets of his dirty jeans. He looked at Thor, saw the black smudges on his face, and asked, "You okay?"

"Yeah," growled Thor. "Fuckin' gun jammed when I shot him the first time. Shot me in the face when I didn't have a gun to shoot back with, the yellow bastard. It took me this long to get the damn thing cleared."

"It's okay, Thor," burbled Danny. "I got him. I got him! Blew his brains out, man! Hey, where'd you hit him, huh? Huh?"

Belatedly Danny Queen saw the look of fury flicker across the face of Thorvald Van Houten.

"Oh, shit, man," he bleated. "I didn't mean it that way, man! I saw blood on his ear...you musta got him in the ear, Thor! You done good. Musta been one strong bastard, take a shot like that an' keep goin', huh?"

Thor's face remained impassive, but the muscles rippled as if stimulated by electricity. The tableau was broken when Rhino and Danny's brother, J.J., came down the hill.

"Ain't good, man," Rhino growled. "Jack's dead. The gook got him. The nigger's dead, an' the gook took off into the woods. We hit him, though, hit him good. Blew his gun to shit, an' he's bleedin' like a stuck hog. You want we should follow him?"

Thor shook his head. "It's still early in the evening. We've been lucky there hasn't been any traffic through here so far through any of this. We got the money, so let's take it and run."

"Money and more, Thor," J. J. Queen interjected. "Look what we found! The coon and the slope had night-vision binocs, man! And a subgun and a 12-gauge in the back of their car. And a SIG 9 mm, man. Two of them, in fact, but one was all shot to hell."

In the darkness the Armorer's eyes gleamed. "Then let's do like Thor says. Throw it in the car, take what we've got and get the hell out. We gotta patch up Harold."

"And," said Thor, "we've got to explain it to Will."

2

Harry Wolfe was standing in front of the Palm Beach County grand jury, about to be sworn in, when his pager went off. His left hand reflexively went to his belt and killed the sound.

"If that's important, we can take a short recess," said the tall, sandy-haired prosecutor who was holding the Bible for the oath.

When Wolfe shook his head, the prosecutor asked, "Do you swear to tell the truth, the whole truth and nothing but the truth, so help you God?"

"I do," Wolfe answered. His voice had gone from soft to firm. It was his courtroom voice, and he did it well. Wolfe was a law school graduate.

"Please state your name and occupation," the prosecutor said, motioning for Wolfe to sit down.

"My name is Harry Wolfe. I belong to Centac, the central tactical unit within the Drug Enforcement Administration of the United States Justice Department. I am presently in charge of AISI, the agent-involved shooting investigation unit, which coordinates with OPR, DEA's Office of Professional Responsibility, our internal affairs unit."

"As you know, sir," the prosecutor began, "this grand jury is investigating the shooting death of Jonathan Kines of Delray Beach, Florida, at the hands of Centac agent Timothy Sears this past November 14. I understand you may have information that would be of assistance to the grand jury in this regard. If that is the case, I would like you to share that information with the grand jury. You may speak in narrative form if you like, and we'll do the questions and answers later. With me is Harold Meyer, from the trial section of the Palm Beach County State Attorney's Office, who will be assigned to prosecute this case if the grand jury should choose to indict."

"Thank you, Counselor," said Wolfe, and he began to speak.

"Ladies and gentlemen, first I want to thank you and the prosecutor for having me here today. In many jurisdictions, the accused is not afforded the opportunity to bring in defense witnesses or expert witnesses on his behalf. The legal office of DEA felt that it would be of benefit to you in your decision-making process to know the parameters of judgment our agents are taught, as well as some of the dynamics that occur in violent encounters, dynamics that can easily be misunderstood.

"I was flown to West Palm Beach the day after the shooting to investigate. I have examined the witness statements, the reports from the Delray Beach city police and the county sheriff's office, and in addition have personally interviewed all involved personnel, as well as visited the scene and examined all evidence. I was present at the autopsy of Mr. Kines at the Palm Beach county medical examiner's office the day after the shooting."

Wolfe allowed his eyes to take in the members of the jury, then he went on to outline the events leading up to the final action. "Briefly, there was sufficient evidence implicating Mr. Kines in multimillion-dollar cocaine trafficking that he had become the object of an intensive investigation, titled Centac-281, and the local authorities had issued our agents a warrant for the search of the premises of Mr. Kines's beach house in Delray Beach on the day in question. We had evidence that several kilos of cocaine would be present. Eight kilos were in fact recovered.

"Agent Sears was the pointman of an eight-person raid team. All were wearing raid jackets and black caps with the letters 'DEA' printed in large, bold white lettering. By all accounts, Agent Sears shouted 'DEA! Police!' repeatedly as he and the other agents entered. Within twenty feet of the alcove they were confronted by Mr. Kines, who was wearing only khaki shorts and was holding a 9 mm Beretta semiautomatic pistol in his right hand.

"Agent Sears shouted 'Drop that weapon!' Mr. Kines's response was to raise the gun toward the clearly identified agents. At this time Agent Sears, who was in front of the other agents in the narrow hallway and blocking their line of fire, opened fire with his issue weapon, a Colt 9 mm submachine gun. He fired one medium-long burst of fully automatic fire, which turned out to be nine rounds, striking Mr. Kines seven times in the torso and neck area. Mr. Kines dropped his pistol and fell to the floor. He was pronounced dead at the scene by Palm Beach County emergency medical service personnel."

For a second Wolfe paused to let things sink in, then continued in his firm voice. "After concluding the investigation on behalf of DEA and Centac, it was my official opinion that this shooting was well within the parameters of the deadly force policy promulgated by our agency. Our personnel are taught that they may use deadly force—the degree of force a reasonable person would consider likely to cripple or kill a human being—only in a situation when they, or someone they have the right to protect, are in immediate and otherwise unavoidable danger of death or grave bodily harm from the individual who winds up being shot.

"We tell them about the three criteria that create that situation of immediate, otherwise unavoidable, deadly danger. They are ability, opportunity and jeopardy.

"Ability means the opponent possesses the power to kill or cripple. A deadly weapon, for instance. The Beretta pistol in Mr. Kines's hand was fully loaded with sixteen rounds of Winchester Silvertip hollowpoint ammunition, including a cartridge in the firing chamber, and the safety off. He had the ability.

"Opportunity means the opponent is capable of immediately employing that lethal power. If he's a block away with a knife, he has the ability but not the opportunity. The pistol, of course, is a remote control weapon. Mr. Kines was about eight steps down the hall, twenty-four feet away, when the shots were fired, based on testimony, blood-spatter evidence and the location of the body and the spent cartridge casings from Sears's weapon. Therefore, Mr. Kines had the opportunity to kill Sears and the other agents.

"The final factor is jeopardy. This means that the opponent is acting in such a manner that a reasonable and prudent person would conclude from his actions that the opponent intended to kill or cripple. Mr. Kines had stated to the undercover officer that he would murder anyone who tried to, I quote, 'send his ass to prison,' and this was known to all the agents on the raid team, including Sears. He was pointing the gun at the agents and screaming 'motherfucker.' I believe any reasonable and prudent person would have come to the same conclusion as Sears.

"At such times, when those three elements are present, our agents are instructed to fire. They are taught to shoot to neutralize the threat and to cease fire when the threat is over. Every bit of evidence I have seen indicates to me that this is exactly what Agent Sears did.

"What I am about to say is something I would never, and could never, say in front of the petit jury. The regular jury decides the ultimate issue, guilt or innocence, and the witness may never address it. However, the grand jury has much more license in seeking the truth. Therefore, I can tell you this.

"Everything I know, every bit of experience and training I have in this area, tells me this was a justifiable homicide. My report to headquarters states that the investigation I conducted shows it to be a justifiable homicide. The conclusion of Agent Sears's superiors, and my superiors, is that it is in fact a justifiable homicide, and the DEA and the Department of Justice will stand fully behind Agent Sears in his defense if he should be indicted."

Wolfe came to a full stop, then said, his voice very clear and soft, "I would be happy to answer any questions."

For a moment the room was silent. Actually it didn't look like a courtroom. It was more like a classroom. Some eighteen grand jurors sat six across in three rows of chairs at long tables, all with yellow legal pads in front of them. Unlike regular juries in most jurisdictions, they were encouraged to take notes as they heard the testimony. Also unlike the regular trial jury, they were allowed to ask questions. Wolfe noticed that most of the jurors were faintly smiling or even nodding. It was nature's way, he thought, of showing that they accepted the truth of his testimony.

Then Meyer, the trial lawyer, spoke up. "I have a question," he said, and Wolfe couldn't help noticing the regular prosecutor roll his eyes disgustedly as Meyer came forward, his eyelids narrowed over small, piggy eyes.

"You say it was a justified shooting," the attorney sneered, "but you haven't bothered to tell these good people what was justifiable about shooting a wounded man in the back." The lawyer's rubbery lips spread, creating a predatory grin.

Wolfe was back in his hard voice, not angry, but firm. "Counselor, the suspect was struck by several bullets, only two of which entered behind the lateral midline. In a rapid-fire shooting, it happens all the time. It's a function of what the doctors call agonal response. As the body is struck by the first of one or more bullets, it may twist away involuntarily from the source of the pain. It happens rapidly, in a fraction of a second. Meanwhile, the defender is still firing, has already had his brain tell his trigger finger to shoot the armed man facing him, and by the time that psychomotor response is carried out, the offender's body has turned in time for the bullet to enter behind the lateral midline, what you call being shot in the back."

The lawyer reddened. "And I suppose," he said angrily, "that you have some excuse for the number of times the deceased was shot?"

"Counselor," Wolfe replied coolly, "Agent Sears was the pointman on a very dangerous entry. He was armed with the gun the DEA tells the agents to use when doing that job, the Agency-issue Colt submachine gun. The Colt SMG fires at a rate of more than 600 rounds per minute when it is set on full automatic. That is ten shots per second or more. Agent Sears fired for less than one second when the deceased aimed the pistol at him."

The red-faced attorney glared at Wolfe, breathing heavily. A couple of the grand jurors snickered and covered their mouths as they watched him. Finally the trial prosecutor snarled, "No further questions... at this time."

The other prosecutor looked at the foreman of the grand jury, a distinguished-looking black man sitting in front at the far right, and asked, "Are there any other questions?" The foreman glanced around, smiled and shook his head.

"You're excused, Agent Wolfe," the prosecutor said. "Thank you for coming." Wolfe smiled and nodded at the grand jury as he rose. Most of them smiled back. Then he was out the door, walking toward the bank of pay phones. He punched in the secure number, waited for the tone and quickly punched in the number for his issue phone charge card.

The director's secretary picked up immediately. "Wolfe," he said simply. "Harry," she said, "the director said to tell you Code Zero. Three agents shot in eastern Washington state, two dead. Centac people. Hang on, I'll transfer."

Three minutes later Wolfe strode quickly down the hall of the courthouse's first floor. He stopped in the secured alcove by the metal detector in the front lobby and produced a key from his pocket. The green-uniformed deputy looked at the key and nodded. His possession of the key meant that his ID had already been checked.

Wolfe unlocked the cubicle in the bank of steel boxes, about the size of safe-deposit units. He withdrew a small revolver, a customized Smith & Wesson .357 Magnum no bigger than a snub-nosed .38, and slipped it into the Ken Null ankle holster still strapped under his left sock. The Glock 17 pistol, with the wedge-shaped +2 magazine extender protruding from the butt, went into the Milt Sparks holster snapped to his belt, holding the lightweight pistol inside his waistband. Counting the one in the chamber, the streamlined pistol held twenty cartridges. A spare magazine went into the sheath behind his left hip under his suitcoat. Finally a lightweight black Spyderco Clipit knife, folded so its wicked three-and-a-half-inch serrated edge was no longer visible, went into his right-side trouser pocket.

He had been the final witness in the Kines shooting. The prosecutor had felt no need to give the grand jury a summation before he turned the case over to them.

Wolfe had not yet reached the parking lot of the Palm Beach County courthouse when the grand jury voted No True Bill, automatically ruling the shooting a justifiable homicide.

CARMELITA MORALES, summoned to the director's office in downtown Washington, D.C., had made the trip from the FBI/DEA Academy in Quantico in about twenty minutes. A fashionably casual Banana Republic khaki shirt covered the yellow polo shirt on which were embroidered the DEA seal and the word, Instructor. A black jogger's fanny pack was slung across the middle of her flat abdomen, unobtrusive against the black slacks of the training uniform. The pack was actually a De-

Santis Gunny Sack, and a hidden pocket contained her compact Smith & Wesson service automatic.

The director's secretary looked up as she walked purposefully in the door, her shiny black hair cascading across her shoulders. A white-toothed smile flashed across Carmelita's tanned-looking face, and the secretary was smiling back when the director's door opened and he called out, "What have we heard from the karate kids?"

The secretary's pale countenance reddened. The director followed her eyes and saw Carmelita standing in the doorway to the reception area, looking at him quizzically. Carmelita could have sworn it was the first time she'd seen a black man blush.

"Oh... uh... come on in, Agent Morales," the director stammered. A solidly built man with graying hair, he was seldom caught off balance and wasn't used to it.

He closed the big oak door of his office behind her. Carmelita said, "Uh, sir?"

"Yes?"

"Karate kids?"

The director cleared his throat and tugged at his tie in a diversionary gesture. "Well," he said, "you are both practicing martial artists, after all, and you work so well together as a team..."

"You mean Harry Wolfe and I?"

"Right. We've had a shooting last night in the Northwest. Two Centac agents dead, one wounded. He may lose his arm."

"Score for our side?"

"Not good. One DOS. One more apparently wounded, judging by the bloodstains found at the scene. Two carloads of bad guys, three in one and at least that many in the other. Heavy weapons, high-powered rifles and at least one submachine gun. One agent was killed by a shotgun slug, and the bastards emptied a submachine gun into him while he lay dying."

Carmelita looked him in the eye. "Code Zero?"

The director returned the stare. "Any reason not to?"

"None, sir," Morales replied instantly. "Any specific reason you need a woman?"

The director looked surprised. "No. What I need are at least two of my very best agents with Code Zero clearance. You and Wolfe work well together."

"Thank you, sir," Carmelita said softly, with a modest downward cast of her eyes. "It was a dumb question."

"Not at—"

The buzz of the intercom interrupted the director in mid-sentence, and they heard the secretary say, "Sir, Agent Wolfe is on the special line, from Florida."

3

The house on the double lot on a side street in Post Falls, Idaho, looked like any other, except for the steel grates on the windows. Even that was not terribly unusual. People who relocated from New York or Miami often had the grates installed as a conditioned response when they moved in.

Beneath the house, however, was a hidden dwelling that was not just a full basement, but half again as large as the good-sized Cape Cod that stood above it. The walls were reinforced concrete. They were lined with racks of weapons and cases of ammunition.

Posters almost covered the walls. D.A.R.E., was the message on one, and next to it was Hugs, Not Drugs. Another one commanded Just Say No! There were also various Christian messages, and a giant poster on the far wall depicted a huge, white, clenched fist, its knuckles scraped and bloody. The legend beneath it, in huge letters was White Power!

Seated by a computer on an expensive office chair was a small man, about five-six, with a slight frame. He wore gray suit pants, a white dress shirt, red "power tie" and dark suspenders. A suede holster, held inside his belt with a metal clip, contained a stainless-steel Walther PPK .380 automatic. The man's thinning hair was grayish white. He was perhaps fifty-five. His fingers danced across the white plastic keyboard.

A beep sounded. He glanced at a panel to the side of the desk. A light was flashing.

The man rolled his chair back along the clear plastic carpet protector and reached behind a file cabinet alongside the computer table. He lifted a lightweight Remington 20-gauge automatic shotgun with extended magazine from behind the cabinet, then stepped behind a big bookshelf facing a large steel door.

There was a buzz. He touched a button on the wall, his other hand holding the gun to his shoulder, the barrel steadied against the steel door. "Go ahead," he snapped into the intercom.

"It's us," came a terse voice. "We've got a wounded patriot here."

He recognized the voice. It was Thor. He flicked the shotgun's safety back on, set the weapon down and walked toward the heavy metal door. Putting his body weight behind it, he shoved open the massive bolt that held it in place and pushed the door out, away from him.

Thor came first. Behind him was Rhino, carrying a wounded Harold Howe in his arms as lightly as a father holding a small child. The older man could see that Howe's face was chalky white and that he was shivering. He was clutching his upper right arm. There was blood on his jacket, but not much.

Next Danny and J. J. Queen came in, carrying long guns. Danny pulled shut the door behind him and shot the bolt closed.

There was a sound from the control panel near the desk. It told the white-haired man that an authorized person had disarmed the alarm system, rearmed it and passed through the front door of the house with a key.

The white-haired man frowned. "Dammit," he snapped angrily, "Jack and the Armorer aren't supposed to come through the front door together! How many times have I told you, Thor and the Armorer only, and then only one at a time! Why didn't Jack use the hidden tunnel like the rest of you?"

There was a pregnant pause before Thor said quietly, "He's dead. Fucking gook dope pusher shot him."

"My God," the white-haired man said softly. "The Team's first martyr."

"Yeah," grunted Rhino, "and we're gonna have another one if we don't fix up Harold. I think he's goin' into shock."

The older man shook his head as if to clear it. "Set him down on the couch. Spread a blanket first so we don't get blood everywhere. Danny, get me the trauma kit."

Harold Howe lay on the couch where Rhino put him. He shivered, more from fear than loss of blood. His shock was psychological, not hemorrhagic or traumatic. The bullet had passed cleanly through flesh and muscle, somehow missing the brachial artery and the humerus.

Then the white-haired man was bending over him, a concerned look on his patrician face, reaching down with a pair of scissors to cut through the sleeve of his jacket to get at the wound.

Harold stopped shivering. He closed his eyes, and a warm peace came over him. He felt as safe as if he were in the arms of Jesus. As far as he was concerned, that was just where he was.

Will was here, hovering over him. Will would take care of him, and Will would make everything all right.

WILL'S HANDS worked automatically. His mind was elsewhere. He had passed a milestone. The first martyr! It was a momentous day.

William Holmes had grown up an atheist, the son of a pretentious junior-college professor who gambled away half his money but made a point of living a politically correct leftist lifestyle. The father had been head of the local chapter of the Communist Party in their midwestern town until the McCarthy hearings had come along. By the time McCarthy had been discredited as a monster himself, it had been too late for Holmes, Sr.

Had a psychologist diagnosed the young William Holmes, he would have confirmed a sociopath. From his earliest memories, he had never felt compassion for any living thing or cared about anything but himself. Coming of age at the beginning of the first generation of Americans who would be totally shaped by the electronic media, he had studied communications in college before there were degrees in broadcasting science. He sold advertising for local TV stations when he ran out of money for college, and seeing it as the wave of the future, soon began to sell air time for a nonexistent station. Before long he had been convicted of felony fraud and sentenced to the state penitentiary in London, Ohio.

It was there, with TV permeating even the recreation room, that it had occurred to the warden that he'd be doing a good deed if he ran evangelical programs every Sunday morning.

Will was sure that it had changed the lives of numerous inmates.

It had certainly changed his own.

Watching the television preachers plead for dollars had been, in the truest sense, a revelation for Holmes. Where had this been all his life? Suckering money from those whom his father had called the mindless believers. It was a victimless crime, in Holmes's opinion; what was the harm in taking money from people so they could feel good about themselves? Wasn't that what entertainers did? And if he didn't believe in what he was saying, so what? Professional wrestlers on TV weren't serious, either, but they entertained the public and made them feel good and were rewarded with large sums of money.

At about the same time, fellow convicts turned Holmes on to the easiest way to get an early parole. There were missionary ladies, zealous and devout Christians, who would come by the prison offering Bible-study classes. Most of them were widows or spinsters. All he had to do, the cons said, was convince one of them that he had seen the light and fallen in love with them. They would mortgage their souls to convince the parole board that the errant one had a home and family and a job to go to, a job they usually arranged with one of their relatives. The next thing you knew, she was in there testifying to the board as a character witness for you, and bingo!, you were on parole.

It worked like a charm for William Holmes. He made his moves carefully, and within three months, a heavyset lady named Charlene had taken him to her bosom in everything but the physical sense. She had arranged with her father to get him a job at one of the family's chain of hardware stores.

Holmes endured the boredom of his job and the marriage to Charlene. He could force himself to make love to her if he closed his eyes and thought about dusky-skinned Polynesian or mulatto women, firm and lissome.

He became fervently active in the Fundamentalist church Charlene's family belonged to. He volunteered for every work party and tithed enthusiastically. He witnessed to his salvation from prison and from sin in front of the flock, and soon the minister had made him a deacon.

He basked in the glow of his redemption and took his time as he earned the minister's confidence and learned the ways of the church. He became a master of church financial management, learned to spout relevant portions of Scripture at will and perfected a technique that allowed him to twist any parable into a justification for whatever he had done.

After about thirteen months, when he felt he was ready, he convinced Charlene to sell their house and close out their accounts without telling her family and to go off together to the West to spread the Gospel and save souls. On the prescribed day, with the money in a cash box between them on the front seat of Charlene's new car, they had driven out of Dayton, Ohio, forever.

Six days later, in a remote corner of the New Mexico desert covered by scrubby brush, William Holmes stabbed Charlene seventeen times with a hunting knife. He took three hours to carefully pull all her teeth with a pair of pliers and to slice off her fingertips to be buried later, down the road, and then dug a shallow grave to bury her under the tumbleweeds. To the best of his knowledge, the body and body parts and generic tools he'd used had never been uncovered from any of their separate burial places. He never knew what Charlene's family thought about what had happened to her, and he soon ceased to care.

He went to the Northwest, figuring that he had a good voice if not a commanding physical presence, and he could get on evangelical radio if a TV ministry was too much to hope for. He made a small living for a few years, but there was something in him that did not ring authentically to the true believer. The riches he sought eluded him.

It was when he combined the great hatred of his life with the great hypocrisy that he found his niche.

William Holmes hated blacks passionately. In prison three hulking black men had held him down, laughing and using words like *petite* to describe him as they forcibly sodomized him in the prison showers. Eventually he had become the concubine of a huge black man named Ike, who protected him from the others. The submission filled him with shame. By the time of his release, he considered blacks the curse of the earth. He felt that the Bible's treatment of Ham and his descendants supported his belief.

He had another revelation in the late 1970s, when he learned of the White Christian Patriots' Defense League and its associated church. Supposedly complete with a black auxiliary, doubtless the same size as the black auxiliary of the Ku Klux Klan, the White Christian Patriots allowed full membership only to white Protestant males, with their womenfolk acceptable as voiceless participants. The annual meetings included small-unit urban guerrilla warfare tactics and the combat use of the submachine gun.

Well, well, Holmes had thought. Yea, verily, brothers and sisters, Brother Johnny Bob is onto something here!

Of course, affiliating with Johnny Bob was out of the question. William Holmes was an alpha male, and would never again be subordinate to another man. Besides, Illinois was uncomfortably close to Ohio for a man who had jumped parole and murdered his wife for her money. But Holmes figured ideas were not patentable and that the Lord helped those who helped themselves.

Johnny Bob Harrel told his followers that God had come to him in a vision and shown him the coming apocalypse, in which Russia and the forces of the Antichrist would attack the God-fearing West. The Mongol hordes, said Johnny Bob, would drive the true believers to a stronghold in the Midwest, the faggot Californians and the heathen Jews of New York all being gobbled up by the Soviet Bear. But, through divine intervention, Johnny Bob would lead the real Americans to victory, and would, as a benevolent dictator, lead America as the dominant force on earth.

Not bad, Holmes had thought, not bad at all. Before long he had his ads out in every right-wing hate journal. By now the ubiquitous home computer had replaced the television as the final arbiter of public opinion in William Holmes's view. He soon established his own computer nets around the country, and hate-mongers lined up to send money to subscribe to his electronic newsletter. Realizing that pure racial hatred had been overdone and that he needed a shtick, William Holmes hit on the idea of tapping into the War on Drugs. What were the biggest hit movies? Chuck Norris and Charles Bronson and Mel Gibson blowing the shit out of dope pushers. Here was a heroic mold that William Holmes could get behind.

In only a few years William Holmes had socked away more than a million dollars in buy money taken from dope dealers he and his team had ripped off and often left for dead, sometimes kidnapped and held for ransom. Much more had gone into the purchase of weapons, the buying and renovating of the safehouse. He had watched white supremacist groups like the Bruders Schweigen go down the tubes when they did stupid things like murder radio commentators who challenged them, or held up Brinks trucks to fund their revolution against ZOG, the Zionist Occupation Government.

Holmes didn't believe in God or in people. He believed in himself, and in money, and in power. Seeing the necessity of changing his name, he had become Will Pelham. He had picked the surname at random from a telephone directory. As a boy he'd been Billy, and Bill as a man; he knew the first name didn't mean much, but he knew the importance of an iron will. Will. It was him.

He still did the radio interviews with talk-show hosts, who, maddened by his white supremacist and anti-Semitic statements, goaded him mercilessly. When that happened, Will Pelham simply put his saintly voice in gear and spoke of how Christ had endured the taunts of the unbelievers and the tortures of the damned before his truths had become self-evident. When they asked him how many followers he had, he replied seven hundred. He told Thor and Rhino and the rest that because each of them was worth a hundred ordinary men it was not a distortion of the truth.

Now, finally, one of his own had fallen. Jack would be the first martyr of his tiny army, the army he called the Team.

God, the atheist but self-proclaimed prophet told himself, was good.

"THE WOUND IS CLEAN," Will proclaimed to his followers as they stood around inside the underground citadel. "He'll be fine. We'll get him home tonight. Harold, you can tell your mom you had an iron rod go through your arm at work. If you told her the niggers and slants did it, she'd call the police, and that wouldn't do. If she asks about the medical bills, tell her the shop is paying for it. Call into the shop and tell them you're sick as hell, and you're taking some sick time."

He turned to the others. "Jack lived alone," he said, "so we won't have much problem explaining his absence for a while. We can come up with a cover story later. What did you do with the body?"

Thor and Rhino, his two lieutenants, looked at each other sheepishly. Will's eyes narrowed. "You didn't!"

"We had to get out," Thor mumbled, chagrined at his own lack of foresight. "Jack was dead, man. Nothing we could do for him. Harold was hit. We had to get him out of there."

Will stamped his foot like an angry mother. "Dammit! And what do we have to show for it?"

"Fifty grand, cash," Danny Queen blurted eagerly.

"And guns," his brother added. "Lots of them! A SIG, a Ruger 9 mm, a shotgun and a machine gun! Then there's a 9 mm Colt, like a little M-16, and the Armorer says it's got a silencer built in. That'd cost us three, four thousand dollars if we had to go out and buy it under the counter. And night-vision binoculars. You gotta see 'em, Will!"

"And trouble," the Armorer intoned from where he stood in the corner. "Big trouble, I think."

The others turned and stared at the tall, cadaverous gun expert. He was turning the Colt submachine gun over in his hands. Through his grizzled black beard, the Armorer continued, "I didn't have a chance to really look at it until now. The gun's a Colt SMG, integral sound suppressor. Colt doesn't sell that as a regular item, even to cops. It's a special-purpose deal. They made it for the Drug Enforcement Administration."

Will's voice tensed. "What are you telling me?"

"I think," the Armorer said nonchalantly, "what I'm telling you is, we just blew away two or three DEA agents."

There was a long silence before Will Pelham, leader of the Team, composed himself enough to say in a strangled voice, "It must have been God's will."

4

"Please make sure your seat belts are fastened, and return your tray tables and seatbacks to the upright position," the stewardess announced to Wolfe and the other passengers as the Boeing 737 began its final descent into SIA. Spokane International Airport was the nearest to the shoot-out scene, perhaps a little less than three hours' drive away from the Colville National Forest.

Wolfe prepared himself to meet his contact, a Centac man from Seattle. DEA had an office in Spokane, but Centac, with only about a hundred operatives total, was more thinly spread, and the shooting of the three agents had maimed the personnel roster in the Northwest.

The contact would be meeting the man who investigated agent-involved shootings for the agency. He'd be thinking of it as the Warren/Passeretti Case. Wolfe knew better, no matter what the official name was.

In Washington, it was Centac-298, almost the three hundredth major operation since the re-forming of the subunit.

And, in one particular office in the nation's capital, it was Operation Barbary Coast.

The director had his own sense of style. When most people, even most cops, thought of "drug pirates," they pictured dope smugglers boarding pleasure boats, slaughtering the legitimate owners and turning the craft into drug boats. But within the hard clique of Centac, "pirate" also meant a criminal whose modus operandi was to rip off other criminals, specifically drug dealers. It was amazing, Wolfe thought sometimes, that it wasn't done more. The victims couldn't complain to the police. Wolfe suspected that the reason there were relatively few pirates of this kind was that scumbags could make more money in the long run dealing with the dopers than ripping them off one time. Also, the dope dealers themselves were such a violent and heavily armed subculture that those who would survive by robbing them were likely to have a short career.

Wolfe wondered idly why "Barbary Coast." The nearest coast, the Pacific Northwest, was at least four hundred miles from where the rip-off had gone down. Perhaps the director had a limited background of pirate phrases. In any case, "Barbary Coast," once the haunt of swashbuckling pirates of legend, was the code name for what he was doing now.

The code name smacked of glamor and adventure. His job, Wolfe knew, did not.

It was a Code Zero operation, a working level so secret that you could practically count on your fingers the number of living people who knew it existed. When the director's predecessor had been murdered along with his family by a Colombian cartel at the height of the drug war, his successor—Wolfe's current commander—had been authorized by the President himself to take a harder line than ever before.

The CIA had called it "termination with extreme prejudice." Centac, arguably the most elite unit of the DEA, had been reactivated after the previous director's death, with perhaps a hundred handpicked agents, within which were precisely seven with Code Zero clearance. Wolfe was one of them. Carmelita Morales, who had left ahead of him from D.C. and should be on the ground by now, was another.

Everyone in Centac knew what a Code One operation was. It was an investigation so hot, so important, that all the stops had been pulled out. Unlimited funding and military and diplomatic cooperation were available, an authorization that had come from the White House itself.

Code Zero went a step further. The same money and power were in place, through the director, who functioned with almost total autonomy from DEA's director and even from the attorney general, but there was something more.

In Code One and lesser missions, the goal was the capture, trial and conviction of the suspects. In Code Zero the mission was to punish the target without resort to the judicial system.

Code Zero meant that the perpetrator or perpetrators were to die.

So far, to the best of Wolfe's knowledge, the concept had been activated only to avenge the deaths of Centac agents murdered in the line of duty. But he couldn't be sure of that. He knew only three of the other six agents with Code Zero clearance, and he was sure the reverse was true. The existence of Code Zero, because it was authorized by the President himself, was a potential scandal of Watergate proportion. The director was the only person who knew the identity of every Code Zero operative. Wolfe wasn't even totally certain that the number was limited to seven agents, though he was reasonably sure.

A light, cold rain was falling. Wolfe watched the raindrops tracking crazily backward and upward on the Plexiglas window, the sky a hard and solemn gray in the background. The color of the sky reflected his feelings about what he was doing. Cold and gray.

Wolfe had been a lawyer. Then he had been an idealistic young agent. Then a go-getter, a veteran, the kind of agent the others only half-jokingly called a supernarc.

At the beginning it had been a game, like gentlemen's warfare. Then the constant contact with dirt and evil had somehow begun its insidious erosion. The enormous potential for graft had never tempted him. But instead, one terrible violent night when grief and injustice consumed him, he had set aside his duty and carried his own sense of justice far beyond what the law allowed. In retrospect, he still felt a chill when he thought of what he had done.

He should have been fired. He should have gone to prison. But instead, because what he did had happened in the very short time between when the director was killed and when Code Zero became a reality, he had been among the first drafted into the deadly new squad. The new director, he knew, had a very good reason. Wolfe was one man he had something on, something the agent could never claim he'd been forced to do.

What Wolfe had done had been forgiven, but with the unspoken caveat that it was forgiven so long as he worked Code Zero ops for Centac. At first Code Zero had been exhilarating. He had been a combat soldier in battle for his government and his people against the deadliest soldiers the other side of the drug war could put in the field, and he and his people seemed to be winning.

But that was then, and this was now. He had become a law-enforcement officer for that most clichéd of reasons: to help people. He had gone from being Officer Friendly to being Dirty Harry. Now, with Code Zero, he had gone one more step. He had become the village executioner.

A trained lawyer, Wolfe knew exactly what the law considered his job to be. He was a murderer, a killer for hire, who happened to work for the United States government. The legal side of his mind said, Plead the defense of collateral estoppel! But what good was it to say, I did it because my government told me to, when he knew the selfsame government would deny any involvement? He thought wryly of the old TV show, "Mission Impossible," which began with a tape-recorded assignment ending with the statement, "If you are caught or captured, we will disavow any knowledge of your existence. Good luck!"

His life had been like a video game. Exciting, and jumping into a new dimension, a new level of play, each time he seemed to have maxed out at what he was doing. The excitement was still there, and he was almost ashamed of it. He was becoming inured to it. Next to fears he had lived with, the fear of being killed was easy to handle.

The bump of the wheels on the tarmac jarred him back to reality. It was no time for angst, he thought bitterly. He'd gotten himself into what he was doing. He was a big boy. Somewhere out here, beyond these beautiful mountains that bounded the airport, was a gang of killers who had murdered two of his colleagues and crippled another for life. He would find them and bring them to justice. He would make absolutely sure, as he always had in the past, that they were in fact the perpetrators.

And then, and only then, he would sentence them to the prison of no parole.

CARMELITA MORALES WAITED just beyond the metal detectors. She was dressed in jeans and a warm sweater, under a fleece-lined corduroy jacket. The weather changed around here, back and forth from brisk spring to vicious winter, even though it was still early March.

Her Smith & Wesson automatic was tucked into her jeans on her left, butt forward, clipped in place in an Alessi Talon holster. A spare magazine sat behind it. In her coat pocket was her backup gun, a Smith & Wesson Bodyguard Airweight. She'd been issued the all-steel version of the 5-shot, shroud-hammered .38 revolver on her last Code Zero, and had liked it. When it was over, she'd bought her own, a lightweight version with aluminum frame, to use as a last-ditch hideout.

She didn't recognize Wolfe at first. She spotted him by his walk before she connected the face. Above the straight shoulders and the confident walk was a different Wolfe.

When they'd last worked together, the assignment had required him to shave his head. She didn't know until now that when it had grown out, he'd grown a beard, too. The hair and the beard were the same length, a close-clipped three quarters of an inch or so, and coupled with the tailored blue pin-striped suit and the subdued red necktie, it came together with the look of a college professor.

He had already recognized her. There was something in his smile, something almost wistful.

She had planned to restrain herself and shake hands. Instead, when she saw him she ran forward. He caught her in his arms, spun her in the air, hugged her.

"Harry," she said when he put her down, "you look great! That tan! All those Florida assignments, huh?"

Wolfe grinned. It felt strange. He hadn't smiled much lately. "Let me look at you," he said softly.

His eyes took her in. Carmelita was five-three or five-four, with a body that was a contradiction in terms. She was slim, yet she was full breasted, petite yet solid—solid without being chunky. Her weight training had brought her up to nearly a hundred thirty pounds, but it was all dense muscle, sculpted into a beautiful, graceful form under skin the color of a tanning lotion advertisement.

The glossy black hair tumbled to her shoulders. She parted it on the side to cover the bullet scar that would always be on her forehead. The plastic surgeons told her that her skin was too dark to heal scar-free. Besides, the hair covered the very slight dent she could feel when she touched the scar, the place where the .45 slug striking on an angle had gouged bone from her skull before caroming off.

Whenever she thought of the man who had shot her, she smiled. She couldn't remember thinking about what he had done to her without also thinking of what she had done in return. What she had done was worse.

Wolfe looked into her glistening brown eyes. "Hey, don't cry," he whispered.

She wiped her eye. "Hey, yourself. I can't help it. It's been a long time, all right?"

Before they broke the embrace, he felt her press something hard against his belly. It was the .38 snubnose. She knew that he generally flew with his guns in checked baggage to save the hassle of being armed in the passenger compartment. Even though they were technically authorized to carry as Federal agents, it was always the airline pilot's prerogative whether they or FBI or anyone else would be armed in the cabin. Wolfe's plane had changed pilots during a stopover at Chicago's O'Hare. If the new pilot didn't like cops or guns, it would have been too late for Wolfe to get his two weapons into checked baggage.

This was one reason Morales had come carrying the two guns and had waited outside the departure lounge area. The theory so far was that whoever had shot down the three agents were doper pirates, but no one knew that for sure yet. If there was something afoot, something by the Medellín or Cali cartels that had a long-standing offer of hundred-thousand-dollar bounties for the murders of any DEA agents in the United States, they could all be at risk. What better place to kill an incoming senior agent than the one place in the city he was likely to be unarmed: the departure/arrival area of a major airport, where everyone beyond a certain point had been ascertained to be unarmed? If she had checked through to the gate with her weapons on, Carmelita would have had to flash her ID card and sign forms, and any scout from the other side would have seen it in time to do something about it. This way, she was armed and ready if an assault came.

But none did, and as she and Wolfe walked to baggage claim, she filled him in on what had happened. "Survivor is Ichiro

Komeito, thirty-four. Two years with a municipal police department in California, then ten with DEA, the last two with Centac. Shot in the gun hand, probably going to lose it. High-powered rifle. He tried to return fire with his other hand, but the bullet had smashed his gun, and he wasn't carrying a second. He killed the one bad guy. May have hit some of the others, too, but we don't know. The guy didn't leave much blood.

"No less than half a dozen weapons used, maybe more, judging by the empty casings. At least one M-1 Garand rifle, fired at least sixteen times. Ballistics guys from Washington State Patrol say the Garand has a unique 8-shot clip that ejects itself when the gun is empty—they found two of those and sixteen empty .30/06 shell casings from it. The bad guys had a twelve-gauge, a couple of .45s, a .380 that was fired at least once and a .45-caliber submachine gun. About fifty spent casings left from it, but no empty magazines on the scene. Ballistics says the extractor marks and primer indents indicate it was a MAC-10.

"Guns moved around. Interesting. Both the dead agents stripped of their 9 mm pistols, a SIG and a Ruger. Komeito's wrecked gun had been left there. Took two guns out of the truck Warren and Komeito were in, both DEA weapons. Remington pump gun, and Komeito's SMG, silencer equipped.

"Now, the other side left some hardware, too. The dead guy had a Springfield Armory .45 automatic. It was found a few feet away from him in the underbrush, cocked and off safe with a few rounds left in it. Looks like he jerked and flung it when Komeito got him in the chest.

"Another .45, down by Passeretti's car. I thought you'd be interested—it's a custom pistol. Ballistics says it's a Colt on top and a ParaOrdnance on bottom, whatever that means."

Wolfe nodded. "A regular Colt .45 is an 8-shot gun. The ParaOrdnance frame takes an extra-big magazine, brings it up to fourteen rounds capacity. Guy probably knew what he was doing, or stole it from somebody who did."

Carmelita continued. "No prints to speak of. They're working now on IDing the dead guy. No paper on him. Some tire tracks, but nothing that'll help until we get something to compare them with."

Wolfe's luggage had arrived by now. He picked up the big hard-shell suitcase and the small one—one with his clothes and guns, the other with his toiletries and ammo, which had to be separate from the weapons, according to FAA regulations—and they headed for the parking lot. DEA had been short of car-pool vehicles in the area, and she'd used the Agency-issue American Express card to rent one. It was a white Dodge Diplomat four-door.

"State police has set up a command post for the investigators at Colville, little town on the edge of the forest," said Morales. "Want to head there?"

"Makes sense to me," Wolfe replied.

INSIDE the run-down bungalow on the 1900 block of East First in Spokane, Harold Howe paced the threadbare carpet of his bedroom. He was almost insane with fear. The MAC-11 mini-subgun on his bed, fully loaded with a stick magazine of .380 cartridges, gave him little comfort.

He had violated one of Will's laws, and now he was paying the price. The leader had said, "Never take a personal weapon with you on an operation! It's too likely that it will be lost and traced to you." But from the beginning, Harold had liked to have a little something extra. And the .45 automatic the Armorer had built for him, with its special bright-colored gunsights that lined up so fast, and the new frame that held the 13-shot magazine and the fourteenth round in the firing chamber... who could *not* take a gun like that with them into battle? Especially when the gun Will had issued him for the job in the national forest had been a worn-out relic from World War II?

But it was done. Harold had no felony record, and he had been legal to buy the gun. He'd purchased the frame at a gun show, and the Armorer had built the whole gun for him, charging only for the Colt slide, BarSto barrel and other parts. It was a beautiful handgun.

And it was totally traceable to Harold Howe.

His mind raced feverishly. Harold was a thirty-year-old man who worked at a metal shop as a semiskilled assistant, and lived at his mother's home. Intelligence and decision making had never been his strong suits. His father had died when he was a boy, and his mother had no work skills. Since that time, she had worked as a maid at the Holiday Inn to support herself and her son. Harold had dropped out of school. The neighborhood had deteriorated around their little house in the past few years. The area was now predominantly poor and predominantly black.

Harold had feared the blacks with a terror that had grown to hatred. When Will Pelham had come along with his message of white superiority, of a God-blessed armed retaking of his birthright from the blacks, Harold had embraced him as a true savior. He would die rather than fail Will or disappoint him.

The gun. The gun! What could he do?

Report it stolen. That was it!

He gathered his thoughts for a moment, then dialed 911. When the emergency operator answered, he blurted, "Somebody ripped off my gun outa my car!"

It took the operator a while to get the caller calmed down. Good Lord, she thought to herself, these gun nuts carry on about a stolen pistol as if someone had kidnapped their child. The guy sounds like he's going to cry.

THE HOMICIDE investigation command post had been set up in a mobile emergency unit that looked like a giant Winnebago bristling with antennae. Phone banks lined an entire wall. The little rolling building bustled with uniformed Washington State Patrol troopers, local county deputies and so many detectives from different jurisdictions that you had to look at the badges clipped to their belts in front of their pistols to see what jurisdiction they represented.

Harry Wolfe, his tie loosened and his sleeves rolled up, sat at one of the flat boards that jutted out from the wall and served as a desk, with an ancient dial telephone in front of him. He was correlating his notes when a state patrolman came up behind him and said, "Agent Wolfe, I think we might have something."

Wolfe looked up expectantly. "BATF says the gun was sold last year to a dealer from Everett. The Everett guy checked his 4473 forms. The ParaOrdnance frame was sold to a Harold Howe in Spokane. We've got an address."

The Bureau of Alcohol, Tobacco and Firearms often provided the best leads. Harry copied the address onto his notepad. "Okay," he said, "who do you know in Spokane PD that can cut through some red tape and pull this guy's background for us quick?"

"Let me call my lieutenant," the trooper said. "He used to work the Spokane post. He knows anybody who's anybody there."

Three minutes later Wolfe was on the phone with a gruff-voiced chief of detectives, who insisted on taking a number and calling him back. Wolfe gave him the number and set the old Civil Defense telephone receiver in its cradle. He understood the cop's concerns. No seasoned investigator took someone's word over the phone for who they were. Disclosure of material in the files to the wrong person could result in a massive lawsuit against both the department and the individual officer.

The detective was on the line again in less than five minutes. It hadn't taken him long to call state patrol headquarters to get the emergency phone numbers that had been set up at the murder scene command post. The chief of detectives called that number and asked for Harry Wolfe, and when he got him said, "Sorry about that, but you know how it is."

"Sure," said Wolfe sympathetically, surprised that the response had been that fast, even for a cop-killing investigation.

"Thank God for our computer system," the Spokane detective commander told him. "The address you've got for Harold Howe seems current. Minor arrests, assault-and-battery plea-bargained down to simple assault, that sort of thing. Doesn't seem to like black people much, from the profile I've got so far. By the way, would the gun you're looking for by any chance be a ParaOrdnance .45?"

Wolfe felt his blood pressure pick up. "Yes," he said. "What've you got?"

"Mainframe says he reported it stolen just today. We haven't even had a chance to get someone by to take the full report. Want us to pick him up?"

"I'd rather you didn't just yet," said Wolfe. "Let me coordinate with the others here. I'll get back to you by the end of the day."

As soon as he hung up, Wolfe stood and grabbed his jacket. He beckoned to Carmelita and said to the state patrol commander, "We'll be back later this afternoon."

HEADING SOUTH on Highway 395, Wolfe and Morales pulled into a rest stop to don their Second Chance bulletproof vests underneath their regular clothes. Had they done so at the command post, it would have been obvious that they were on to something. Discretion had to be maintained. The other cops' job was apprehension, not termination. Beyond the bounds of police duty and police morality itself. Carmelita and Harry had to work separate and apart from the cops.

"We'll need him alive," Wolfe said.

"Then why are we doing this alone?"

"If we all arrest him and take him downtown and read him his rights," Wolfe said, "he'll invoke those rights. If we have him off with us, we can interrogate him much more efficiently."

Morales looked at him in horror. This was not her first Code Zero assignment. She had done brutal things during desperate struggles for survival, mangled men with her trained hands. But torture was something else again.

Wolfe caught the meaning in her glance and laughed without humor. He reached into his attaché case as they stood at the open trunk of the rented Dodge and extracted a small leatherette container. He opened it and showed her the syringe and ampoules.

"Amytal," he said. "The improved Mark II version of Pentothal. Truth serum. No pain, no aftereffects. Of course, the results are court admissible only if both sides agree, which never happens, and not at all when taken under duress."

Morales shrugged, relieved. "I don't see court admissibility as a problem," she said sweetly.

HAROLD HOWE HAD BITTEN his nails down to the quick. Would the police send an investigator to take a report on the stolen .45? He didn't know. What if they didn't believe the story and came to take him away? If they arrested him, they'd find the wound in the shoulder. He reached down to his bed and clutched the little submachine gun. It was illegal as hell, he knew, and his possession of the fully automatic weapon could get him sentenced to years in a federal prison. But if they connected him to the killing of the agents, they'd send him to prison *forever.*

He wasn't going. He ran to his closet and dug out the shoulder harness the Armorer had sold him, the one that held the MAC-11 under his gun arm, muzzle down. His right arm was too stiff and sore for that to work right. He turned the harness inside out and hung it under his left armpit, affixing the MAC to it. He practiced for a few minutes working the latch from Safe to Fire with his left index finger instead of his right, and rotated the separate selective fire switch to Full.

Because it had a light bolt, the MAC-11 cycled incredibly fast, at a rate of nearly 1200 rounds per minute. It shot twice as fast as most standard submachine guns, like the DEA Colt. It would empty its 32-shot magazine in a second and a half.

HARRY AND CARMELITA drove in a cautious circle around the block, scoping out the ramshackle little house. The tiny patch of front yard had only little scrubs of grass scattered over the frozen dirt. The paint was peeling, and a rusty roof gutter hung precariously from a single support. An old red Ford pickup and a battered gray Chevy subcompact stood in the driveway. The pickup had bumper stickers that depicted a Confederate flag on one side, and on the other the bold-lettered statement, They'll Get My Gun When They Take It From My Cold Dead Hand.

It would be dark in another hour. Lights were on inside. The two cars meant their target was not alone. Damn.

Wolfe, the senior partner, saw three options. The logical thing was to hit it with a full entry team, but that was out of the question. It would take a good part of a day to marshal that many DEA agents, and in any case, neither they nor the Spokane Police SWAT team could be called in on a Code Zero op. The next possibility, more sensible in Carmelita's view, was to stake the place out and wait for Harold Howe to emerge. They could follow him and grab him at leisure.

Harry disagreed. The little bastard was scared, and he could hole up in there forever. With only two agents, neither of whom could stay on a near-condition-red alert more than a few hours, it wasn't viable. Harry pushed for the third option: go to the door, talk to him and grab him. By the time the family and the lawyers found out where he was being held, the Amytal would have done its work.

Carmelita didn't like it. The plan meant they'd have to identify themselves when they made the arrest, and the only ID they had was their real identification, the dual and separate Centac and DEA badge and card wallet. They were in their own names.

"Let's just do it," Wolfe said. He seemed impatient and tired, not like himself at all. The new attitude, the new beard . . . this wasn't the Harry she knew.

But he was the senior partner, the more experienced. "Okay," she sighed, "let's do it."

Wolfe pulled the car around the corner of First and Magnolia and parked on Magnolia, facing south. Sprague Avenue, the nearest main thoroughfare, was one block behind them. Driving through the neighborhood, they had noticed a tiny police station on Sprague, a block over and almost parallel to the Howe house.

They walked west on First Street, Wolfe unbuttoning his leather car coat and his suitcoat so he'd have access to the Glock behind his hip. Carmelita undid the front of her corduroy coat to allow an easy reach to her service automatic and kept her hand on the little Airweight in her jacket pocket. Its shrouded hammer wouldn't foul in the lining; she could fire right through the coat pocket if she had to.

HAROLD WAS in his little room on the second floor when he heard the doorbell. He screamed, "I'll get it, Ma!"

Harold grabbed his Army fatigue jacket and threw it on over the shoulder-slung MAC. He grabbed another 32-round stick magazine and shoved it into his belt at the small of his back.

As he ran downstairs, his frustration grew. His mom was already at the door, heavy and stooped, fifty and looking fifteen years older in her worn pink housedress. He'd told her he'd get it! Didn't *anyone* ever listen to him?

The people were in the doorway. Average-sized guy, older than him, short hair and a trimmed beard, leather jacket, suit and tie on under it. The woman . . . beautiful . . . dark skin, though, kind of small, corduroy jacket. The woman was talking in a clear voice, no accent, asking politely, "Is Harold Howe at home?"

His mom looked over her shoulder at him. She thought they must be the insurance company, come to settle with Harold for getting his arm hurt at work. She smiled, but the smile froze when she saw the look on her son's face.

It was the expression he would have as a child when she caught him doing something bad. A mixture of shame and fear. She knew it well, and she knew suddenly that something was very wrong.

"Mr. Howe," Carmelita said sweetly, flashing her badge wallet open and shut quickly before anyone could read what the ID actually said, "we're here to take your report on your stolen pistol."

HAROLD WENT THROUGH the discussion as if in a trance. The man and the woman sat on opposite ends of the couch across from his rocking chair while his mother got coffee. He hoped they hadn't heard the clanking sound of the muzzle of the submachine gun under his coat hitting the wooden seat of his chair. The woman was doing the talking. For some reason, they weren't taking notes. He had always thought detectives took notes in little leather-covered pads.

"I'm afraid," the lovely Hispanic woman was saying, "that your pistol was used in a recent felony. Mr. Howe, do you have any knowledge of people who might have known you kept a gun in your trunk, and might be involved in the drug trade?"

"It's about the narcs that got shot, right?" Once he'd blurted it out, Harold couldn't help saying, "It wasn't my fault. I didn't shoot anybody. I didn't do anything!"

This one would break quickly, Wolfe knew, and he decided to speed things up. "Mr. Howe," he said, "I think it would be a good idea for you to come downtown with us to talk about this some more."

His mother cried, "Is he under arrest? My boy didn't do anything! Is he under arrest?"

Carmelita stood. So did Harry. It was time to get out of the tactically unsound sitting position anyway.

"Not at all, Mrs. Howe," Carmelita said, her voice calm and low. "We'd just like Harold to look at some pictures, some suspects."

But the older woman was becoming hysterical. "He told you he didn't do anything! How would he know who the suspects were? They just stole his gun! How would he know? Oh, Jesus..."

The rising pitch of his mother's voice was driving Harold to the edge. "Yeah," he said, suddenly finding strength in his voice as he stood up himself. "How the fuck would I know who—"

His mother snapped, "Harold! Don't you dare use that kind of language in this house!"

"For Christ's sake, Ma—"

"Hey, let's everyone calm down," Carmelita said soothingly. She just wanted to get this kid out of the house without the mother calling the whole damn bar association to find out where he was. "It's just that whoever stole the gun may have known Harold and known he kept a gun in his truck. That person may be one of the suspects in the shooting. You see? Harold isn't in trouble at all."

The mother looked at Carmelita dubiously. Harold looked at Harry.

The man's eyes were on him intently. Like a predator. At that moment, Harold knew.

Pictures of suspects, shit. It was him they'd come for.

He swallowed hard. If he'd had the courage to move quickly, he might have gotten them both. Instead, his first move was hesitant, slowly creeping his left hand under his fatigue jacket.

Harold was watching the bearded man, and he saw the recognition in his eyes, saw the man's own hand start to react. Harold had not practiced left-handed with the shoulder sling, but this man must have trained like hell with his pistol, because the arm merely flashed and an ugly black gun appeared in his hand, in both hands, leveled at Harold.

The bearded man's voice roared, "Don't move!" Harold, his hand on the submachine gun, froze without raising the muzzle from under his coat. His bowels contracted in terror.

He caught a movement from the side as the woman came toward him. There was a silver-colored automatic in her hand.

He'd forgotten about his mother.

Mrs. Howe saw guns pointed at her only child. She lunged forward with a scream, putting her considerable bulk between her boy and the strange man and woman with the pistols.

"Don't hurt him," she shrieked hysterically. "Put those guns away! Put them away! This is my house! This is my—"

Harold knew what he had to do. Thanks, Mom.

His mother's back was to him, her arms out to the sides. He swung his sore right arm over her shoulder and around her neck, pulling her tightly to his chest as a shield, and he swung the MAC-11 out from under his coat and up toward the two strangers with the guns.

As Wolfe saw the hand movement, he was ready to fire when the pink blur of the woman came between him and Howe. Damn!

Behind him was a doorway into a bedroom. With a long sliding step, Wolfe was behind it, in a right-hand barricade position, the heavy beam of the door frame shielding his head. The walls, he knew, were the kind of light plasterboard that a submachine gun bullet would pass through as if it were fog, but at least his vest was on and his head was protected. The woman was squarely between him and the suspect. The ugly square gun protruded past her left arm. Wolfe could see it was some sort of a MAC.

He wanted this guy bad. It had to be the one who'd emptied a MAC into the dying agent as he lay in the lonely dirt of the forest logging road. But it was obvious that the woman in pink wasn't putting up an act. This was the guy's own mother that he'd taken hostage.

Wolfe had killed more criminals than he wanted to remember. But he hadn't killed anyone's mother yet. And he wasn't about to now.

Carmelita's voice came from Wolfe's left. He had seen a cast-iron wood stove over that way. His partner must have taken cover behind it. Good, thought Wolfe. She's behind the one bulletproof thing in the whole damn place.

"Easy, Harold," she was saying. "You haven't killed anybody yet!"

The hell he hasn't, Wolfe thought. A MAC had been hosed into Passeretti, and a MAC was what this man was holding now.

"Fuck you," Harold shrieked. "Drop your guns! Drop 'em!"

"You know we can't do that, Harold," Carmelita said, calmly but firmly. "But that's your mom. You don't want your mother to get hurt now, do you?"

Harold stammered, trying to think what to do. His mother didn't say anything. She was gasping like a fish.

"Harold," said Carmelita in the soothing voice, "your mom is turning blue. I think you're holding her too hard."

Reflexively Harold loosened his hold on his mother's neck. The gun was still pointed in Wolfe's direction. Harry stayed where he was, his right eye barely peeking around the corner. The three dots of his gunsights remained steady on the little bit of Harold's head that he could see behind the mother's puffed gray hair.

He let Carmelita keep talking. Two hostage-negotiators at once was a bad idea. And Carmelita was doing well. Voice, Wolfe knew, followed voice. Speaking slowly and softly, Carmelita was calming the panicked gunman. Wolfe didn't want to distract from that.

Another rule was to get the hostage taker thinking about something to slow his reaction time down if the rescuers decided to act. Carmelita said, "Harold, you know we can't put down our guns. But tell us what you do want. Let's get this resolved without anyone getting hurt."

Before Howe could answer, his mother gave out with a loud, choking cry. "Harold," Mrs. Howe shrieked. "Harold! What are you doing? Oh, my dear God, stop it! Stop it!"

Her keening shout brought Harold back to the edge. "Shut up, Ma! Just shut up!"

He was losing it. "Harold," Carmelita said, "just ignore her. This is between you and I. If you put your gun down, we'll put ours down."

"Bullshit," Harold squealed. The tension and fear had tightened his throat and turned his voice into a falsetto. "I know what you're gonna do! You're gonna off me!"

Unconsciously he had turned his body to face Carmelita. This opened his left side up a little more to Wolfe, who was on Harold's left. He steadied the gun.

I could kill him now, Wolfe thought. Just squeeze the trigger and put one right through his ear, separate the medulla, and drop him like a sack of rags without a single reflex to the trigger finger.

Yeah, he thought. I could blow his brains all over his mother's head.

Wolfe lowered the pistol until the sights were squared on the point of Howe's left shoulder. From this angle, a bullet that went all the way through the shoulder would continue into the spine and still kill or paralyze the target. Wolfe hoped it wouldn't be fatal. He needed this guy to talk.

Howe, confused and desperate, made a sputtering sound. "Drop the guns," he screamed at the agents again. "Drop 'em, or I'll shoot!" His face was dark red, suffused with blood and rage.

"Please listen, Harold," Carmelita said in her most soothing voice.

Totally focused on Carmelita now, Harold Howe turned more toward her. His left side was now toward Wolfe.

"I'll kill you, you bitch! You spic bitch, don't order me around no more! You ain't even white!"

It was going downhill too fast. Wolfe knew it was time for a resolution. He could see the cornered gunman's finger turning white from its pressure against the trigger of the little submachine gun.

In a clear, crisp voice, Wolfe said one word.

"Enough!"

The effect was electric. Harold Howe's face snapped toward him, contorted by fury, the lips drawn back from the teeth. As his head turned, the MAC turned, too. Wolfe was aware of a flash at the muzzle of the submachine gun, but his primary visual focus was on his front sight as he calmly, smoothly pressed the trigger.

IT WASN'T THE WAY it felt a couple of nights ago when he'd been shot. Then, there had been a hard slap and a hot lance of pain as the bullet from Passeretti's gun had torn through the muscles of his upper arm.

This time it was more a hammer blow than a slap. Howe felt instantly the deep agony of crushing bone hurt. The room was turning, he was turning, he was falling away from his mother.

He was holding the trigger back, but nothing was happening, no bullets coming from his submachine gun.

Then his face was pressed against the carpet, even though he didn't remember hitting the floor, and there was more pain in his arm. He opened his eyes and saw a black shoe standing on his wrist. The pain was unbearable.

In the distance, Harold could hear his mother screaming. Jesus Christ, Mom, don't you ever lighten up? Something hard was against his face. It was a gun muzzle. He turned his eyes and saw the dark eyes of the black-haired woman, her face tense and angry.

Harold Howe fainted.

MRS. HOWE RAN OUT the back door, screaming wordlessly, like a siren. Carmelita had time to think that the woman must have tremendous lungs to scream that long without taking a breath.

They were alone with Harold, who was unconscious on the floor. Wolfe's bullet had caught him in the shoulder as he turned, exiting the left shoulder blade. Reflexively, from his time investigating so many shootings, Wolfe glanced at the area behind where Howe had been standing. He could see, shoulder high, a hole in a dictionary on a bookshelf. Well, at least Harry's bullet hadn't gone out of the house, even if it did go through Harold.

Carmelita barked anxiously, "Are you all right? Are you hit?"

"I'm all right."

"Can we get him out, take him with us?"

"No good," said Wolfe. "He's bleeding too much. They'll have to get inside him to stop it."

"There's a couple of throw pillows here on the divan," Morales said. "I'll get this one under the shoulder, so his body weight puts pressure on the exit hole. Press this one down hard on the entry hole."

Wolfe said, "There's a phone on the table. Better call in to Spokane Police and ID us. Tell them we need the meat wagon ASAP."

As she went to the phone, Wolfe kept his eye on the area of the hallway Howe had emerged from when he'd come downstairs. The house hadn't been cleared. There was no way of knowing if there were accomplices still there. They'd have been pretty damn stupid to still be there after all the yelling. Only now did Harry realize he could have been shot in the back the whole time he was tunneled in on Harold, but then, you could never be sure.

He kept glancing over at the hallway as he searched Harold. No other weapons. A spare magazine was stuck in the back of the belt. Wolfe left it there.

He saw the MAC and the leather straps attached with snaps to the back of the weapon's frame. He didn't unbutton it. Instead, he shifted his Glock to his left hand, thumbed open his Clipit knife and cut the two straps halfway up. He pressed the bladelock release and closed the knife against his thigh, then shoved it in his pocket.

Morales was on the phone identifying them, giving their descriptions as arresting officers to the dispatcher so that the arriving uniformed cops wouldn't see people in plain clothes with guns and shoot them by mistake. Wolfe picked up the MAC his knife had freed. He realized instantly that it was the small one, the scaled-down MAC-11, not the full-size MAC-10 that had been used in the massacre of the agents. Maybe this was the wrong guy, after all.

He had been aware of a single flash at the muzzle. Why not a burst? He looked down at the weapon. The selector switch pointed to full automatic.

Then he saw it. A tiny .380-caliber shell casing was sticking out of the ejection port. Suddenly Wolfe knew what had happened.

The basic mechanism of a Military Armament Corporation submachine gun, any of the MAC variations, was inside a rectangular box of folded sheet metal. Spent shells ejected from a port on the right side and flew out of the gun directly sideways rather than up and over in an arc like most automatic weapons. It had been designed for right-handed personnel. Firing with his left hand, from the hip, either Harold's body or his mother's had been against the side of the weapon and blocked the ejecting shell, jamming the feed mechanism and keeping the next cartridge from chambering.

The sirens were coming already. The little COPS office was only a block away. COPS—Community Oriented Police Services—had been introduced to Spokane by its progressive chief of police. Little storefronts in each of the crime-plagued neighborhoods put cops on view and accessible instead of leaving them as remote figures enclosed in passing patrol cars, seen only when they came to make an arrest. The concept in urban policing had begun with the police commissioner in Houston and later New York, and had evolved from the street corner Kobans, or mini-police stations, of Japan.

Wolfe put his pistol back in his right hand and, careful to keep his finger off the trigger, thrust it back into the Summer Special holster behind his right hip. He saw that Morales had already put her Smith & Wesson away. Lower profiles were less antagonizing when the uniformed cops got on the scene.

From a side window, Wolfe heard a masculine voice command firmly, "Police! Don't move!" He froze obediently. From the corner of his eye, he saw a trim cop in a blue-and-black uniform covering him with a Glock 17 identical to his own. There was another in the doorway.

In moments the uniformed officers took charge. They put the Glocks away in their lightweight black nylon holsters after checking IDs. One of them secured Wolfe's Glock and Morales's S&W 9 mm, and another gingerly prepared the jammed MAC-11 for the evidence technicians who, the radio dispatcher said, were on their way.

Paramedics were rushing into the crowded living room, men in dark blue pants, with T-shirts the same color under light blue uniform shirts and leather equipment pouches hanging down at their sides. "We'll be out here by your patrol cars," Wolfe told a sergeant, who nodded.

The cold air was refreshing after the smell of the blood. Wolfe could see the anger in his partner's flashing eyes as they stood in the gathering dusk between the blue-and-red flashing roof bars of the white patrol cars and the reflected red lights of the huge lime green step van whose reflective white letters read Paramedic Unit.

He said sheepishly, "Blew it, huh?"

The expression on her face was puzzled. "Harry, it just wasn't you. We went in there with no real plan. We were flying by the seats of our pants. And I know how well you shoot under pressure. You were *aiming* for his shoulder, weren't you? Not his head like you were supposed to."

Wolfe took a deep breath of the icy night air. "We're supposed to shoot them in the head when they're holding hostages they're going to kill. Not when they're holding their mother," he said quietly.

Carmelita winced. She put a hand on his arm. "You're right," she said. "Okay. You're right. Besides, we needed him alive. But the guys we were working with at the command post aren't going to like this. It wasn't exactly team playing."

"It couldn't be," her senior partner said, and she could have sworn he said it sadly. "We aren't working with their team, remember? The difference is, they take prisoners."

In the eerie half dark amid the swirling emergency lights, Wolfe looked terribly tired and strangely alone. Carmelita felt a deep surge of compassion. He had, after all, just shot a man who was probably getting ready to shoot her, and here she was criticizing him for not having his act together.

"Hey," she said quietly, "I'm sorry." Impulsively she embraced him. As her arm went around him, she caught it short. Something didn't feel right. "What—"

She looked down at what she had touched, and said softly, "Oh, my God..."

There were two holes in Harry's leather car coat, one in the right breast and one at the corresponding point in the back. The .380 bullet from the MAC-11 had torn through the garment. It had to have passed a fraction of an inch from his liver as the jacket hung away from his body while he stood in that awkward barricade firing position in the doorway.

The paramedics were rolling Harold out now, one standing beside him holding the bottle of Ringer's Lactate as two others pushed the gurney to the ambulance. One of the officers went with them to the paramedic unit. Hey, thought Wolfe, good policy. They've got their act together up here.

He didn't realize Carmelita was no longer by his side. She had gone back into the bungalow. She wanted to know where the bullet from Howe's gun had gone.

It didn't take her long to find it. A devout Catholic, she crossed herself when she saw it. The bullet, fired by the man who followed the self-proclaimed prophet of Jesus, had ripped through her partner's coat an inch from his ribs and liver. It had gone on down to shatter the plaster Christ on the Cross that hung in a place of honor at the end of the Howe family's hallway.

5

Spokane Police had taken both agents' service automatics for ballistics testing, routine procedure in any police-action shooting in the city. After leaving the routine detectives' interrogation—with the head of the Spokane office of DEA at their side, per departmental regulations—they returned with him to Spokane DEA headquarters at West 920 Riverside.

DEA was involved in more shootings than any other federal law-enforcement agency. It had long since become policy to keep a stock of spare weapons in each office to issue to agents after the guns they'd used in shoot-outs were submitted to the lab for evidence and investigation purpose. The local SAC, or Special Agent in Charge, who looked for all the world like the head of the local Kiwanis Club, ushered them into the locked armory area of the evidence room. A tall, good-looking young agent followed with a clipboard that held the weapons requisition forms and receipts.

"We don't keep as many on hand as some of the other offices," he said almost apologetically. "Not that many shootings in Spokane."

There were two Glock 17s in their plastic boxes. Wolfe checked them both. One had the standard sights with white enamel, a dot on the front and a three-sided outline in the back, and the old smooth grips. The other was like Wolfe's, with the three glowing night-sight dots of tritium on the sights and the new-style checkered grip panels. He chose that one and began to fill out the requisition form.

Carmelita found two Rugers. They were big in her small hand. There was nothing in the inventory that resembled her compact Model 6904. There was disappointment in her voice as she asked, "You wouldn't have a Smith & Wesson, would you? I'm used to the mechanism, and the Glock works so much different."

The SAC shook his head sympathetically, but the tall young agent blurted, "I've got a Smith! It's a .45, but the compact one, the Model 4516, works just like yours."

Harry turned away to hide his smile. Carmelita had that effect on men.

Carmelita smiled demurely and cast her eyes downward. She had grown up in the barrio of East Los Angeles, and had learned that few men could resist a pretty girl who looked helpless. "Oh, I couldn't," she said sweetly, at the same time giving a longing look at the pistol in the young agent's black nylon hip holster.

The agent looked pleadingly at his boss. "I can lend her a personally owned gun, can't I? I mean, it doesn't say in the regs that an agent can't lend another agent a gun, does it? I've got a .38 in my locker that's authorized on my card, so it's not like I'd be going without a gun or have to requisition one, sir...."

The SAC sighed and nodded. He sympathized with both of them. People who'd just been in a shooting needed a gun they were familiar with, if only to give them a grasp on security. As for the smitten young man, well, if the SAC had been younger himself and hadn't been drilled in the dangers of sexual harassment suits that come from consorting with women of lower rank on the same job...

Harry and Carmelita left carrying a new Glock 17 with an issue box of Winchester 147-grain subsonic hollowpoint 9 mm ammo marked Law Enforcement Only, and a model 4516 S&W with an extra magazine and fifty rounds of Remington 185-grain hollowpoint. Those were the Agency-issued loads for the standard 9 mm, and for the .45 automatic that had been optional for individual agent purchase since 1990.

They drove to the Embassy Suite hotel on the edge of Spokane, and used their DEA charge cards to check into adjoining rooms. Carmelita dumped her suitcase in her room and went next door to give Harry moral support for the call to the director that they both dreaded.

Wolfe used the bedside phone, and Carmelita spoke on the extension on the desk on the other side of the partition. The discussion was everything they had feared.

"Goddammit," the director roared after they'd finished the explanation, "I cannot *believe* that you screwed up this badly! Why the hell didn't you call me for authorization to get some other Centac people in there, pull a stakeout and take this son of a bitch on our terms? You're both damn lucky that you and the old lady aren't lying in the Spokane morgue right now."

"It was Code Zero," Carmelita said protectively, even though it had been Wolfe's idea. "We didn't think you'd want any more personnel involved than necessary."

"For Christ's sake," snapped the director, his exasperation evident in his voice, "you wouldn't have had to take them along to... to finish the assignment. Just to grab the little bastard."

Wolfe felt he had to speak. "If you want to take me off it, sir, that's always your privilege." There was no sarcasm in his voice, no anger, no challenge. He said it flatly, Carmelita realized, as if he didn't care anymore. Perhaps, she realized, that was the problem.

There was a pause before the director growled, "No, I'm not taking you off the goddamn case! What I am doing is sitting here waiting for you to tell me where you're going from here."

Wolfe was silent.

Morales said, "Sir? I remember when you explained to me the difference between Code Zero and Code One, the emphasis was on the one place where the first one went beyond the second. But if Code One is unlimited funds and unlimited resources, that's still true of Code Zero, too, right?"

"Of course," snapped the director. "What are you getting at?"

"I think, sir, that I may have a plan," Carmelita Morales said.

6

The white Dodge Diplomat pulled into the area reserved for doctors in the parking lot of the sprawling Deaconess Medical Center on West 805th Avenue in Spokane. A man with a close-cropped beard and a dark-skinned, raven-haired woman, both wearing business suits, stepped out and walked briskly toward the main entrance.

A receptionist looked up at them expectantly. Harry Wolfe smiled and said, "I'm Dr. Jerome Bossler and this is Dr. Anna Castille, Walter Reed Medical Center. We've been sent to do a consult on one of your trauma patients, a Mr. Harold Howe. Do you know if the attending physician is handy?"

Impressed enough to momentarily lift her eyebrows, the receptionist immediately picked up her phone. In a moment she purred, "Dr. Cynthia Paytelle is the one you'll need to see. I'm told she did the surgery on Mr. Howe yesterday, and she's making her rounds right now. She'll meet you in the recovery room. Fourth floor. I'll show you how to get there...."

They waited for Dr. Paytelle at the desk that was the hub of the different recovery wings for Deaconess, the region's premier trauma center. In moments a slim woman, medium tall and wearing scrub greens, approached them with a confident stride. Her silky blond hair was drawn up in a bun, and she held an oversize manila portfolio.

"Doctors," she said, extending her hand. She shook hands first with Carmelita and then with Harry. He gave her a limp hand, not thinking surgeons would crunch each other's fingers, and was surprised at the strength of her grip.

"Walter Reed," mused Dr. Paytelle. "To what do we owe the honor?"

"We do a good deal of work with the Drug Enforcement Administration," Carmelita said. "As you may know, Mr.

Howe is a suspect in the shooting death of two DEA agents and the wounding of a third. He was shot yesterday by another DEA agent who was investigating the case. Apparently there is some concern in Washington about the propriety of the second shooting, and DEA wants us to examine Mr. Howe with a view toward angles of entry, the damage done, etcetera."

Dr. Paytelle furrowed her eyebrows. "Why send physicians to examine hands-on for that? I would have thought the reports, the X rays and the photos the detectives took of the entry and exit wounds at the emergency room would have been more than sufficient."

Of course, she was right, but Wolfe said smoothly, "Apparently there was some question of the agent who shot Mr. Howe using particularly destructive, nonapproved ammunition. Dr. Castille and I specialize in the forensic aspects, as well as the treatment, of handgun wounds. Apparently the Agency thought there would be things we might pick up that would help them in their internal affairs investigation."

Dr. Paytelle made a face. "Very well," she said. "I assume you want to go over the charts and the pictures before you examine my patient?"

"Please," said Morales, and the doctor beckoned them to a small room just off the hub. As the doctor clipped the pictures—the X rays—to the lightboard, Morales asked, "Is the patient sedated?"

"Not fully, Dr. Castille. He's in a lot of pain, and it's not surprising. This wound is an orthopedic surgeon's nightmare. He's lucky he's alive. The bullet missed the internal jugular and the left subclavian by centimeters. There was a good deal of collateral bleeding, of course, but the paramedics stabilized it immediately. He's in and out. He'll be crying for more painkiller within the hour, I suspect."

Wolfe frowned. He'd thought from the blood volume that the bullet must have cut the subclavian artery or one of the other great vessels. Not severed it—it hadn't been pumping—but opened it up enough to bleed him out without surgical intervention. They could have kidnapped him and kept him alive long enough to truth serum him after all. Aarrgh!

Carmelita, on the other hand, was thinking positively. If he'd been awake, he would have recognized them both, when the time came for them to enter his room, and started screaming. Howe was doubtless under police guard. This was why time had been of the essence, so that they could get to him while he was still under and doped up from his surgery.

"You can see the level of destruction here," Dr. Paytelle was saying, pointing to the radiograph. "The greater tubercle of the humerus has been shattered to dust, the kind of comminuted fracture I'd normally associate with a rifle bullet instead of a pistol slug. The coracoid process has been separated completely from the scapula at the base of the suprascapular notch—we can see the multiple fractures of the head of the humerus, and the clavicle has been separated from the scapula at the juncture of the acromion process."

The agents nodded sagely. Morales knew her narcotics well enough to talk shop with any physician or pharmacist, but the fine points of skeletal structure were considerably beyond her. Wolfe had seen enough autopsies as an investigator of the agent-involved shootings to have a somewhat better idea of what the surgeon was talking about. He resisted the urge to say, "Blew the shit out of him, huh?"

Dr. Paytelle said, "You know, I assume, about the other wound? The older one?"

Morales and Wolfe looked at each other. "No," said Carmelita. "We weren't told."

The surgeon shuffled the papers and produced a photograph, a color print. It showed the dark-edged, discolored wounds in the arm. "We don't usually take pictures, unless it's something unusual we want for briefing or study. I don't know what you do at Walter Reed. The police investigators usually take any forensic evidence pictures of patients, unless, of course, they go to the medical examiner's office."

Wolfe was studying the wound photo intensely. "Anterior to posterior," Paytelle said. "Distal to proximal. Very little internal bleeding, no important vessels struck, never touched the humerus. Nice and clean. Apparently whoever shot him was using regular bullets, not whatever the agent used to blow this guy's other shoulder up."

Harry tried to keep his face expressionless. Whichever agent at the scene had shot Howe would have been using the same Agency-issue rounds Harry had used. 147-grain subsonics. It was all in where you hit them, Wolfe thought. An inch one way or the other was the difference between a boo-boo that caused not much more pain than an inoculation and a shattering injury that crippled for life.

Wolfe asked, "Do you have the blood screen, Doctor?" The blond surgeon shuffled the papers once again and produced an official-looking sheet. Wolfe scanned it quickly. The blood type was AB Positive. The same as the blood found by the Jeep Wagoneer where Passeretti had been shot down. None of the agents had that blood type. One more solid reason to believe the little bastard had been there shooting down Wolfe's brother agents.

"What's your prognosis, Doctor?" Morales asked.

The blond looked at her coolly. "You're the gunshot expert from way back east, Dr. Castille. What's yours?"

Caught off guard, Carmelita needed only a second to regroup before she said quietly, "Doctor, we were *told* to come here. That's one. Two, I never give a prognosis without having seen everything there is to see, let alone before examining the patient. Third, I trust the attending surgeon who was inside the wound when it was fresh to have a better perspective on where it's going than I can have, seeing it after it's undergone the initial repair."

After a long moment, the surgeon looked Carmelita square in the eye and said, "I'm sorry. I deserved that. It's just—look, Mr. Howe is my patient, like any other. I did the best I could on him and I'll continue to do that.

"But Dr. Castille, you and Dr. Bossler haven't asked me a word about my other patient from that night's incident, the DEA agent, Komeito. You tell me you're just concerned that the agent who shot the man who may have shot Komeito might have used too nasty a bullet.

"I'm sorry about that. I know you do what you're assigned to, just as I do. But, you see, I amputated Ichiro Komeito's right forearm halfway from the elbow this morning. We tried and tried to save it, but it was an explosive wound from a high-powered rifle. We couldn't keep the tissue from going necrotic.

"He didn't say anything when I told him, but I saw the tears coming up in his eyes. I read in the paper how he tried to shoot back with his other hand, but his gun was broken, and the only time he cried out loud was when the nurse told him the other two agents were dead.

"I worked on your Mr. Howe last night. For all I know, he's the one that did that to Komeito. I looked at the Swastika tattooed on his right forearm, and the Iron Cross tattooed on his left, and you'll have to forgive me, Doctors, I found myself judging my patient just a little subjectively. But all that time my scalpel was working around his subclavian artery, I never let it slip once, and I'm kind of proud of that under the circumstances.

"Prognosis? He'll keep the limb, but he won't do much with it. They can try to rebuild the socket, but with the structural damage done to the surrounding bones, it will always be weak and have very limited rotation. The other arm will heal, even though whatever idiot tried to treat him at home just poured sulfa powder in it and left it in a rotting bandage. But the infection is responding to treatment. Who knows? If the government sent you here to do your gunshot wound treatment on Mr. Howe, and if you're a hell of a lot better than I am, maybe in a few years you'll have him up and running so well he can hold his Uzi again, or his Magnum, or whatever it is he blew that young agent's arm off with.

"And now," Dr. Paytelle said, taking a breath, "let's get you down to prep and put you into some scrubs and I'll introduce you to my patient."

A MUSCULAR young police officer with a thick but trimmed dark mustache was standing at semiattention in the recovery room the surgeon led them into. He looked sharp, Carmelita thought. Brown curly hair, the almost-black uniform cops called "midnight blue" crisply creased and perfectly tailored, the light black ballistic nylon gunbelt and black athletic shoes looking casual and professional at the same time.

He and the suspect, Howe, were in the far right corner of the room. There were no single recovery rooms at Deaconess, and each was designed for four patients. A large, opaque, movable screen had been set up around Howe.

"Officer," Dr. Paytelle said in a voice accustomed to command, "these are Doctors Castille and Bossler. They're consulting on this patient and will need to take him to the examining room." It was not a request for permission; it was a flat statement.

The cop stepped to the side, his hands behind him in parade rest like a soldier. Stepping into the cubicle, Morales and Wolfe could see that the patient's eyes were closed. A bottle of solution was attached to him, and there were tubes in his nose. The right arm was heavily bandaged, and the entire left arm was encased in a heavy cast that encompassed the chest and both shoulders, as well. The officer followed as Paytelle and Wolfe pushed the bed down the hall, with Morales bringing along the rolling rack that held the bottle of solution fed into his veins. All three were wearing green surgical masks.

"You may remain here, outside the door, Officer," the surgeon said crisply. She undid her mask's top string and let it fall around her neck. "Good luck, Doctors. You may leave the case file for me at the main desk when you return him. Take your time. I should be around for at least two more hours. If you need me for anything, have me paged."

She walked away, and the patrolman stood at attention as Wolfe and Morales rolled Harold Howe inside the examining room. They had him alone now.

Wolfe unzipped the small leatherette carrying case he'd brought with him and removed the syringe. There were two ampoules next to it. One would make the patient tell the truth. The other would keep him from ever repeating it.

Wolfe held the ampoule up to the light and punctured it with the tip of the needle. As he drew the fluid into the syringe, Harold Howe opened his eyes.

"I hurt," croaked Howe. "It hurts! Gimme a shot!"

Carmelita didn't speak. She'd done almost all the talking back at the bungalow. Even as groggy as he was, Howe was likely to recognize her voice and start screaming. It was Wolfe who said, in his soft voice, "One shot, coming up."

Harry had an overwhelming urge to rip off his mask and reveal his face and watch this son of a bitch scream. But he knew that even if he held his hand over Howe's nose and mouth long enough for the drug to take effect, it would never work as well on an agitated man as on a calm one.

Wolfe contented himself with the grimace of pain as he stabbed the needle into Harold Howe's buttock and rammed the plunger home.

TWO HOURS LATER, back in Wolfe's hotel suite, they picked up the phones again. They reached Centac's director on the secured line almost immediately. Code Zero personnel usually did.

Wolfe and Morales briefed him quickly. The drug had taken effect almost instantly. Howe's weakened condition, the painkillers in his system and the residual effects of the anesthesia for his emergency surgery the day before had all contributed to the effect.

There were names, but only first names. J.J. and Danny, spoken together as if they were one. Armorer, unlikely to be a name, probably a title or nickname. Thor, apparently a code name of some sort. Jack, dead Jack, the martyr. That was confirmed when prints had come back identifying the dead killer as one John "Jack" Murphy, a small-time hood with more time served for nonsupport in the county jail than for his one armed-robbery conviction. A name that sounded like "Reinhold" or "Rheinholt." And, again and again, someone named Will. The tone of Howe's voice, even deep under the drugs, changed to something between reverence and fear when he spoke the name.

The Team kept coming up. The guy wouldn't say what the team was, just the Team. They kept asking whose team, and Howe kept mumbling, "The Team. The Team!"

Howe was obviously a weakling, mentally and physically, Carmelita interjected, but the one place he was strong was his refusal to give last names or addresses. It was as if he had been programmed to withstand hypnosis or even truth serum in that regard. An incredibly powerful command had been planted in his mind by someone. It was like asking a Catholic to deny Christ or the Pope, she told the director; even under truth serum, and for that matter, with bamboo slivers shoved under his fingernails, he wouldn't have done it.

They'd asked him about the shooting. He had cried through his drugged haze, told how ashamed he was that he hadn't gotten a shot off. The Armorer and J.J. and Rheinhold, apparently, had done the killing. Thor had failed. They couldn't penetrate the pharmaceutical fog deeply enough to get the details, but somehow Thor had failed to hold up his end of the firefight.

Who had bandaged him? Will. Who was his boss? Will. Who set up the shooting? Will. Was it a drug money rip-off? Yes. Why for the crummy fifty grand in buy money when there were supposed to be bigger dealings down the road?

It was going to be a rip-off and a kidnap, Howe told them. It always worked before, but this fucker had backup. They saw Howe and the others coming, came up with guns, and Rheinhold and the others had opened up on them, and everything had gone to shit quickly. The dude pulled his own gun.

Did they know these were drug-enforcement agents? No, Howe had cried miserably under the truth serum. Who would ever bring down heat on themselves like that? They thought it was one asshole cocaine dealer, one more to take off the streets. And besides, they were drug fighters themselves.

What? Of course, Howe had moaned. The Team. Fighting drugs was what the Team was about. Stopping the nigger Jew Commie dope pushers that were rotting the souls of American white kids. They never meant to shoot any drug agents. In a way, now, Harold was glad he didn't get a shot off. Shooting another narc would have been like shooting his brother. He only faced the white narc, though. If it had been the nigger narc or the gook narc that shot his brothers, that would have been different.

When Carmelita and Wolfe finished their recount, there was a long silence. Then the director said, "I don't know what group he's talking about, but in that Washington and Idaho area, there are enough white supremacist groups it could be any of several. I'll get our people to work with it tonight and touch base with FBI.

"No addresses," he went on. "What did you get from him that you can work with?"

"I asked him how many were in this team he kept talking about. He said seven hundred. But the only names I got were the ones I told you. I asked him where to find Will. He said wait awhile and we'd find him in the White House. I asked him about the Reinhold guy and he said, find him in the jungle, and laughed like it was a joke. The only one we got a line on was the guy he called an armorer. He said, 'Find him at the range, where else? He rules the range. He's the best. He's the champ.'"

Twenty-five hundred miles away, the director grunted. "'Rules the range.' Do you think it could be a cop? A police rangemaster at a firearms training center? He wouldn't be the first cop to get hooked up with right-wing weirdos."

"Maybe, but I don't think so," answered Wolfe, who had been a law-enforcement firearms instructor himself. "The rangemaster is in charge of the shooting, and an armorer is a gun mechanic, working at a tool bench rather than on the range. Howe said, 'Find him at the range. He's the best. He's the champ.' Maybe he means the guy is a good shot, shoots in competition or something."

"You used to shoot a lot in combat matches," the director said. "You know the turf. Check out the scene out there and see what you can find. I'll check on the white supremacist angle and get back to you."

The conversation ended. Wolfe stood and stretched wearily after he hung up the phone.

"You're upset," Carmelita said suddenly.

"You noticed, huh?"

She frowned. "C'mon. This is me, all right? You don't have to be sarcastic. I can see there's something on your mind, something beyond the case."

He just looked at her and waited for her to continue.

"The ampoules in your bag," she said quietly. "There were two of them. Two different colors. They weren't both Amytal. You only used the one. I'm curious. If he had told you he'd killed our guys, would you have used the other?"

Wolfe looked her straight in the eye and said simply, "Yes."

"Cyanide?"

Wolfe shook his head. "It's a cocktail of two or three different things. We got it from CIA. Supposed to be totally untraceable even if the toxicologists and pathologists know what to look for. Complete cardiopulmonary shutdown in ten to thirty minutes, depending on the dosage. With the drugs he's got in him now, the full ampoule would have done him before we were back in the parking lot."

Carmelita nodded quietly. "You could have anyway. There was nothing to stop you."

"*I* was there to stop me."

"You didn't ask him if he'd killed any of the dopers they'd been ripping off."

"Did it matter?"

"No," she sighed. "Ironic, isn't it? We're assigned to put dopers out of business. These guys are putting dopers out of business. Why not just let them keep going? We're doing the same job—really, that part of it at least."

Wolfe made a sound that was half laugh, half snort. "When I went to Josh Hooper's gunfighting school, Colonel Hooper talked about how the people who want to ban guns distort all the facts, and that includes in the statistics for the number of people being killed by people they know, an awful lot are instances of dopers blown away by other dopers. He suggested airdropping AK-47s and lots of ammo into the drug neighborhoods, and letting the problem solve itself. Maybe he was right."

Carmelita smiled sadly. "But we still haven't talked about what's bothering you, have we?"

Harry walked to the window and looked out into the blackness of the northwestern night. After a long moment he spoke, very quietly.

"I was ready to kill him, Carmelita. Because Centac said he was my enemy, because he may have hurt men I never knew who do the same job I do. He was lying there helpless, the pathetic little loser, and I was going to put him to sleep like a stray dog nobody wanted anymore. When I found out that whoever he may have killed wasn't one of mine, I let him live. I didn't like any of that. I shouldn't have that power. Nobody should. Men shouldn't play God."

Carmelita's voice was still gentle. "Did any of the others bother you like that?"

Wolfe closed his eyes, wincing at the pain of the thought. Only two instances had really troubled him at all. The first was the one involved in the situation that had put him at the mercy of the director. The other had been an assignment last year. He'd done that job with Carmelita, but he'd been alone when it had happened.

The man he killed was an evil man, a brute killer. He had known that from the beginning. If he hadn't, he couldn't have done it at all. But the others in his clique of scumbags had turned on him, and Harry was undercover with them, not yet accepted as one of them, and the cunning bastard who was their leader had decided there was one way for Harry to prove himself.

To murder the errant one in front of them.

What had troubled Harry most about it was how little time he'd needed to make the decision. There had been multiple Harrys at that moment. The craven one that honestly wanted to live, that knew even with the loaded gun he could take out a couple of them at most, but the others would kill him right there if he didn't pull the trigger. There was the Harry of the job, of Centac, who knew that this would open the door to put him inside the gang he was investigating, that it would give him the goods to wrap up the mission, to do justice. And there was the pragmatic Harry who'd said in essence, what the fuck, the rat bastard deserved to die anyway for the monstrous things he'd done.

Harry Wolfe could recall the moment as if it was last night, as if it was ten minutes ago. The look of pleading terror in the big man's eyes as Harry raised the Colt .45 automatic. The blast of the shot, which Harry couldn't really remember hearing at all. The suddenness with which the man had fallen when the big bullet from Harry's gun tore into his brain, so fast that his body seemed to disappear from in front of the pistol. A human life, gone so quickly and so irrevocably... and so against his training. Everything he'd learned, from law school to the DEA Academy and beyond, had told him that you only used the gun on a man who put you in immediate danger. He had violated his own law—as a lawyer, as a lawman, as an instructor... as a man.

"Yes," Wolfe said. "Yes. One or two have bothered me like that."

"It's getting to you, isn't it, Harry? The whole Code Zero thing."

He nodded his head, affirming.

"You did them because you had to," she said, because she didn't know about the two Harry was thinking about. Only the director knew about the first one, and no one was left alive except Harry Wolfe who knew about the second. He was his own accuser in those. The others who'd gone down? They'd deserved it.

But Carmelita didn't know about those two. Her mind was racing. She knew that she wasn't aware of all there was to know about her partner, but she remembered the case that had brought them together, the case where he had rescued her, severely wounded, from her captors. Harry had taken one of them off guard, by surprise, killing him as swiftly and efficiently and horribly as a Green Beret "silencing" a sentry. My God, she thought, is any of this from *me?* Is any of this baggage he's carrying on his soul from what he did for *me?*

She went to him instinctively and hugged him. "It's a war, Harry," she whispered urgently. "The President himself calls it the War on Drugs. We're soldiers, and they're soldiers. You kill the other soldiers in a war because they're going to kill yours if you don't get them first. You kill the other soldiers in a war because they already killed your buddies. You don't wait for them to point the AK-47 at you before you shoot them. Every one you stop is one that won't hurt you and the other good guys anymore, the way they were going to.

"A sniper shoots the enemy soldier while the enemy's minding his own business. That doesn't make him a murderer, Harry. The sniper works alone, against an enemy force that outnumbers him. So do we. The difference is, we don't take them on sight. We don't take them in advance. We shoot our enemies only when they've already killed one of us.

"Soldiers aren't immoral," she whispered fiercely. "Soldiers aren't murderers. We're soldiers, too, in our war. Why should anyone judge us any different? Why should we of all people judge ourselves harder than the bastards we're hunting are ever judged?"

There was nothing more to say. He hugged her, hard. A part of him wanted to do more. A part of him had wanted to do that with her since he'd first seen her, helpless and hurt and vulnerable, and had wanted it more and more as he'd come to know her, to appreciate her inner strength and fire.

But not now, not like this. Not when sympathy—no, he couldn't bring himself to say *pity*—might be motivating her to be this close to him, as personal as they'd ever been.

He couldn't remember the last time he'd wanted to cry. The last time he actually had wept was when he was in his early teens and his parents had died in a car crash. But he wouldn't cry now. By God, he wouldn't!

He gently pulled away from her and kissed her primly on the forehead. "Thanks," he said. "That helped. Believe me."

They separated. It was late. They could deal with this in the morning. Alone in his room, the snub .357 revolver on one side of the bed and the newly issued DEA Glock on the night table on the side where he slept, Wolfe stretched out nude under the crisp sheets, too tired to shower.

He thought about the woman one door down. He loved her, he realized. He felt good whenever he was around her. He was protective toward her while at the same time he recognized her enormous strengths, physical and mental, that went far beyond her beauty. The compassion he'd seen her express tonight reinforced that.

She had been lucky, he knew. Carmelita had killed men. He had seen her do it. They had both been tournament fighters at one time, he in shotokan karate and she in professional kickboxing, but she had won higher titles in her game than he had in his, and had gone further. He never would have made it as a professional fighter. She could have, he knew, easily. She could have been the woman's world champion if she'd chosen that direction.

But she had never had to commit murder. As a law-enforcement officer, as a lawyer, Wolfe knew beyond doubt that by the standard of the law, he himself *had.* If he was the judge in a bench trial and knew all he knew about Harry Wolfe, he would find himself guilty under the standards of the law. Harry and Carmelita had both been forced to kill human beings in the line of duty. In the semantic sense, you could say that they were both killers. But only Harry, he knew, was a murderer. A murderer approved, indeed created, by the highest arms of the United States government, but a murderer nonetheless.

She had gone through more horror in her life than he had in his longer time on earth, his longer time with DEA. She had come through it harder, stronger. Some people broke under suffering, and some were made better by the experience. Carmelita was one of the latter. Like scar tissue—tougher and stronger after the healing of the wound was done.

She had not yet become a murderer, at least. He didn't want her to. There was an innocence there inside her strength that he didn't want to see lost, a tremendous integrity he didn't want to see compromised the way his own had been. He wished, at this moment, that he had never recommended her for Code Zero.

He was the senior partner, the streetfighter so hard that one gang he'd been undercover with had nicknamed him "Bonebreaker" after seeing him in action in a bar. The pistol shot so good he could win shooting tournaments with a street-duty gun instead of a target pistol.

But, he realized at this moment, it was Carmelita who was the stronger of the two of them.

CARMELITA MORALES stepped out of the streaming shower. The cool air of the room felt cleansing. But neither the chill of the air-conditioning she'd turned up nor the heat of the shower she'd just left could cleanse the things that preyed on her mind.

She hadn't been able to really work out since she'd left Quantico, but she did her stretching exercises before she went to bed. As she went through the moves, she thought about Harry Wolfe.

He was the kind of man her mother had always told her to marry: responsible, successful at what he did, strong. A man of few words, but when he spoke, you listened. Funny when it was time to relax, and kind, and gentle. A good man. That's what her mother would have said.

It was Harry, she knew, who'd gotten her into Code Zero, given her a chance to prove herself. He'd been the senior partner, the idea man. She was proud of her idea that had worked so well today, boldly infiltrating the hospital and probing the brains of the enemy without anyone knowing who they were, even the man they'd put in that hospital.

She remembered the moment when Harry had shot him. She'd seen Harold Howe turning savagely toward Wolfe, the submachine gun coming up in his hand as he spun. She couldn't fire because the woman's body had blocked Howe completely. She'd looked instinctively toward Harry in that split second, seen the nasty little muzzle-flash spit from the front of the MAC-11, and all she could see of Harry—the gray-black pistol in his two hands—had never twitched, never flinched as he'd fired the shot exactly where it had to go.

Carmelita had never seen him frightened. He seemed always cool, always calm. She'd lost it once or twice, succumbing to the Latin rage that she considered a curse of her heritage, even though that was the kind of stereotype she herself had worked so long and so hard to wipe out.

So many men were threatened by her strength; Harry took pride in it. So many men made fools of themselves over her because of the way she looked; Harry seemed not to notice her beauty and cared for her because of what was inside her, not how the outside looked. It wasn't that he was uninterested in women. She'd seen the proof to the contrary. One woman she'd introduced him to had given her glowing reports.

She guessed it was the respect thing. That made it harder for her to help him come to terms with what he was going through now. He didn't seem to want to open up.

He'd been working Code Zero longer than she. She wondered if it would affect her the same way in a few years. Too long on what the kids called "the dark side of the force." Well, life wasn't *Star Wars*. Someone had to do it, and she had found the strength in herself to be one of them. But part of that strength she'd drawn from Harry, and it pained her to see him this way.

It also frightened her, because if the self-doubt could happen to him, what was to keep it from happening to her?

After all, she knew, of the two of them, he was the strong one.

7

It was Carmelita's turn to drive. As she guided the vehicle east on I-90 toward Coeur d'Alene, Harry leaned back against the seat to reflect.

The case was growing cold. The task force had located the dead Jack Murphy's tiny apartment, but it had been ransacked by the time they got there. No leads. Neighbors and people where he worked said he was quiet, kept to himself, occasionally muttered about the goddamn niggers and Jews and cunts that were running the world, and that was it.

FBI research with the specialists who followed white supremacy groups aggressive enough to be classified as organized crime had turned up little on the Team. That part of the country was a national hotbed of white racist activity, centered around places like Hayden Lake, Idaho, not far away. The Order, the Aryan Nations, and the supposedly wiped-out Bruders Schweigen had all been headquartered there in the past or present.

The Team, FBI's researchers said, appeared to be a paper tiger. It had an "electronic newsletter" that circulated around the country and was protected by a labyrinth of computer codes it had taken the Bureau's technicians ages to solve. Its big theme seemed to be that the drug problem was part of the nigger Jew Communist conspiracy that controlled ZOG, the Zionist Occupation Government, that the master plan of ZOG was to weaken the white race and its Aryan bloodlines with narcotics so the Jews and the mongrels could more quickly rule the world. The bizarre editorials were always signed, the Team. Will and Rheinhold did not compute; they'd never been mentioned. There was, however, a column in the computer newsletter titled "Aryan Gunrack," written by someone who called himself the Armorer, with advice on things like how to turn hollowpoint bullets into exploding slugs by filling the cavities with lead azide and epoxying over the tips. The Bureau had not taken the Team seriously until now and had kept them on the back burner. FBI's contacts with Centac promised an accelerated investigation, using their latest technology to attempt to trace the source of the computer net "broadcasts."

Harry said idly, "I'm going to have to buy some clothes today or tomorrow. What I had in the suitcase isn't enough for long-term."

Carmelita answered, "Think we're in for the long haul, huh?"

"Looks like. The trail's damn cold. If the Feds don't come up with something on the computer trace, and if we can't find a line on this Armorer guy from the gun people, which, no pun intended, is a hell of a long shot, I don't see too many more leads."

"Why do you think it's a long shot from the gun angle?"

"Because," Harry began, "if I'm interpreting what Howe said correctly, this guy is some sort of a shooting champion. The organized gun sports is something I know. I shoot in competition to stay sharp for the street. Gun people are like motorcyclists: ninety-nine percent or better are legitimate, and they have no use at *all* for the one percent of outlaws and scumbags. They figure they don't deserve the redneck image shooters have been given, and they ostracize people who perpetuate the stereotype. It's hard to believe somebody who's a loser like Howe, the kind of guy who belongs to the racial hate cults, would still be around in that environment."

"Maybe someone will remember him from before he got kicked out," Carmelita said hopefully.

"I think that's the one chance we've got," said Wolfe, "but I'm not holding my breath. These people are losers across the board. That's why they go with racial hatred and a weird, inflated sense of racial pride—to have something to hang on to. That's not the kind of guy who can win in an open competitive environment. If and when we break this, we'll probably find out he was just the best shot on the Team or something, intramural competition, something like that."

"This match today," said Carmelita. "Are you actually going to compete or just watch?"

Wolfe shrugged. "I don't know yet. The folks at the gun shops I called said the only combat shooting match they have this time of year is the pin-shooting championships for Idaho, at this little range on the forest preserve in Coeur d'Alene. I do okay at the practical shooting events, the simulated gunfights, but I've only shot pins a couple of times."

Morales looked puzzled. "Pins," she said. "You lost me."

"Bowling pins," said Wolfe. "Five of them on a table, twenty-five feet away. Whoever shoots them off fastest wins. Like shooting tin cans off a fence, only tougher."

"Why is it tougher? Bowling pins are bigger than cans. They should be easier to hit."

"Yeah," said Wolfe, "but they're heavier. You've got to blow them all the way back off a three-foot table. That's another problem. My 9 mm doesn't have the momentum, the bullet weight, to do that. You need a .45 or a Magnum."

Carmelita grinned smugly. "Oh, you poor little thing! Well, tell you what. Now that I've got this .45, I'll let you use it. If you're sure you can handle it, that is. It's a real man's gun…." Her voice trailed off impishly.

Harry laughed good-naturedly. "I used to buy into that too," he said, "but the more I've actually had to do it, the more I've been convinced it doesn't matter a damn if you're shooting a 9 mm or a .45. It's where you hit them that makes the difference."

"Tell that to your bowling pins," said Carmelita.

"Bowling pins," Wolfe said, "don't have any blood or nerve endings. Bowling pins don't scream. And they don't shoot back."

"In that case," Carmelita teased, "logic indicates you should get a cute little .22, maybe one of those pink ones. Stick it in your sock or something. You won't pay all those tailor bills, getting your suits cut to hide your Glock and all those spare magazines."

"I'm keeping my spare magazines, thanks." Wolfe smiled. "I've run out of ammo twice. You remember the first one—thanks again, by the way—and I don't want to go through that again. Starting off with twenty bullets makes me a lot more comfortable."

"Yeah," said Carmelita with good-humored smugness, "let's see if you still say that when we get to the range and your competitive spirit takes over, and you come crawling to me to borrow my Testosterone Special .45!"

THE FRIGID WEATHER had broken for a while. It was about fifty degrees and sunny on the grassy firing range near Fernan Lake. More than a hundred shooters milled around in the welcome Saturday sun, waiting their turn to fire at the rows of white pins on the dozen or so heavy wooden tables. At the booth set up between the range and the parking lot, huge white scoreboards clocked the times of the contestants.

The tall, rangy man with the unruly black beard was edgy. It had been a rough week for Walter Leonard, and here in what should have been his last refuge, he felt like Heinlein's stranger in a strange land.

Killing a pig, one of the KGB agents of ZOG, qualified you for the coveted title of Aryan Warrior. In a ritual ceremony in the underground bunker of Will's headquarters in Post Falls, Rhino and Danny Queen had been solemnly elevated to the title, as Will quoted from the Bible about Jesus telling his flock to sell their cloaks and buy swords. Yet he, the Armorer, who had pumped out twenty-five rounds, had been denied the honor because the *Idaho Statesman,* the *Spokane Chronicle,* and the *Spokane Spokesman-Review* had all reported that the narc Passeretti had been killed instantly by the shotgun blast, and all the machine-gun bullets had been fired into him after he was already dead.

How could Will take their word? Wasn't it Will himself who told them that ZOG and the Jews ran all the newspapers in the country? And then, for Will to say it was too bad that the ZOG agents who died had been narcotics agents, because they shared the Team's holy mission of eradicating drugs and dope pushers. You couldn't have it both ways! He didn't understand Will at all sometimes.

Then there was Harold's gun he'd made for him. Jesus Christ! How many times had he and Will told them all to never carry a weapon, wallet or anything else that could be traced to identify them or any other member of the Team? Fucking weakling, fainting from a chicken-shit flesh wound in his arm and probably spilling out his guts in the hospital. He knew everyone, knew the location of the bunker in Post Falls. The Aryan Warrior ceremony had been the last thing they'd done there before Will ordered them all to go to ground. Most of them were staying at Will's cabin in the mountains beyond Coeur d'Alene. He had resented at first that Will had never told them of the fallback citadel, but he quickly understood. Will had planned for just this contingency, one of the Team being captured by ZOG and tortured, revealing the headquarters location. Will planned ahead and he was glad of that, at least.

Will had also told them to stay away from their local haunts. Well, screw Will! If he was going to elevate a fat, vicious idiot and a drunken fool who was lucky enough to be in the right place at the right time to the lordly status of Aryan Warrior, and leave the smartest man on the Team out of it, he had no right to tell Walter Leonard what to do! He could accept Thor as a squad leader, before at least, but to give Rhino the same authority and leave him out, just a peasant? Will gave him some bullshit about a technician like himself being on a career ladder, the same as in the Army, and in truth his share of the Team's rip-off earnings was the same as Thor's and Rhino's, and more than the others'. Still, he hungered for the recognition.

That's why he was here. Everyone from his mother on down had told him he was mean and crazy and good for nothing, for as long as he could remember. Guns were the one thing he'd ever been good at. Making them, fixing them, shooting them. Rhino got Aryan Warrior for shooting one big nigger who was a sitting duck? And for shooting a whole clip from a damn M-1 at one little Jap, less than thirty paces away, and only hitting him in the hand? With an infrared nightscope? He was disgusted. He himself would have killed the gook and the coon with one shot apiece!

In this place last year, he had won the match, become state champion. It was the most important thing he had ever done in his life. The gun people didn't like him. All the tight-ass Ward Cleavers, coming home from the range to work at their factories and garages and banks, sneering at him behind his back, not letting him wear his camouflage to the range because they said "it wasn't the image the shooting sport should project."

Dumb-ass yuppies. Same for the Army and Marines, the one Section Eighting him out and the other not taking him at all when they had the chance. No wonder the U.S. Army was so wimpy it couldn't whip anybody but rag-heads and Third World countries, and the Marines got their asses blown to shit by one little camel driver in a truck full of dynamite.

But here, last year, he had shown them. He wouldn't shoot in the open class, where the fancy-britches punks who called themselves "sportsmen" shot their trick pistols with recoil compensators. He had entered the tactical class, for street guns like cops and soldiers carried for real. He used the Colt automatic he'd built himself, grafting its superstructure to the ParaOrdnance frame so it held fourteen .45 slugs. It was identical to the one he'd built for Harold Howe, except his own had a hair trigger that fired as easily as touching an electric typewriter key. Harold would have blown his own ass off with a trigger like that. In retrospect, maybe he should have given him one. Then they wouldn't be hiding out like dogs, wondering what the little pussy was going to say. He'd told Will that he should go down there to the hospital, and either snipe the little bastard through the window with his match rifle he'd built himself, or just walk in and dust him and the cops that guarded him, too. But Will said no because the cops were sticking to him close, and there'd been enough cop-killing already to call the hounds to their trail.

The Armorer felt free and proud for the first time this week. If the pigs of ZOG were waiting for him at the match, well, let them be ready to fight. His 14-shooter was unloaded in its carrying case, the way the wimpy "sportsmen" required, but to hell with their chicken-shit rules about no one carrying loaded guns on the property. His regular .45 was in his belt, under his loose red-and-black lumber jacket. Its eight bullets were enough. If Howe had ratted him out and ZOG was waiting for him, they'd shoot him down by the time he'd fired the eight, anyway. But he'd take eight of them with him, for sure. That much, he swore to himself.

"Next relay," a rangemaster announced over the loudspeaker, and he heard his name called on the list. His heart convulsed in his chest. He was ready to defend his title.

WHEN THEY ARRIVED, Wolfe gave in to an impulse and decided to shoot the match. He was relieved that they had a tactical weapon class. Carmelita had been right about "the old competitive instinct": shooters called their customized target pistols "race guns," and firing a street-duty gun designed for concealed carry against such a precision high-performance machine was like taking a family station wagon or a police cruiser to the starting line at the Daytona 500. Against other street pistols, he should have a fighting chance.

Carmelita's borrowed .45 shot well for Harry. They let him start with the hammer cocked, since pin matches began with drawn instead of holstered guns, so he didn't have to struggle with the long, heavy pull of a Smith & Wesson's first shot. That way, it felt a lot like his familiar Glock. The three-dot sights were similar, too, except that they didn't glow in the dark, but that didn't matter in the bright sunlight.

His turn came, and he shot well. The martial-arts training helped. He tried to zone everything out of his consciousness but the front sight, raking across the table and firing as soon as the middle dot, the front sight, seemed on top of the big white pin. Bruce Lee had called it the empty cup. Empty your cup of thought and of need, he had said, and let your body do battle by itself, doing what it knows it has to do. Western man's own aggressive thoughts, Lee had said, got in the way of his ability to do battle under stress.

They shot in a round-robin format, man against man, until only a handful remained who had not yet been beaten. Wolfe felt good. The exhilaration of competition, and of holding his own, helped burn away the frustration of the screwup at the Spokane bungalow and the investigation that was going nowhere. Gun as catharsis, he thought. Whatever you say about a gun, it's a hell of a stress reliever.

As he waited for his relay to shoot again, he watched the others. There were some good shooters. The guy to beat seemed to be a gangly fellow with an unkempt black beard, shooting a ParaOrdnance .45. There was an intensity on his face that made it seem as if he was taking it too seriously, as if he was shooting in something much more important than a pistol match.

WALTER LEONARD fought the shakes. His mouth was dry, and he kept swallowing involuntarily. He was still undefeated, but the match wasn't over. He was one of four people left who hadn't been beaten in head-to-head competition yet. Bates, a deputy from down in Ada County, was using a big Smith & Wesson .45. He was smooth, Leonard knew, and consistent. Massey from Boise, a holster maker, was quiet but deadly accurate, and quick with his Government Model Colt .45 automatic.

And there was the new guy. Leonard had never seen him before. Pressure didn't seem to get to him when Leonard watched him shoot. Ordinary-looking dude, jeans and running shoes and a plain gray sweatshirt that didn't tell anybody where he was coming from. Short hair, short beard. He could be a regular guy, could be a yuppie. He was shooting with the smaller version of the Smith .45, the 4516 Compact, which was a hard gun to master compared to the Colt. Leonard felt a grudging respect.

But he'd take them, take them all! Just like he had last year. He'd learned the secret.

When he'd first showed up at the range, the yuppies had frozen him out. Told him politely not to wear his cammies anymore, or his T-shirt with the rag-head in the cross-hairs of a scope that said, Terrorism Ends Here. He had burned with the shame. But he'd shot their match last year, and beaten them all, because he'd found the secret.

The secret was not to give a shit. The others got rattled by the pressure, made little mistakes like pressing the trigger too soon instead of waiting one more fraction of a second to be sure the sights were in line. It was the caring that got to them, the caring about what the others thought of them. Hating them, Walter didn't give a damn what they thought. His hatred made him concentrate on the job, on the gun. Every one of those bowling pins was his mother or his teacher or his boss or his sergeant or the Marine recruiter, and he focused on the job of venting his rage on them with righteousness and fury. It worked. He felt the muscles twitching in his face, the way he always did when he was psyched up.

They called him to the line for the semifinals. He felt short of breath. They paired him with Massey, and issued the command to load.

On the whistle, the Armorer tunneled in so hard on what he was doing he didn't even hear the gunfire. He raced the pistol across the table, firing when the bright red gunsights crossed the white of the target, and swept back to shoot anything still on the table. But there was nothing there. He couldn't help looking to his left. Two pins still stood on Massey's table, and the man was struggling with the slide of his pistol. A defective cartridge had jammed a bullet in the breech, and Massey had only gotten three shots off. A wave of relief flooded him. He heard the rangemaster on the loudspeaker intone, "Winner to the right, the defending state champion, tactical class."

One run left, the finalist duel. Clearing his pistol, Walter Leonard shambled back behind the firing line to refill his magazine. The next shoot-off would decide whom he'd face at the climax.

WOLFE HAD WATCHED the last duel. He turned to a pleasant-looking middle-aged man standing next to him and said, "Excuse me, I'm new here. Who are these guys shooting now?"

The man smiled warmly. "I've watched you shoot today, and you're doing great for a newcomer," he said. "The man on the left is Earl Massey, makes holsters for a living, down in Boise. Guy on the right, I forget the name, Leonard something I think. Won tactical last year. The look on his face when they gave him the trophy, you'd have thought he'd been elected President. Takes this stuff real serious. Strange dude. Look how nervous he is, like the fate of the world was riding on it. Heck, it's just a pistol match. But look how wired up he gets."

Wolfe watched. The tall, hollow-faced man seemed to be trembling, tiny fine motor tremors. His eyes were narrowed behind the mandatory shooting glasses, and he kept licking his lips. Standing ready on the firing line for the command to load, the man kept wiping his sweaty palms on his grease-stained jeans and his red-checkered lumber jacket.

Harry felt something that had been gone from him for what seemed too long—pity. Shooting at the range was like golf or tennis, pleasant recreation, a chance to meet good people. He wondered how empty a man's life had to be when recreation, a simple sporting game, became the reason for life itself.

If Harry won the next heat, and the lanky defending champ won his, they'd shoot against each other for the title. Would Harry care if he won? He didn't know a soul here. A pistol trophy meant nothing to him. Carmelita had joked about "the old competitive instinct." Maybe it was time to put it back on the shelf. If it was so important to this poor guy, what the hell.

It was Wolfe's turn to shoot. He didn't care about winning anymore, and the cup was more empty. He actually felt lighter on his feet. He loaded on the command, and the cop on the line next to him did the same. At the whistle the little .45 seemed to move by itself, its sights magically finding each target, and almost going off by itself without Harry's conscious thought. Five shots, five pins gone, and he heard a shot to his right. He'd been a fraction of a second ahead of the cop. "Winner to the left," the loudspeaker said.

Now the finals, him against the nervous guy. Harry felt good. The man came up to the right, glaring at him as if he was an enemy. Harry brushed it off. The guy had a right. Harry *was* an enemy, someone who came into this man's game not giving a damn about it, and threatening the position of a man who apparently lived for this little measure of glory.

"You may handle your weapons and load," the loudspeaker said. Wolfe's borrowed pistol was open, its slide locked back. He shoved a magazine into the butt and let his thumb trip the latch above the trigger, slamming the slide forward. Wolfe held the gun firmly in both hands, his trigger finger outside the guard. He glanced over. The gaunt man had loaded his big .45 and had his finger on the trigger, ready to go. Wolfe saw that the man was trembling slightly. He knew he wouldn't want that man behind him going in on a raid. Probably no one else wanted him, either, Harry reflected, and shooting at overgrown tin cans was the only thing he'd ever do with a pistol.

"Stand by," the megaphone ordered. "Ready." Then came the shrill whistle.

Wolfe raised his pistol with exaggerated deliberation. He didn't want to make it obvious that he was throwing the match; that would hurt the poor guy's feelings more. He heard the first shot next to him, and in his peripheral vision saw that the five pins were still on his opponent's table. The man had missed the first shot.

With icy coolness, Wolfe squeezed off his first shot. His pin flew back. And the second. The gunfire was more rapid on the table next to him. The guy was losing it. One pin was still standing, and two or three were rolling around. The man was firing madly. Wolfe slowly blew his third pin off the table, still looking out of the corner of his eye. One pin was now left in front of the tall man. Wolfe shot his fourth pin dead center, blasting it backward. There was a flurry of shots to his right, and he saw the skinny guy's slide lock back empty on his pistol as his last pin rolled off the table. He'd made it. Wolfe fired his fifth shot, driving his own final pin backward, and pumped a sixth into it as it hovered in midair before falling to the ground.

There was applause in the background. "Winner to the right," the man on the microphone repeated, "And tactical-class state champion for the second year in a row, uh—" the man on the mike was obviously fumbling for the list of shooters' names "—Walter Leonard." There was another flutter of perfunctory applause.

Wolfe cleared his borrowed .45, showed the line safety officer it was empty and thrust it into its case, then walked directly to his right to the gaunt man, whose own trembling hands were putting his empty Colt into its black plastic carrying box.

Wolfe offered his hand. "Damn good shooting," he said. "Congratulations."

As the gaunt man turned suddenly toward Wolfe, he seemed to change into a whole different person.

A wide grin split the scraggly dark beard, revealing teeth that were brown and ugly. Moments before, he had been taciturn, but now he virtually gushed as he thrust his hand toward Wolfe.

"Hey, bro," Walter Leonard said, "that was some fine shootin'. I thought you had me there for a minute."

Wolfe shook his hand and smiled easily. "So did I," he lied. "I'd been watching you shoot and I knew how good you were. I figured my only chance was kind of like hoping the dealer'd go bust...for me to shoot slow and steady and hope you'd go too fast and screw up."

"Shit," said Leonard, "that's just what happened!"

"Yeah." Wolfe smiled, still in his white lie. "But I guess I was a little *too* slow and steady. You whipped me, fair and square."

The tension had left the thin man's body. "Man," he said effusively, "this has been a hell of a day. It's been a hell of a week, tell ya the truth. Listen, amigo, I think I'll go have a few brewskis and celebrate. What do you say you join me?" His tone of voice made it almost a plea.

Damn, thought Wolfe, making the poor guy feel good was one thing, but how do I get out of this?

"Well," Harry began, "I'll tell you, uh, it's Mr. Leonard, right?"

"Walter Leonard," the gaunt man said happily, "but nobody calls me that. All my friends just call me the Armorer."

8

Carmelita Morales wheeled the white Dodge into the parking lot of the shabby roadhouse and parked near the sign that said Stumble Inn. Things were moving fast since the range.

Wolfe had come up to her and whispered insistently, "The Armorer. I've got him with me. You're my girlfriend. Watch what car we get into, and follow us. We're going into town for a drink. Just watch me for cues and play along. You know the drill." He'd slipped her the Smith & Wesson .45 automatic she had lent him to shoot the match.

She checked now to make sure it was still loaded and slipped it into her waistband on the left hip, butt forward. It was bigger through the frame and slide than the 9 mm Smith & Wesson she'd turned in for the ballistic check, and it wouldn't fit her holster, but the tight jeans held it securely in place.

She could see Harry in the rearview mirror now as she parked, already entering the tavern with the tall guy who looked like a mountain man. She put the keys in her pocket and locked the door behind her.

Country music was blaring over the jukebox as she entered the windowless cinder-block building. The stench of cigarette smoke assaulted her nostrils as a nasal voice bemoaned the heartache caused by fickle women.

Wolfe and the cadaverous suspect were already at a table in the one uncrowded corner. The tall man had his back to the wall, and Wolfe was seated to his right. In turn, she pulled up a chair close to Harry's right side, putting her directly across from the Armorer. Before she sat, she leaned over and kissed Harry on the cheek.

"You weren't kidding," the Armorer crowed. "She really is docile and affectionate."

"Told you," said Wolfe, ruffling her hair like a child's. "Latin women are where it's at." Carmelita obediently dropped her head on his shoulder for a moment.

A fat barmaid came by for their order—light beers all around. As she was walking away, the Armorer said, "So, John, what brings you to these parts?"

"Wrong color to stay where I was," Wolfe said. "All set up to be regional director of sales, an' lost it 'cause the boss said we needed more black supervisors. Son of a bitch who stole the job from me's got shit for brains, and he's making damn near twice the money I was. I wasn't gonna take that."

"Know what you mean." The Armorer nodded eagerly. "They're takin' over everywhere. Fuckin' niggers!"

"What do you mean, 'taking over'?" Wolfe sneered. "They already took over, in D.C. at least. That's why I got the hell out."

"You come to the right part of the country," the Armorer said. "Don't no white folks take shit from niggers up here."

"Why do you think I came here?" Wolfe asked. "I've been reading some things on the computer message board. I figure this is where it's at to get away from the damn seagulls."

The gaunt man looked puzzled. "Seagulls?"

"Sure, that's what I call 'em," said Harry. "They cruise all night, they scavenge all day, they breed out of control and the good ol' U.S. government says they're a protected species."

The Armorer howled in laughter. "Seagulls! Oh, man, that's good! I got some buddies gonna laugh their ass off when they hear that." They all fell silent as the waitress arrived with their beers.

"So, whatcha gonna do for a livin' up here, John?" the Armorer asked when the barmaid left.

Harry took a long swallow. "I've been thinking about, ah, alternative life-styles."

The Armorer glanced pointedly at Carmelita. Harry said, "Hey, Consuela, go powder your nose five, ten minutes, okay?"

Burning with anger, Carmelita stayed in character. She smiled demurely, casting her eyes downward like a proper Mexican maiden, and kissed Harry's cheek before she stood and walked to the corner where the ladies' room was.

"Sorry, man, but I don't like to talk business in front of, you know..." The Armorer was hunched forward as he spoke.

"No problem, man," Wolfe answered. "Connie's cool. What's on your mind?"

"You said 'alternative life-styles.' You mean like, survivalism, or what?"

Wolfe glanced around conspiratorially before he answered, "Hey, man, you look around, you can see where this country's going. Few years, between the rag-heads and the Commies and the rest of 'em, only place a white man's gonna survive is gonna be in a self-contained white community. In a place of his own, with his own kind. Some place small, like up here in the forest, where you can seal off the roads when the filth from the cities runs out of food and comes after you for yours."

"Amen, brother," the Armorer breathed enthusiastically. "A survivalist community, is what you're sayin'. I hear ya. There's a whole lot of folks up here think just the same way as you do about it."

"S'why I'm here," said Wolfe. "I've read about groups, the Aryan Nation, and the Team, and the Covenant, Sword and the Arm of the Lord. I figure maybe I'll find a community I can be comfortable in. Community that's got a place for a white man with a strong back and a fast gun, who's fed up with taking shit from lower forms of life."

The Armorer chuckled. "I hear you. Oh, man, I hear you. But, you know, you think about a survivalist community, you're talking about goin' back a hundred years in time. Raise your own corn, raise your own chickens, build your own barn. You got any background in farming, livestock, anything like that? Some kind of trade you can make a living with, an honest white man's kind of living, after the balloon goes up? You said you was in sales. Time's gonna come, after the apocalypse, a man won't be able to sell nothin' less'n he made it with his own hands."

Harry looked away, trying to project weakness. He wanted to make the Armorer feel strong. If you made a man feel strong, he liked you, trusted you, opened up to you.

"Well, hell, Walter, not like you. What you tell me, you could probably make a gun from scratch. Time comes, guns are gonna be real important to everybody, somebody like you, can keep 'em up an' runnin', is gonna be pretty damn important. Me, I can't do much with my hands 'cept fight an' shoot. That's why, y'see, I gotta make my money and pile up my gold before society gets turned over on its ass."

The gaunt man smiled sardonically as he sipped his beer. "And how you figure to do that?"

Harry leaned forward as if to whisper, and the other man reciprocated and bent toward him. "I figure I'll just take it back from the lowlife bastards that took everything away from me, that's how."

The Armorer raised an eyebrow and looked all-knowing. "Tell me more."

"Real simple," Wolfe whispered. "All them seagulls, filthy with drug money? They pay a million dollars cash bond when they get arrested, and then just walk away. The cops confiscate a few million bucks in cash, then piss it away on high-tech snooping devices and shit, so they can fuck with decent people and take away their rights? I figure there's a whole lot better use for all that money. I don't see any reason not to set some of those dope dealers up, and just take 'em off. What're they gonna do, call the cops?"

"Well," said the Armorer condescendingly, "I dunno. Them dope dealers, they're supposed to be pretty tough, all carryin' Uzis an' everything."

Wolfe snorted. "I doubt like hell there's one of 'em can shoot as well as me. An' from what I've seen today, I'll bet my *ass* there ain't one at all can shoot *half* as good as *you.*"

The Armorer's grin widened, showing his decaying teeth. "That's just what you'd be betting, ol' son. Your ass. But I'll tell you what. I like your style. I'm gonna see about gettin' you in touch with some good ol' boys I know."

"I'm up for it," said Wolfe just as Carmelita came back to the table.

She asked in a soft child's voice, "Is it okay to sit back down yet?"

"Sure, honey," the gaunt man said cruelly. "Me an' John here was just talkin' about why spic gals are better'n white bitches, weren't we, Johnny?"

"They damn well are," Wolfe forced himself to say, grinning lecherously as he put an arm around Carmelita's shoulder and pulled her toward him possessively. "They don't give you no shit at all. When they get slapped around, they know they deserved it and they get back to behaving real good. And in bed? Ay, Chihuahua!" He kissed the tips of his fingers like a gourmet. Carmelita just flashed her white teeth modestly.

They left together. Before he walked to his car, the Armorer said, "Stick around your hotel tonight. I might just be gettin' in touch with you. Job offer, maybe. Who knows?"

Once he was out of earshot, Carmelita said, "John?"

"John Patrick," Wolfe answered. "It's the name on my 'clean card,' the AmEx I used to rent the car at the airport. I figure he's gonna memorize the license, find some way to check it. I wanted the story to jell. You're my mistress, Consuela Delgado. You played it beautifully in there, by the way."

"Yeah, right," said Carmelita as they pulled out into the traffic. "You just seemed right down home and natural talking that crap, Billy Bob John-boy."

"Hey." Harry laughed. "Gimme a break. We lucked into something here."

"Of course I'll give you a break," she answered solicitously. "Tell you what, find a camera store and buy some kind of a Polaroid."

"What for?"

"To photograph your private parts."

"Wha—? Why?"

"So you'll have something to remember them by," she said sweetly, "'cause if you make me put up with that kind of bullshit much longer, I'm gonna rip them right off your frame!"

9

"I'm not angry," Will Pelham began angrily.

The Armorer had just told his story. He'd gone to the match and successfully defended his title, and he'd met a hell of a cool guy who was perfect for the Team.

"I'm not angry," Will repeated. "It's good, in a way, that you were dumb enough to go to the range, where they would have been looking for you if Harold had talked. If he had, they would have been all over you."

"I would've taken about eight of 'em with me," the Armorer growled.

Will shook his head, exasperated at the man's machismo. "Spare me that bullshit, Walter," he sighed. "You're sure you didn't pick up a tail?"

"Positive. I was watching for one."

The whole Team was gathered at Will's cabin in the mountains. None of the others had spoken since the Armorer's arrival until now.

Thor said, "Watching for one? Fuck, maybe you brought one back! How do you know this guy ain't another narc, or DEA?"

The Armorer snarled back, "You think I'm a fuckin' idiot? I'm tellin' ya, this guy is one of us! He came out here from the east coast to get away from the niggers. He's been reading about us and the Nations and all on the electronic message boards. He come out here to join up with an outfit like this. He's *great* with a gun, too. Damn near beat *me.*"

The Armorer didn't notice Thor and Will rolling their eyes at his last statement. He continued. "And, get this—he's thought up a way to make his living off the niggers." He paused triumphantly.

After a moment Will said impatiently, "Well?"

The Armorer burst out laughing. "He's gonna set up dope dealers an' rip 'em off," he brayed.

Rhino looked at Will through his thick glasses. "He'll fit right in, then."

Jesus Christ, thought Will. God save me from these idiots. Aloud, he said, "Gentlemen, does it occur to either of you that this is awfully coincidental? It doesn't sound just a little too pat? It doesn't sound a little like some damn government narc from ZOG who knows a little about us and wants to infiltrate us, for Christ's sake?"

After a moment Thor said, "Let's give it a little more thought, Will. We're short two men. We could use another good recruit. Besides, what's to infiltrate? We killed two of their agents and chopped another one in half. If they had a line on us, they wouldn't be trying to sneak a mole in. They'd be outside right now with helicopter gunships, fixing to shoot us into about a thousand different pieces."

Thor turned to the Armorer. "Tell me, careful. This guy talked about niggers, wantin' to off 'em, like we been?"

"Yeah," said the Armorer. "But get this. He calls 'em sea-gulls. Says it's 'cause they cruise all night, scavenge all day, an' the government protects 'em."

Rhino, Danny and J.J. brayed in laughter. The brothers were half in the bag anyway, both swigging from beer cans.

Thor turned back to Will. "There you go," he said. "If this was some narc tryin' to bust us, he'd have to testify about talkin' that trash in court. There'd be coons an' kikes on the jury, an' it'd turn them right against the guy. Even if he denied it, after all of us said he said it, wouldn't no jury believe him. It don't sound like a narc to me, Will."

The white-haired man frowned. "You've got a point," he admitted grudgingly. "And we do need fresh blood. Still, I don't want to touch him with a ten-foot pole until he's proven himself."

Rhino perked up. "Wanna take him on a mission?"

"No," said Will immediately. "It's way too soon. Besides, we don't have anything lined up yet."

Danny Queen's eyes narrowed. "Hey," he said, "why don't you take him out, have him trash a nigger?"

Rhino beamed. The thought of hurting people, especially black people, always pleased him. "Hey, yeah! I can take him out an' do it, Will! Run him over to Spokane, maybe Seattle or someplace."

"He'll do it," said the Armorer solemnly. "Wait till you meet this guy. He hates niggers as much as we do. He had any money, he'd probably pay us for the chance."

"If he's for real," said Will, "he'll ask us what's in it for him."

Thor shrugged. "So we'll have him take off a crack dealer or somethin', give him a piece of the action."

"Let me think," said Will. "The bitch. You said she was a spic?"

"Yeah." The Armorer leered. "Good-lookin' head, too. He says she takes real good care of him."

Will leered. Brown women were his weakness. White ones were connivers, and he wouldn't touch a black one, and yellow ones faked it, but those brown bitches made a man feel like a man. Maybe, if this all worked out...

"Okay," said Will. "Go see him. Set it up for tomorrow. Rhino, you'll go along. Take Danny and J.J. out tomorrow morning, steal a couple of cars. Thor, you'll stay with his brown bitch the whole time. Don't say it to him in so many words if you don't have to, but she's a hostage. Rhino, make sure you pat this guy down for guns and wires and everything."

The Armorer grinned, showing his brown teeth. "You won't be sorry, Will," he said earnestly. "He's gonna work out for us. You'll see."

"Yes," said Will. "I'll see. We'll all see. Walter, you'll see something tonight. You felt it was cool to go out to that damn pistol match where you could have been arrested.... Well, I guess you can head into town and see if the Post Falls house is safe to reoccupy, then."

"I ABSOLUTELY HATE doing this unarmed," said Wolfe as he secured the Glock, the spare magazines and his holster and magazine pouch into the suitcase.

"Then why do it?" Carmelita asked simply.

"We don't have the clean guns," Wolfe replied. "This is a DEA-issue Glock. If these guys have gotten control of a copy somewhere, anyone with access to a National Crime Information Center computer can trace the gun. It'll burn me in a heartbeat. Same with my little ankle gun. They'll trace it to a gunsmith called Trevor Strachan in Georgia. He is an honest guy. A cop asks for info on the serial number, he'll tell him the truth. He custom built it for a DEA agent named Harry Wolfe who was working out of D.C. at the time."

With a sigh, Wolfe ripped loose the Velcro strap that secured the object of the discussion to his leg. He withdrew the snubnose .357 Magnum, looked at it wistfully, then put it in the suitcase.

Carmelita asked, "Do you think I should lose mine, too?"

"No," said Wolfe emphatically. "Keep yours. Keep them both. If they went to search you, putting their hands on what they think is my woman would be a sign of disrespect. It would show that they never intended to accept me. If that's the case, we're both as good as dead if they catch us *both* without guns.

"What I'm expecting, though," he continued, "is that they'll pat me down before we go out on that 'little job' the Armorer called to tell me about last night. Maybe they'll take my guns and maybe they won't, but they'll damn sure memorize the serial numbers, and if they've got a way to check it, we're dead. Remember, that happened to me once before."

Carmelita nodded. "I remember. Thank God BATF got us untraceable guns for that one. Too bad we couldn't have gotten a couple this trip."

"No time," Wolfe answered, closing his suitcase. "I didn't know about this deal until two this morning when the Armorer called, and it's 10:00 a.m. now. We can't risk letting any of the local office people here catch on to a Code Zero operation. If we'd known beforehand that we might be going undercover, sure, we'd have had them. But it looked like a routine chase."

"A routine hunt," Carmelita observed.

Harry looked at her. "You can call it that if you want."

Her eyes met his. "Well," she asked "isn't it? They murdered two of our agents. They crippled a third for life. They deserve Code Zero. You bet it's a hunt."

"It's a job," Harry said. "Not a hunt. Not even a mission. Just a job that has to be done."

She faced him full on. "Still bothering you, isn't it?"

He asked, "What do you mean? Is what still bothering me?"

"The whole thing. The whole Code Zero thing. I mean it, Harry. I sense a real depression in you. That scares me. Depressed people don't care anymore."

"I care."

"Yeah, right," Carmelita said intensely. "That's why you say you hate going to do this unarmed, but you just throw your guns in the suitcase and go on your way. Off with those vicious, murdering assholes."

Wolfe forced a grin. "I don't need a gun for assholes," he said. "That's the good thing about knowing disarming. If I need a gun, it's only as far away as the nearest armed man."

Carmelita made a face. "Ooh, *muy macho, muy macho.* Dammit, Harry, I'm serious! I'm worried about you. You don't even have to do this! Why can't you just meet him alone, the three of us, we'll cuff the ugly bastard and you give him some of your truth juice, and then your special cocktail after we find out where the rest of them are, and do them one by one? Why not do it that way?"

Harry counted off on his fingers. "One, he wouldn't give me a phone number. I can't arrange to meet him before he shows up at the other hotel with the other scumbags. Two, the last one who was administered the Amytal was programmed enough that he couldn't give us last names or addresses. He was all shot up, all doped up, and I have a feeling he was the weakest link in the chain. That means the truth serum may not do everything we need on Walter Leonard, either. Three, if we overpower Walter Leonard and inject him and he doesn't talk, we've lost our lead.

"I didn't like this turning into a dead-end case," Harry continued, "and I liked it even less when I screwed up the one lead we had before. I don't want to botch it. I think what we've got today is our best shot to get inside, find out who and where all these people are. Then we'll do what we have to do."

"I still don't like it."

"I know," Harry said gently. "We don't have to like it. It's not in our job description. Now, pick up some clothes and throw them in with mine in that duffel bag. When we get to that motel we're supposed to have been staying the last couple of days, I want the room to look lived-in."

THE TWO CARS PULLED UP to the Sundown Motel on the edge of Spokane just before noon. Wolfe answered the knock on the door.

Three men stood in the portal. "Hey, Armorer," Harry said. "Good to see you."

"You too, Johnny," the gaunt man said, pumping his hand enthusiastically. "I want you to meet two of my buddies. Teammates, you could say. Rhino, Thor, this is Johnny."

Rhino. That explained what had sounded like Reinhold. And Thor. He was shaking hands with the murderers of the agents. Half of them were right here. If he could just signal to Carmelita to throw him her second handgun, they could get the job fifty percent done right here....

He dismissed the thought, submerging himself in his undercover role, taking the chance to size up the men he knew would soon be his opponents. He shook hands with each of them.

Rhino. Huge. Hard. The hands were thick and callused. The piggy little eyes behind the thick glasses were hard to read, as if there wasn't much behind them. Maybe there wasn't.

Thor. Bodybuilder. He saw the man subconsciously start to pump, defining the muscles, posing. A monumental egotist, Wolfe thought, and a dangerous one. He felt Thor's strength as the big blond man clamped down during the handshake, trying to crush Harry's fingers. He'd been through that before. Harry tightened his own hand, grinned, stared the man in the eye. He didn't win the short contest of strength, but he didn't lose, either. After a moment Thor let go. There was a look of grudging respect on his face.

As Wolfe closed the door behind them, the Armorer said, "Bro, I'm gonna tell ya the score up front. My buddies here had seen a lot of good white men get ratted out by their own kind, and the fact is, they don't trust a whole lot of folks anymore. They said they'd like to pat you down, make sure you didn't have a weapon or anything, before we went out."

Harry shrugged. "No problem, man." He raised his hands submissively. Thor expertly patted him down. All he came up with was the black-handled Spyderco knife. He drew it, opened it two-handed and gently touched the blade. "Neat knife," he mused. He closed the blade and handed it back to Harry, then turned to Rhino and said, "He's clean. Don't sweat the knife."

The Armorer looked at Harry apologetically. "Johnny, I hope you understand, but we thought it'd be a good idea for Thor to stay here. Remember, my buddies don't know you yet, and like I said, they got hurt a few times, trustin' people. If it's okay with you, we'd like to leave Thor here with Consuela. Don't worry," he added hastily, "she'll be okay."

Wolfe forced his face into a knowing leer. "Sure, bro, so long as your buddy Thor realizes she's private stock."

Thor just grinned evilly and flexed his muscles.

"Trust me, man," the Armorer said hastily. "On my mother's grave. She'll be fine."

AFTER THEY'D LEFT, Thor just stared blankly at Carmelita for a while, his acne-scarred face devoid of any expression.

Carmelita asked, "Would you like a drink?"

Thor shook his head. "Don't drink."

"Wanna watch TV?"

Thor said flatly, "I don't give a shit."

She moved to the television, turned it on. She was going to make it CNN, then realized that hard news wouldn't fit her new identity as an airhead. She spun the channel selector to MTV.

Suddenly Thor said, "What do you see in that guy?"

Carmelita put on her demure look, gazing at the floor. "He takes care of me," she forced herself to say in a tiny voice.

Thor despised any sign of weakness. He snorted in disgust. He sprawled into the room's one easy chair.

Carmelita sat primly on the edge of the bed, several feet away from him. Her borrowed .45 automatic was between the mattress and the box spring, more toward his side than hers, but the Airweight .38 Special was tight inside her panty hose, easily hidden by her jeans and baggy sweatshirt. She saw the outline of what looked like a .32 or .380 automatic in his pocket.

If he went for it, she was sure she could get hers out first, could put five plus-P hollowpoint bullets in him before he ever got his out of the pocket.

He didn't say another word, just sat there flexing his muscles and watching MTV.

It was shaping up, she thought, to be a long afternoon.

THE ARMORER was seething inside.

He had wanted to do it in Seattle. No, Will had said, it's five hours each way to Seattle from here. Just go over the state line into Spokane, get it done there.

The Armorer had said that night was the logical time to do it. No, Will had said, if this guy was undercover ZOG, they had to find out now. Go, he said. Get it done.

So here they were, running in the stolen black Chevy hardtop through what passed for the red-light district in Spokane, Washington, in the middle of a weekday afternoon. Harry, Rhino and the Armorer. They'd parked the maroon Ford wagon, also stolen, about ten blocks away in a market parking lot. If they were seen doing anything in this car, they'd have long since changed cars by the time the Spokane cops found the hardtop.

There wasn't much hunting here. Mostly pale, furtive-looking white guys cruising for hookers and slinking in and out of the adult bookstores with the peep shows in the back. The Armorer curled his lip in disdain. He knew what went on in those peep shows, the ones that were pitch-dark inside, with glory holes drilled through the partitions of the film cubicles, groin high. But none of them were the right color. Too bad.

Rhino stopped at a light, looking around, squinting like Mister Magoo. Suddenly he pointed across the street. "That one," he said. "What about that one?"

Wolfe and the Armorer looked. "Shit," said the Armorer, "that's just some nigger whore. We don't wanna do no bitch. That don't prove nothin'."

The light changed, and the car rolled on.

WOLFE LEANED BACK against the cushions of the right front seat. They'd been cruising for more than an hour, and were starting to look conspicuous.

He was struggling with mixed feelings. He knew he was going to have to do it again. Like on his last Code Zero assignment.

Prove himself. Prove himself to assholes, to be an asshole like them. It made him want to vomit.

It also made him scared, because he wasn't sure he could do it.

Hurting people was something he could handle if they deserved it. Killing people, for that matter. But these two wanted him to just beat up on the first black person he saw. Damn it all, he was dealing with monsters.

"Look," Wolfe had told Rhino, "if I just walk up to some black dude and nail him in this neighborhood, you're going to have more of them on you than Tarzan calling the apes for backup."

Rhino had giggled. The Armorer had grunted, "We can handle 'em."

"Yeah," Harry had forced himself to say smoothly, "but you're also gonna have ten of 'em chasing us afterward, and another ten calling the cops with our license tag. Look, there's enough black scumbags around. We'll catch one in the act, do him up righteous. Hell, the other ones'll probably give us a standing ovation. Give it another couple of minutes. We'll find a black scumbag. God knows, there's enough around." He didn't add out loud, "There's sure enough white ones."

The Armorer said, "He's got a point, Rhino. We're gonna do it, let's do it righteous. That's what the Team's all about."

And now they were cruising in silence, going past the musty bars and the X-rated bookstores for what seemed like the twentieth time when Rhino said, "Over there. On the left. Check it out."

Wolfe sat bolt upright, looking left as Rhino slowed. "Lower your window, so we can hear what they're saying," Wolfe snapped.

Across the street a tall black man in a knee-length black leather coat was holding a pretty black woman. His fists were wrapped around both her upper arms, and he was shaking her like a terrier shaking a rat. As the window came down, Wolfe could catch snatches of what he was shouting at her.

"Fuckin' useless bitch," he was saying. "No good to me, no good to nobody else. I pay your lawyer, I keep your nose fed, you don't do nothin' all day but nod off on the fuckin' corner.

You best peddle that ass, bitch, else you ain't gonna have no fuckin' ass to peddle!"

"Pimp," said the Armorer sagely. "Givin' one of his whores a hard time. Whadda ya think, Johnny? That look righteous enough for ya?"

For the first time that day, Wolfe's anger extended out of the car and away from the two killers he was with. He had always felt a contemptuous rage toward men who brutalized women, toward people who had power and abused it with people who didn't.

"Yeah," said Wolfe, not realizing that his voice was beginning to deepen into a low growl. "Yeah. That's just about righteous enough."

The Armorer asked, "Need a gun, Johnny?"

"No," said Wolfe. He unbuckled his seat belt and started to reach for the door handle when Rhino gunned the accelerator and swung the hardtop into a hard, screaming U-turn toward the pimp and the helpless prostitute. Caught off guard, Wolfe had to drive his foot into the floorboard to keep from being thrown out of the car.

The car squealed to a loud, conspicuous stop a few feet away from the black man in the leather coat.

Wolfe thought, Idiot!

He had planned to quietly slip from the car, smash his fist down once or twice on the pimp's neck with a brachial stun, and drop him helpless in the street. The man would have recovered within an hour. But now surprise was gone. The fat, myopic cowboy next to him had drawn the attention of everyone within three blocks, including the big dude in the long leather coat, who now thrust the woman away and turned toward the car, fists on hips, staring at Wolfe defiantly.

So much for the element of surprise. Now it was going to be tough.

Wolfe stepped out of the car.

The tall black man yelled, "What you want, asshole? You fuckin' got somethin' to *say* to me?"

Behind him, Wolfe heard the left car door open as Rhino began to get out, and the right front seat bump forward as the Armorer struggled to bail out of the two-door vehicle. Glancing around, Wolfe could see a lot of angry black faces.

If the crowd thought three white guys were beating up a black man, they could turn quickly into a mob. Maybe Wolfe and Rhino and Walter Leonard would all be killed. Maybe one of the other two would pull guns and kill somebody. Most certainly they'd be surrounded by a riot squad of cops before they could ever get out of there.

Wolfe yelled over his shoulder, "Stay back. Stay back! He's mine!"

The two Team members froze. So did the gaggle of spectators on the sidewalk. Thank God for that, Wolfe thought. Only one to deal with now.

"Hey," yelled the pimp. "Answer me, you fuckin' whitey! You got somethin' to say to me or not?"

"Yeah," answered Wolfe, his voice clear and hard. "I got somethin' to say to you. I don't like to see women getting shoved around."

"None of your fuckin' business!" the pimp spit back. "You just wanna show off for your white friends. You just wanna gimme a hard time 'cause I'm black!"

Wolfe moved steadily forward, watching the man's elbows and knees. These median joints would give him the first warning that his opponent was going to launch a punch or a kick.

"Bullshit," Wolfe barked at the pimp, loud and clear for the witnesses. "I don't care that you're black. I'm gonna slap you down 'cause you're yellow!"

Rage contorted the pimp's face. He swung his foot up in a straight-legged kick, the pointy toe of his alligator shoe homing for Wolfe's crotch.

Harry pivoted easily at the hips, pulling himself out of the way as the foot went past, missing him by inches. Finishing the pivot, he threw himself into a spinning back kick. His heel crashed into the chest of the pimp, who was already off balance from his own missed kick. The pimp grunted harshly at the impact, stumbled backward and sprawled on his back in the street.

Wolfe moved slowly forward, a mocking grin on his face. From the corner of his eye, he could see that the crowd hadn't moved. A few were smiling. He heard an old black man cackle with laughter and cry, "This like that Iraq-Iran war. Shithead against shithead. Who cares who wins?"

The pimp scrambled to his feet, his eyes narrowed with fury. He lunged at Wolfe, swinging wildly.

Harry ducked under a looping left hook and countered with his own left, digging his left heel into the ground so his whole body weight was behind the uppercut that caught the bigger man in the solar plexus. He felt the air come out of the pimp in a rush.

Wolfe followed with a right cross, what his sensei called a reverse punch. The pimp's mouth was open from the shock of the blow to his diaphragm, and as Harry's fist connected with the side of the man's chin he could feel the jaw snap loose.

The man stumbled back, starting to fold. Wolfe saw his opening. He raised his right knee to his own chest, "chambering" the leg, then let drive with a powerful side kick that caught the other man square in the center of the black leather topcoat. He could feel the cartilage give way as the pimp's ribs broke. With a strangled sound, the man fell onto his back in the middle of the street, then rolled slowly onto his belly, starting to curl into a fetal position.

Wolfe glanced around. The woman the pimp had been slapping around was surrounded by two or three other black girls, also wearing cheap too-tight clothes, and overly made-up. The other hookers were pulling her away from the scene. Wolfe started to breathe easier. Throughout the fight, he'd been afraid that she'd try to jump on his back to rescue her pimp. He hadn't wanted to hurt her, and he was glad she was out of it. Abused women often came to the defense of the abusers. It was part of the syndrome. Wolfe knew it wasn't their fault.

He turned away and began walking toward the car. Rhino and the Armorer were inside, grinning, thumping each other on the shoulder. He moved toward them.

Then he saw their faces change.

Their eyes widened and their jaws dropped. Rhino just sat stupidly. The Armorer gestured wildly. From the sidewalk, Wolfe heard the simultaneous shouts.

"Watch it!"

"Kill him!"

"Cut the honkie bastard!"

Harry pivoted.

The pimp was back on his feet. In his right hand was a knife. Actually, Wolfe recognized, more than than just a knife.

The blade was called a tanto. Harry knew it from the dojo. In the days of the Japanese warrior, the katana, or samurai sword, had been the primary weapon of battle, and the tanto had been its backup. Nine inches long, with a gently curving blade that came to an off-angle chisel point, the lower edge was wickedly sharp. The spine of the blade was thick and heavy. It had enough sharpness and weight to punch through a car door in a stab, and to turn a slash into a cleaverlike chop that could amputate a limb.

Wolfe felt time suspended, space extended. He was weightless. He became a creature of his training.

The big man shambled relentlessly forward, the knife pointed out ahead of him, probing in deadly circles as the sunlight glinted off the wicked blade. Wolfe thought about going for his own knife, then made the conscious decision not to.

God damn you, he thought. You beat up women. You take girls and fill them with drugs and send them out on the streets. I was just going to give you a brachial stun, and an hour later you would have been fine. But you tried to kick my testicles apart, and now you're going to kill me.

They circled each other. Wolfe's hands were out in front of him, loose and ready, and he felt his body dodge automatically out of the way as the pimp lunged.

You cheap excuse for a man, Wolfe's separate consciousness thought as his body moved on automatic pilot. You're going to kill me? It's funny, in a way.

Someone in the crowd yelled, "Look out! White guys in that car got guns!"

Without looking away from his opponent, Wolfe raised his hand, palm toward the car, the universal human gesture for *stop*. "Don't," he yelled. "I told you! He's mine!"

With a strangled cry of hatred, the big pimp lunged at Wolfe. The point of the knife was ahead of him, and he drove forward with his whole body weight, aiming at Harry's heart, intending to impale him like a vampire on a wooden stake.

Wolfe's pivot was reflexive. With his left palm, he slapped the back of the attacker's knife hand, deflecting it past him. He brought up his right hand, locking it in a hard claw around the pimp's knife hand.

Then he swung his left hand under the man's knife arm, catching the inside of the elbow with a cupping slap, and Harry threw his own left leg back as he pulled the elbow toward him, thrusting out and forward with his right hand.

The momentum and leverage were enormous. The movement jerked the attacker forward and off balance, pulling him onto his own knife.

It happened so fast that Harry didn't feel the knife enter the man's chest until the arm and body convulsed in his hands. Harry looked down. The blade had disappeared completely into the pimp's black coat. His hand, and Harry's on top of it, still clutched the black rubber handle.

Someone on the sidewalk screamed, "Oh, Lord, look! The point stickin' out his back!"

They froze together, in a tableau. The pimp's face was inches from Harry's, staring into his eyes with unbelieving horror. A bloody froth began to grow at his lips. Wolfe felt the other man's knees starting to give way.

"No more," the bloody-faced man pleaded through the broken jaw. It was a child's voice now. "No more. Don't hurt me no more."

In the distance Wolfe could hear sirens. It was time to go. Wolfe held the man's hand and arm tight, and whispered, "Remember this. Remember when the girls said that to you, and then remember this, forever. Remember!"

Wolfe shoved the man away. He fell heavily to the pavement, clutching with both hands the handle of the knife that protruded from the side of his chest. Harry turned and sprinted toward the car. The door was open. As soon as he dived in, Rhino put the accelerator to the floor.

There was a heavy blue-steel automatic in the hand of the wild-eyed Armorer in the backseat. Harry ducked as the G-force of the speeding car threw them around inside. He hoped the pistol wouldn't go off by accident. It didn't.

"Hang on," yelled Rhino. He spun the Chevy through the intersection in a racing drift, the tires screaming, as Harry braced himself as best he could. Behind him he could hear horns honking and the sounds of other drivers standing on their brakes. Then the street scene was gone from sight, far behind them, as if it had never happened.

BACK IN THE STREET, the pimp lay on his back, gasping like a fish with the pink froth running down his chin. The sirens were drawing closer.

A slim black woman in an electric blue, skintight dress stepped off the curb and walked toward the man in the street. She stood over him.

"Hey, Leon," she taunted. "How it feel? You remember the night you beat me with the coat hanger 'cause I didn't bring you home enough money? Remember how I begged you to stop, an' you kept hittin' me? How does it feel now, Leon?"

On the sidewalk someone yelled, "Call him an ambulance."

"Shee-it," another voice responded. "You deaf or what? You hear them sirens?"

"Dumb shit," the first voice responded, "that ain't no ambulance, that's the fuckin' police. They won't do him no good. Hey, girl, you in the blue dress! Come on, call him an ambulance."

The woman in the blue dress giggled. "Okay," she yelled back cheerfully.

She hawked deep in her throat, and then spit in the fallen man's face. As the glob of yellow phlegm rolled down his bloody cheek, she shouted at him, "Hey, Leon, you an ambulance!"

10

When one car pulled in instead of two, outside the motel door, Carmelita listened acutely. Thor, who had not said another word in all these hours, jumped to his feet and went to the window, his hand going into his pocket on the pistol as he edged the window curtain open and peered through it.

"They're back," he said, unlocking the door.

Wolfe and Rhino and the Armorer entered. Wolfe smiled at her in a carefree way and winked. "Hi, honey. Did the big guy behave?"

Carmelita knew her role. She smiled softly, looked down and said, "Yes, he was a perfect gentleman. We were watching MTV."

Thor didn't say anything. He just looked at Rhino. The big man with the glasses burbled, "Thor, it was fuckin' *primo!* He knifed a nigger with the nigger's own knife!"

The Armorer reached over and slapped Wolfe on the back. "How'd it feel, huh? One less seagull to trip over at the beach, right?" The gaunt man winked.

Harry just winked back. He glanced at Carmelita. She hadn't missed a beat. Her eyes were still cast to the floor, like an obedient, demure Mexican maiden's.

"Hey, bro," said the Armorer. "We gotta run. We got a guy to see. See about a job. For you, my man. You done fuckin' great!"

Hands were shaken all around. Then the three Team members trooped out. Wolfe stood in the doorway and waved as they left in the stolen station wagon. The other stolen car, the Chevy, had been abandoned in the Spokane parking lot as planned.

He closed the door, locking it behind him. Carmelita started to speak, and he touched the tip of his finger to his lips to call for silence. He made a gesture with his hand like a kid playing guns. Carmelita realized he wanted a pistol. She walked over to the other side of the bed, pulled the compact Smith & Wesson from under the mattress and handed it to him.

They were wordless. Harry pulled the magazine out of the gun, saw that the clip was loaded with seven rounds and shoved it back into the butt. He pulled the slide partway back until he could see the brass case of the ready-to-go chambered round through the ejection port, then eased the slide forward again. Carmelita had left it on Safe. That irritated him. You didn't have to do that with a double-action pistol like this one. He flipped the lever to Fire. Before he put it away, he mouthed the words, "Got your other one?"

Carmelita nodded yes, and he shoved the gun into his waistband behind his right hip, then beckoned her into the motel bathroom. She followed and watched as he turned on the faucets full blast, in both the sink and the shower. Carmelita reached over and pulled the shower curtain shut so it wouldn't splatter on the floor. Harry reached over and pulled it open again, and beckoned to her once more.

As she turned to him, he took her in her arms and put his mouth next to her ear.

He whispered, "Leave it on. Drown out sound. Did the bastard plant any kind of a listening device?"

"I don't think so," Carmelita whispered back. "He came into the bathroom here a couple of times, and I sort of had him in peripheral vision. I don't think he planted anything."

"Let's check," he whispered back, barely audible in her ear over the rush of the water. "Then let's get the hell out of here. We have to talk."

THE TEAM WAS GATHERED around the funny-shaped table in the living room of Will's country cabin, the one that had been made out of a cross section from a big tree. "It was primo," Rhino kept saying. "I'm tellin' ya, fuckin' primo!"

Will looked toward Thor, who nodded in confirmation. Thor was the only smart one in the bunch, and Will considered him his eyes and ears, his information filter, for what really happened when the Team went into the field.

The acne-scarred blond man nodded. "I wasn't there, but it sounds kosher. News oughta be on in a minute. It's almost six. Turn it to the Spokane station."

J. J. Queen got unsteadily to his feet and turned on the television. The Armorer said, "You should've seen it, Will. Nigger pimp was about twice as big as he was. Johnny did that karate shit, kicked him around like a ninja turtle. You could hear it from the car. Sounded like when you hit somethin' with a baseball bat. Then the jig pulled a knife on Johnny from behind when he was walkin' away. Me an' Rhino, of course, we come up with our guns, but Johnny just waved us off. Danced around him for a bit, then just grabbed the black bastard's arm, swung him around and stuck the prick right through the chest with his own pig-sticker. Left him there holdin' it, layin' on his back in the gutter. Slicker'n shit, man!"

"Here it is," J.J. interrupted, turning up the volume on the set.

"In downtown Spokane tonight, what may have been a racially motivated incident left a city man in critical condition at Deaconess Hospital. With more from the scene, here's Jan Brown, 'Eyewitness News.' "

The scene cut to a city street, with an attractive brunette in a beige topcoat standing in front of the camera. "That's the place," Rhino cried. "That's where we done it!"

Will shushed him just as the newswoman began to speak.

"On this Spokane street this afternoon," she said in a clear strong voice, "Leon Baldwin, 31, a black man, was beaten and stabbed. He is in critical condition tonight at Deaconess, suffering broken jaw and ribs, and a knife wound in the chest. A racial incident? An ordinary streetfight that got out of hand? Witnesses say it may be something else."

The camera cut to an elderly black man with iron gray hair. "I *seen* it," the man said adamantly. "The guy got cut, he asked right out, you hassling me 'cause I'm black, and the white guy say, no, man, I'm hassling you 'cause you're yellow. 'Cause, see, the black guy, he was slapping this whore, slapping her all around and shaking her, and this car with white guys swings around and the one with the beard gets out, and pretty soon they're going to town, you know?"

The scene cut back to the reporter holding a foam-wrapped microphone in front of a slender black youth wearing wrap-around sunglasses. "I seen it all," he was saying to the camera. "Man be mindin' his own business, talkin' to his woman, an' this black sedan with three, four big white dudes come up and pull guns, hold guns on that man while one of 'em stomps him an' stabs him!"

Another cut. This time a heavyset black woman was on camera. "The man who was stabbed was beating that poor girl. I know who he is. He's a pimp. One man on the whole street had the guts to stop him. After he beat him up and was walking away, the pimp tried to stab him in the back and the man turned his own knife on him. This wasn't a black or white thing."

Now the pretty reporter filled the screen again. "Racist or rescuer? There are witnesses who claim both," she intoned. "Meanwhile, Leon Baldwin is in critical but stable condition after being stabbed through the right lung, and the investigation, police say, continues."

The station's theme came on then, and as the screen cut to an automobile commercial, Will gestured for J. J. Queen to shut off the television. J.J. scrambled to obey.

The Armorer crowed triumphantly, "What'd I tell ya? He done fine. The place in Post Falls is clean. It's all goin' great, Will! We got us a new recruit who's gonna be super. Man, oh man, the Team is *back!*"

Will Pelham just grunted. He was lost in his own thoughts.

From what his men were telling Will, this new guy Johnny seemed to have half a brain, at least, and all things considered, that would be a refreshing change from what he'd been dealing with. Rhino could keep the peace through intimidation, but Will couldn't avoid facing the fact that the man was incredibly stupid. Thor wasn't stupid—indeed, he had a certain native animal cunning—but Will had long suspected that the pumped-up muscles hid a yellow streak as bright as Thor's platinum blond hair. Besides, he sensed that Thor lacked the fundamental driving hatred of minorities that bonded the others to Will. Thor was out for Thor.

That was fine—Will was out for Will—but another strong, smart man, another alpha male, would always be a contender for leader of the pack. Will longed for a strong man, a fighter, someone as smart as Thor if not as smart as Will, and someone who could command fear the way Rhino did, without sacrificing allegiance to Will.

Perhaps this Johnny was the guy.

"Very well," Will said grandiosely. "Armorer, he's your find. Tomorrow we move back into the Post Falls headquarters. The day after tomorrow, we'll bring him in for a meeting."

None of the others noticed that Thor was frowning.

WHEN THEY'D CHECKED into the little mom-and-pop motel, the old lady at the desk had told Carmelita and Harry how lucky they were to be in the area and how they must see the sights. She had chirped out the directions to places like the falls while Harry had filled out the register with the false names of Johnny and Consuela.

Now, suddenly, he thought of the waterfall the woman had told him about, the one where the explorer Post had signed the treaty with the Indians, the landmark that had given the nearby hamlet of Post Falls its name. Trusting his memory for the directions, Harry drove there as he and Carmelita talked.

"I want to ask you a question," Wolfe was saying as he pulled the car into the parking lot by the power station. They could hear the roar of the falls in the distance. It was twilight now, but there was still enough light to touch the mists of the river like a rainbow.

"Shoot," said Carmelita, stepping out of the white Dodge.

"Hypothetical question," said Wolfe. "Ethics question. You're an undercover narcotics agent. The other side won't accept you until you do drugs with them. Do you do drugs with them?"

"No," Carmelita replied automatically.

"Why not?"

"It's a contradiction in terms to break the law to arrest a lawbreaker," she answered immediately. "Besides, it violates regulations and costs the agent her job. In addition to which, of course, it kills your case in court."

"Right," said Wolfe. "Second hypothetical. You're an undercover narcotics infiltrator trying to get inside a ring. They tell you there's a rite of passage. You have to find some black man and 'do' him. They don't say kill him, but they make it clear they want the guy at least badly beaten. Do you do it?"

"You mean, just pick out some black person on the street and nail him? No, of course not."

They were drawing closer to the thundering falls, walking slowly. "I'll modify the hypothesis now," said Wolfe. "Same situation, but you are with them. You see a black man assaulting someone, say stealing an old lady's purse. Does that change anything?"

Carmelita shrugged. "Sure. I wouldn't let him get away with mugging an old lady, anyway. If I can kill two birds with one stone, what's wrong with that?"

"I'm not sure," said Harry, and he began to tell her what had happened that day.

THOR WALKED ALONE outside, under the pines that surrounded Will's cabin in the mountains, and brooded in the gathering dusk.

He didn't like this Johnny shit at all. The man wasn't afraid of him. He could tell that. Thor didn't trust people who weren't afraid of him. They couldn't be controlled.

The only two on the Team he hadn't intimidated were Rhino and Will. Rhino respected him, though, and looked to him for guidance. That was enough. It gave Thor a sufficient hold on him. If he didn't totally control Rhino, well, at least Rhino was not an actual threat.

Will? First of all, Thor wasn't altogether sure he didn't intimidate the Team's leader. He saw the envious way Will sized him up when he wasn't looking. Puny, potbellied old fart! Of course Will envied the sculpted body of Thorvald Van Houten. A man who envied you was, by Thor's definition, a man who feared you.

Thor knew he was the de facto second in command of the team. He couldn't afford this Johnny to come in and push him aside. He ran his fingers over his rutted cheeks. Goddamn acne! Without it, he'd have a face to match his golden hair and his tremendous physique.

Thor had tried one of the new miracle drugs for acne sufferers, but the medication had provoked a nasty reaction with the anabolic steroids. The inflammation in his joints had been nightmarish. He had felt like a crippled old man for months. He couldn't give up the 'roids; they'd become his life. But he'd had to stop the acne medication, and without it, his pimpled face was more raw and ugly than ever.

Pizza-face. That's what they started calling him in junior high, when the carpet of red pustules had begun to blanket his features. Not just pimples. Not even just acne. There wasn't a square inch of skin on his face that hadn't erupted. His mother and his stepfather told him that it was his hormones and his dirty thoughts. If he didn't stop his dirty thoughts, he'd turn into a pizza-face forever.

He had wallowed in guilt and shame...and, of course, in sexual fantasy. Subconsciously he believed that it was his unrequited lust for the pretty young girls at school that had disfigured him, that had made him have to endure the white-hot rage of being tormented about his appearance.

Then he had discovered bodybuilding at the YMCA. He'd been a beginner in his prime growth years, and his body's response to the barbells had been satisfying. By twenty, now a high school dropout living on the proceeds of minor crimes, he had discovered anabolic steroids.

People had left him alone after the first couple years of developing his strength. But as the steroids exploded his body into something that looked like the cover of a weight lifting magazine, people had not just left him alone...they'd shown him their fear.

No one looked at the pitted face anymore. Now they looked at the shoulders and the neck muscles. Contempt had turned to awe. For him, the steroids had been the miracle drug that had changed his life.

No one had liked him before. No one seemed to like him now. But their fear was so much more welcome than their contempt.

And the 'roids had taken the other thing—the source of his shame. The lust that had tormented him in his teenage years was long gone now.

He didn't need girls. Or boys. Or anyone. All he needed was himself. He'd read that bullshit about steroids killing sexual desire, but he didn't think that's what it was. He was convinced that his bodybuilding had made him so much more of a man that he didn't need the other stuff anymore to prove his masculinity. And that other stuff, about it atrophying your testicles? Well, that was bunk, too.

His testicles hadn't shrunk. He was convinced of it. They just looked smaller, that's all, because of the contrast with his huge, powerful thighs. Yes, that was it.

So why didn't this Johnny fear him?

Well, maybe he did. Maybe Thor had just read him wrong. Johnny was about average size, in what some dumb yuppie would probably call good shape, but his body was no match for Thor's.

Still, the stories of the fight disturbed him. Was this Johnny some black-belt karate jock? They talked about him spinning and kicking this guy all over the place. Well, from the way they described him, the nigger was just a string bean, some tall skinny coon with no strength to him, probably all fucked up on alcohol and drugs anyway. Thor could take Johnny—he was sure of it.

Besides, he had something else to fall back on.

His hand caressed the Walther automatic in his pocket. The stainless .380 was identical to the one Will carried. If his fists failed, this wouldn't. It was the gun he'd fired at the DEA agent. He had wanted to throw it away after it jammed, until the Armorer convinced him that it wasn't the gun's fault, that any automatic would jam if a man was holding it by the slide when it went off. He'd taken Thor out into the woods, and they'd put a hundred shots through the gun, two boxes, before Thor accepted that the gun really did still work. They had to test the gun anyway. The Armorer had put in a new barrel and shell extractor and firing pin, and had filed over the face of the breech. That way none of the marks on the bullet he had fired into the car or the spent shell casing he'd ejected from the gun by hand at the scene while fixing the jam could be traced to the pistol.

Johnny? Maybe. If Thor could bend him to his own intentions, Johnny might be an asset. If not, well . . .

His hand went unconsciously to the pistol again.

THEY STOOD on the cliffs over the river as the white water from the falls crashed to the rocks two hundred feet below. Dusk had turned to dark. In the moonlight Harry finished telling Carmelita about the day's events.

She said, "And you're asking me about ethics? Harry, if you'd been on vacation and you'd driven by and seen that pimp roughing up that poor girl, you would have stopped and done exactly the same thing. Don't tell me you wouldn't. I know you.

"This way, you got a bonus. You got inside these bastards. Ethically it's actually kind of ironic. If the Team hadn't wanted to hurt an innocent victim, you wouldn't have been there to help an innocent victim. God knows what that pimp would have done to her if you hadn't come along. Maybe he would have used the tanto knife on her. What you did wasn't bad, Harry. What you did was good. Good for the girl, good for the mission. Good for the pimp, maybe. If he lives, maybe he'll stop being a scumbag."

Wolfe looked into the foam at the base of the falls below. "Carmelita," he asked, "do you think I'm losing it? Do you think I'm going soft?"

She wrapped her arm in his and pulled it to her tightly. "That's two questions, partner. Have you still got it? Hell, yes! Great timing, great technique—no, don't stop me, I know that's not what you meant, but I'm saying it for a reason.

"Now, the other thing. Do I think you're getting soft? No. I thought for a while that *you* thought you were getting soft, or losing it, or whatever you want to call it. But you can't think that after today. You fought beautifully. And, Harry, you fought justly.

"Some people can't do that," she continued. "They fight for the wrong reasons, hurt people for the wrong reasons. Like the Team. Some people are good, they're righteous, but they can't fight. Or at least, they can't fight effectively. Hey, I know it sounds cornball, but you fight very well. And you fight for right."

Harry squeezed her arm reciprocally. "Thanks," he whispered. "I guess I just needed to hear that. Look, I think I got in the door today. I think something's going to break soon. When it does, we're going in. There aren't that many of them. We should be able to finish it, quick and clean."

Carmelita said, "I wish we could come up with some good excuse, how we knew it was them. Something to get around the Amytal, get around you beating the crap out of the black guy while you were out with the good-ol'-boy white racists. If we could just bring in a full raid team!"

Wolfe nodded. The cool mist rising from the falls felt good on his face. "Yeah, well, if you come up with some great excuse like that, let me know. In the meantime, like they say, 'It's you and me, kid.'"

"Why not at least bring in another Code Zero person? Right now it's five of them and two of us. Even three of us would be a quantum leap in the odds."

Wolfe nodded. "Assignment of more personnel to a Code Zero op is always up to the director," he explained. "If you want it, I'll go along with it. But I'm not sure we'll need anyone else. Once we know where we can get them all at once, you and I can take them easy if we move first. The director doesn't like one hand to know what the other's doing in Code Zero. That may be the single biggest weakness in the concept. If it ever got out that we're doing what we're doing, it could take down the whole Administration. It'd be bigger than Watergate."

Carmelita was frowning now, but she nodded. "I understand. Should we at least get some extra guns? All we've got now are DEA weapons. Our backup guns are traceable to us personally. Your 9 mm and my .45 are listed to the local DEA office. And we don't have shotguns or SMGs."

Wolfe shrugged. "Again, we can if you want. It'll take time, though, and people will know about it. I think we can get in close and do it fast. If we can't, we'll get whatever we need."

"I still feel like we're flying by the seat of our pants," said Carmelita.

"You have good instincts," Harry replied. "That is exactly what we're doing."

11

It was morning of the next day. Light streamed through the windows of the dowdy little motel room. Harry glanced over. Carmelita was sleeping on the far side of the bed, wearing panties and one of his T-shirts.

They'd decided to stay together. The possibility of surveillance was always real, and they'd come too far now to break their cover.

He hadn't touched her. But, God, he had wanted to.

He fought the *L* word. He accepted that he felt a magnetic attraction to her, though. He could see the dark aureolae of her nipples as her firm breasts pushed his T-shirt taut before she slipped under the covers.

There had been silence. She was, he knew, the kind of woman who would leave it up to him to make the first move. The thought of doing so had paralyzed him.

This woman had once saved his life. He had once saved hers. She was the strongest woman he had ever known, and something in him deeply needed her to respect him. If he made a pass at her and she took it the wrong way, a relationship as important as any he'd ever had in his life would be jeopardized. It was a risk he didn't dare take.

His mind took that ball and ran with it. *Didn't dare.* That was the crux of the crisis he was going through right now.

The incident the previous day had taught him a lot. There was no more doubt about ability. He wasn't sure there ever had been. When it had gotten down and dirty with the pimp in the street, his training had taken over, and he was frankly pleased that he had performed well. The man hadn't laid a glove on him. Harry had been too long away from the dojo, and it was good to know that the techniques still worked. There wasn't even any lingering soreness in his hamstrings, the way he would have expected after connecting with a high kick after being away from the heavy bag and the mat and the stretching exercises for so long.

Less totally satisfying was the way he felt about the act itself. Hell, it wasn't as if it had been *his* idea to go out and pound a black man!

The pimp had been shaking that girl violently. He was going to hurt her, that was for sure, one way or another. And Harry had stopped that.

If Rhino hadn't been so precipitously stupid, it would have been clean and simple: one or two economical blows to the brachial plexus, the man down twitching in the street, and Harry walking away like a proud tomcat with his tail in the air. But the man had tried to cripple him for life with that kick between the legs, and things had changed pretty damn quick.

He had deserved everything he'd gotten after that. The kicked-in ribs, the broken jaw. And trying to knife Harry in the back...

Wolfe hadn't been wearing his bulletproof vest. It would have broken his cover. Scumbags generally associated vests with cops. That knife would have skewered him like a shish kebab if he hadn't picked up on it in time. It would have gone through Harry's spine and heart as effortlessly as it had pierced the pimp's body through and through.

And, when he and Carmelita had driven back from their talk at the falls, there had been a note on the door from the old lady who ran the motel. It said, "Be there at midnight. Your friend said he'd call. He wouldn't leave a number." Below it was another note that read, in the same hand, "Please see me in the office—Manager."

Wolfe had walked to the motel office. "I'm sorry, sir," the old lady had said primly but firmly, "but I go to bed at eleven o'clock sharp. When I turn lights out, I turn the switchboard off."

Terrific. There wouldn't be anyone to take the midnight call. Harry had paid her fifty dollars in tens so she'd stay up until half-past midnight.

At twelve on the dot, the phone had rung. It was the Armorer. He was brief. He said, "Remember where we had the drink after the match? Tomorrow night at eight. You passed the hazing, my friend. Now you're in the fraternity. A very special fraternity. The one you came out here for, you might say." Then he'd hung up.

Now it was morning, and Harry sat up looking at the back of the beautiful woman who was sleeping on her side next to him, untouched.

His erection was persistent, not just a morning erection. There was a deeper emotion than lust keeping it insistently up. Still, he didn't dare act on it. He remembered the time she had been kidnapped. He'd never really talked with her about the helplessness she'd felt, drifting in and out of consciousness from a severe injury. He knew, though, that he would never touch this woman until she expressly asked him to.

He slid out of bed softly, so as not to wake her, and reached inside his briefs to try to reposition himself, make the protuberance less obvious as he walked past her. It was useless. He just walked quickly into the bathroom.

As he waited for the tumescence to die down enough to allow him to empty his bladder, he decided a cold shower was definitely in order.

CARMELITA MORALES sensed the movement next to her in the bed, and for an instant she froze, like a rabbit hearing a coyote nearby. Then the training took over, and her toned muscles coiled for the movement toward the .45 automatic on the night table beside the bed.

In one instant more, she had hit full, alert wakefulness and the memory bank told her, It's all right, it's Harry. She relaxed.

The whole procedure, from sleep to the start response to the beginning of the draw to Hey, body, it's okay, had taken perhaps one second.

In the near-total darkness of the room, she watched through lidded eyes as he padded softly around the end of the bed toward the bathroom, not looking at her. The darkness hid her smile as she saw him walking edgeways so she couldn't see his front. Hiding a morning erection, no doubt, she thought.

He looked good in just the white briefs. Lean, a good V to his upper body, a pleasing pattern of body hair. He was better looking every time she laid eyes on him.

She had wanted him to take her last night.

If she'd said that in front of her mother, Mama would have crossed herself and said twenty Hail Marys, then called in the priest to do an exorcism. It was not an appropriate thought for a good little Mexican girl, she thought as she smiled to herself, but it was her thought nonetheless.

She liked men. She enjoyed men. She could feel her biological clock ticking. She also found damn few men she could take seriously.

When they found out what she did for a living, most of them were turned off. Of the rest, well, when they found out that she was an unarmed combat instructor at the DEA school on the FBI Academy grounds at Quantico, teaching men as well as women, a good portion of the survivors lost interest.

And the rest? They would find out eventually that she was *that* Carmelita Morales. The one who had been the sole DEA survivor of the ambush in the Great Lakes where so many agents had died. She had been the one who was shot in the head and miraculously survived, kept hostage for days, naked and helpless with the head wound that had scarred her for life. The object of a nationwide search.

The Carmelita Morales who, having been rescued, immediately left the hospital and went on the trail of the cop-killers. It was she who had killed first one of the criminals, the newspapers had all reported with their sick sense of societal vengeance, and then left the other killer worse than dead.

After that, among the boyfriends, there were no survivors at all.

She could just imagine the dialogue. "Sonny, you don't want to marry that dirty little Mexican girl. She's probably a castrating bitch."

"Castrating bitch? Mom, you don't know the half of it."

Then there were those who wondered if they were getting damaged goods. They couldn't believe that she hadn't been raped. But mainly they couldn't take a woman who was strong.

But Harry could. She knew that he cared for her, but it seemed more as a brother, as a partner. She basked in that. She would not violate that respect for anything.

Last night she had yearned to take the initiative, to reach under the sheets and grab him, kiss him, envelop him. But she was a woman who had fought her way up against the prejudices of a man's world, to survive there in the most demanding atmosphere of such a world. His respect meant more to her than anything. What if he thought she was a slut?

No! She squeezed her thighs, fighting the demands of the insistent wetness between them. She would never make the first move.

WOLFE BRUSHED and flossed and showered and shampooed. The beard was still fairly new, and it felt strange to shampoo his face, but it was the only logical way to keep the whiskers clean. He thought about why he'd grown a beard. All DEA and Centac men were allowed to wear them. Some were encouraged to, for the counterculture look, when they were working undercover. Harry hadn't been UC, though. He'd heard that some men tried to change their appearances radically after something traumatic happened to them. Where had he learned that? Oh, yeah, post-shooting trauma school. Had he grown the beard, he mused, so he wouldn't have to see the same familiar face of the man he'd condemned as a murderer, in the mirror every morning?

He was toweling off when the pager went off in the other room. It had gone into the locked suitcase along with the Glock and the .357—turned off, of course, so it wouldn't beep at an inopportune time—when they'd left the motel. Now it made its importunate buzz, and Harry wrapped the towel around himself and left the bathroom.

He dressed hurriedly, snapping the Glock and its Summer Special holster into his jeans. He saw that Carmelita was awake.

"There's a pay phone outside by the office," he told her. "Gangs like this are into gadgets, and they might have tapped the regular motel phone. I'll check in from there."

Carmelita nodded sleepily and smiled. God, thought Wolfe, her teeth are so white. He felt an almost overwhelming urge to go to the bed, scoop her gently in his arms and kiss her. Instead, he strode to the door. Before he left he said, "Double lock it behind me."

Wolfe jogged across the crushed gravel of the parking lot toward the pay phone. He gave it a once-over. It didn't look bugged, but a pro could have done it. He didn't think these guys were pros.

Time for another calculated risk. If they were sharper than he thought, calling from here could put him in a trickbag. If the call was a seconds-are-of-the-essence kind, on the other hand, he couldn't lose time. It didn't take him long to weigh the balance of competing risks. He knew he'd never won a fight by underestimating the intelligence of an opponent, and he knew he'd never gotten a pager call where seconds had really been essential. Hours, yes. But not seconds.

The decision was easy. The keys were still in his pocket. Wolfe jogged to the Dodge, and in two minutes he was at the pay phone of a doughnut store a couple of blocks away. No one had followed him that he could see. He punched in the numbers for the secured line.

The director was on the line almost instantly. "You two have been hard to get hold of, Harry," he said.

"The pager just went off," said Harry.

"True," sighed the director. "I guess I've been dealing too long with office people who are available by telephone."

"We changed motels," Harry answered, and he brought the director up to speed on where the investigation and the infiltration now stood.

"Carmelita thinks we need more people and more guns," Harry finished.

On the other end of the line, the director snorted. "You know you can have whatever you want. If you think you need other Code Zero people, you've got them."

"Well," said Wolfe, "my own feeling was that the two of us could probably handle it. But then, I'm sure that's what our three guys thought up in the forest that night, too. What do you think, one more?"

"Three of you and, what did you say, five of them? Should be ample. Harry, I know it violates the whole code of FBI, DEA, and all. We're taught at the Academy that the lone agent is the scout, not the fighting force. His job is to get back to headquarters with the necessary Intelligence, and then the colonel sends out the cavalry. Our problem is, we can't have the cavalry witness a Code Zero operation. Will one more do it?"

"I think one will be fine, sir," Wolfe said obediently.

"Now," the director continued, "you said you needed more guns. What do you have, and what do you need?"

"Carmelita's 9 mm, and mine, are still in Spokane from the Howe shooting. I've got a loaner Glock, and she's got a Smith .45, both registered DEA weapons. We've each got a revolver for backup, personally owned, Agency approved, traceable to us. Nothing heavier."

"Okay," said the director. "What the hell, we'll Rambo it. You know Bob Montplaisir, Code Zero out of Chicago. I'll assign him in to help. We've got some clean weapons accessible there through our sources. I'll get you two of everything—subguns, sniper rifles, shotguns, clean pistols."

"Something silenced would be nice."

"I think I can do that. Pickings have been fat around Chicago. We've got a couple of Learjets there that belong to us now instead of the cartels, and people to fly them. I'll assign a pilot, and I'll have Montplaisir liaise with you on the executive jet runway at Spokane International, midnight tonight. If you can't make it, advise on the secure line if possible."

"Thanks," said Wolfe.

"That wasn't actually the reason I called you," the director continued.

Wolfe waited.

"Ichiro Komeito is out of the hospital," said the director. "He signed himself out. The doctors said it wasn't smart, but he's not really endangering himself. The kid apparently has great recuperative powers, and in any case, as horrible as his injury was, it was to an extremity."

Wolfe said, "And?"

There was a pause. "Harry," said the director, "you are there officially to investigate the shooting of the three agents. Komeito is on indefinite medical leave pending hundred percent disability retirement. He is not handling this at all well. He spoke with his supervisors out there, and they told him he was on his way out of the Agency. They also told him that you are the man investigating the shooting, and he is not happy that the lead investigator has not yet been in to ask him about what happened."

Wolfe felt his face harden. "Sir," he said testily, "my job here is to Code Zero the people who did that to him and his partners. That's what I've been working on, night and day. I've shot one of them for him already, for God's sake."

"True, true," the director interrupted, "but the fact remains that your cover story is being the lead investigator on a shooting in which two Centac agents were killed and another crippled for life and lost to us. So far, all you've done to hold up that end—an important end that *has* to be held up if we're to continue operating Code Zero as well as we have in the past—all you've done to hold up that end is utterly piss off every other law-enforcement agency that's working the case. That includes local DEA for that matter, when you went off after Howe and wound up putting him in the hospital instead of the morgue.

"In short," the director went on, "I think you owe Ichiro Komeito a debriefing session. You being the guy who wants to put in the post-shooting trauma counseling program and all, I'm surprised you haven't talked to him before."

"There was no reason to believe," Wolfe said in a hard voice, "that he'd want to talk to me or have anything to say to me. I can't do everything at once, sir. I can soothe him, or I can avenge him, but I can't do them both at the same time."

"Understood," the director answered in a placating tone. "Nonetheless, I think you should see him. Centac field command is concerned that Komeito's upset, and apparently Komeito's a little fucked up. The hospital shrink said he was dangerously depressed, and told Komeito's supervisor that the kid might shoot himself in despair. They pulled all his guns before he got out of the hospital. Sure enough, as soon as he checked out, he was at the boss's desk in the Spokane office of DEA, demanding that he be issued a replacement weapon or that the two confiscated guns be given back."

Wolfe exploded. "Hell, sir," he hissed into the pay phone, "I can't blame him! He almost died for us, he literally gave his right arm for us, and we thank him by disarming him again? Because some hospital shrink, who doesn't begin to understand how a police-action shooting differs from a street killing, figured 'depression' equals 'suicidal'? Wouldn't you be a little pissed off, too?"

"I quite agree," the director said placidly, "and I know I'm dumping a lot on you at once. But first we have to uphold the pretext of you being there to investigate and to manage the investigation of the shooting. Second, you're the one who keeps sending me the memos of how we should be handling post-shooting trauma, okay? Here's one to handle. Third, if I'm to keep these people off your neck so you can do your job, you have to check into the local office at least once in a while, and at least pretend to give them the courtesy of working with them instead of away from them. Okay?"

Wolfe knew he was right. "Okay," he sighed. "When?"

"I wasn't sure how long it would take me to reach you, so I let out that you'd be there at four tomorrow afternoon, at the Spokane office, DEA. I figured that would give you plenty of time to get there, deal with this guy, make him happy...you know."

"Make him happy," said Wolfe gravely. "He gave his right arm for us, and we're throwing him out, and we figured he was nuts so we took all his guns away from him. And I'm going to make him happy."

"Hey," the director said. "You know the motto here. 'The difficult, we do immediately. The impossible takes a little longer.'"

"I don't think," said Harry Wolfe in a tired voice, "that we have enough time."

12

Afternoon found them in the shabby motel room. Carmelita, modestly attired in a gray sweat suit, napped on her bed. Harry, as restless as the creature of his last name, could not sit still.

He didn't want to pace. It might waken his partner.

He didn't want to go for a walk or a drive. When he did either, it was time to think. Thinking was what was getting to him. He needed to take his mind off things.

He remembered the rack of worn paperback novels in the motel office under the hand-lettered sign, To Read Yourself To Sleep. As silently as he could, he padded across the motel room floor, slipping through the door, and strolled to the office.

The old woman at the desk smiled warmly as he browsed through the rack. There was mostly romantic fiction, princes and white horses and hot-blooded virgins. He smiled inwardly. So that was what women read when they needed to fantasize.

A couple of cowboy novels. Three or four murder mysteries. He'd never been able to read that kind of crap without tossing it aside after the first chapter or two. All so violent, and the violence all so pathetically phony.

A well-thumbed green paperback caught his eye. The title was One Lonely Night, and the cover said it was a Mike Hammer thriller by Mickey Spillane.

He started to put it back. He'd seen the Mike Hammer show on television once, featuring a private investigator who didn't handle his .45 automatic correctly. In the one episode Wolfe had seen, the hero was chasing a man who was shooting back at him with a shotgun. Every time the bad guy fired, another car on the side of the road would explode in flames. Wolfe had found himself laughing out loud. Regular bullets or shotgun blasts didn't—couldn't—do that to automobiles.

But he recalled somebody saying that Spillane wrote popular fiction that actually said things about the ways of men and women in a basically violent world. It was worth a try. Wolfe brought the book back to the motel room. Carmelita became alert like a sleeping cat as he entered, then smiled as she recognized him and settled back to sleep. Wolfe curled up in the old-fashioned armchair by the window and started to read.

One Lonely Night began as the hard-bitten private eye walked alone on a New York bridge, listening to the foghorns of the tugboats below as a sleety rain slowly coalesced to snow. Mike Hammer had just skated out of court after killing a man, but he was brooding over the frustrated judge's condemnation of his actions, calling it "the spicy sweetness of murder sanctified by law."

Wolfe set the book down, frowning. This was hitting a little close to home. "The spicy sweetness of murder sanctified by law." Had Harry tasted any spicy sweetness?

Yes. He was alive. That was spicy and that was sweet. If he hadn't killed the man in the desert, he would have died himself. He would be rotting in the ground, instead of sitting here going through self-doubt, instead of being here able to watch that beautiful woman's chest rise and fall beneath her gray sweatshirt as she slept.

He wanted to throw the book across the room. He started to. But then he thought, If I can't read a mystery novel, I'm more screwed up than I thought I was. He picked it up again and started to read once more.

A frightened girl ran to Mike Hammer for help. Behind her on the bridge came a hulking Eastern European type with a gun. When it was over, the girl had plunged to her death and Hammer had killed the man, kicking both his guns and the corpse into the river below.

Wolfe lowered the book again and pondered the sense of righteous indignation that came from firing a bullet into a killer who had taken the life of someone innocent. He didn't like the way the book made him feel, but Spillane was a hell of a writer. He had a way of dropping his commas when he wanted the action to hurl the reader along at a faster pace. If nothing else, Wolfe told himself, he would read it for the good writing alone. He continued.

The detective soon discovered that the European was part of a gigantic Communist plot. Along the way, assorted Commies and bad guys messed with Hammer and Hammer in turn messed them up.

Halfway through the novel, a couple of enemy agents tried to murder Mike Hammer and Velda, his secretary and girlfriend. Mike shot one and Velda blew away the other as he was about to shoot Mike in the back. Then Velda went on to ask whether it was all right for her not to feel any guilt, and Hammer reassured her that there was no sin in killing a killer, in ridding the world of evil.

Wolfe let the book drop into his lap as he closed his eyes and tilted his head back wearily. He thought of Carmelita.

It was she who had given him the pep talk such a short time ago. She hadn't killed as many men as Harry, but she had done her share. There was no sign of guilt or remorse in her at all.

And why should there be? Harry felt no guilt or regret, either, at least not for the ones he'd killed in self-defense. All of Carmelita's had been kill or be killed. Harry wished he could say that. He wanted to keep that purity in her. That was what allowed her to reconcile everything that had happened to her.

No, it was more than that. Her ability to control the violence had been her therapy after the nightmarish massacre she'd survived. She had been brutalized in the incident. Becoming the huntress instead of the hunted had been her redemption. For Carmelita, Code Zero had been positive. For Harry, it had been half and half, and the negative side seemed to weigh more heavily every day.

Carmelita was still sleeping, breathing evenly, like a child. Her lips ware barely parted. The fact that she had killed men did not alter that serene beauty. Perhaps, Wolfe realized, that fact was the only thing that had preserved it.

Wolfe read on. He concluded that Mike and Velda were in love, but had never made love, that Velda was an aging if beautiful virgin. Talk about the improbable. Yet, in 1950, those were the standards. But then, many decades later, wasn't *he* in this hotel room with a beautiful partner he was falling in love with and had never touched? Maybe fiction wasn't so improbable, after all. He decided to finish the book.

It was near the end that Wolfe, the cool and unshakable Harry Wolfe, found the tears coming to his eyes. Velda had been kidnapped by the spies and was being tortured by a gang of them in an abandoned warehouse. Mike Hammer, a Thompson submachine gun in hand, came to the rescue.

Wolfe found himself weeping.

He put the book down and put his face in his hands, biting down on a knuckle so he wouldn't make a sound that would wake Carmelita.

Hammer's final summary of his purpose in life—"I was the evil that opposed the other evil."

Wolfe remembered the man in the desert, the pleading face that haunted him. The man had been responsible for the deaths of Federal agents, responsible for the rape of a young girl and murder. What haunted Harry was that the man had been helpless, childlike himself, begging for his life at the moment Harry had pressed the trigger.

The evil that opposed the other evil. He wondered what other things that man would have done if he'd walked away alive that day. Would he have felt the guilt Harry felt now, had felt ever since, for the killing? Had he ever felt a twinge for the men he'd killed, and for the young girl? Had he thought of them at all, even at the moment Harry put the gun to his head, or had the man in the desert truly cared for no life but his own? How many more would have fallen to his uncaring hands, how many more innocent victims would have died, if Harry had not performed that flick of his trigger finger that he had regretted ever since?

The silent tears had stopped. Wolfe picked up the book. The end was an anticlimax, really, Hammer strangling to death one last Commie spymaster before drifting away into the night. Wolfe closed the book, set it down, stood.

He felt cleansed. Okay, this Spillane guy was so full of hate for Communists that he made the people Wolfe was dealing with look like moderate Republicans. For all that, what he'd written had hit home.

Wolfe had heard about people having a revelation from reading the Bible or some other religious tract. A Mike Hammer novel by Mickey Spillane hardly fit the category.

But then, Wolfe thought to himself, he would take his salvation wherever he could find it.

13

It was not quite 3:20 p.m. when Wolfe left the motel room. He glanced around. No sign of a tail or a stakeout. An old man nodded in the chair of the barbershop across the street, and in the run-down liquor store next to it a couple of bums were drinking from bottles in paper sacks, seemingly oblivious to the world.

Wolfe stepped around the car, performing the routine check for explosives. With people like the ones he was dealing with, you never knew. They seemed stupid so far, but he knew the far-right groups were into deadly technologies and had exhibited cunning in the past. Harry had always figured that as soon as he underestimated an opponent, he was going to lose the fight.

Nothing under the fenders, on or under the tires. Nothing near the hood release. Nothing under the hood itself. No beeper or bombs attached anywhere to the underside of the car or the inside of the bumpers.

Wolfe got into the white Dodge and engaged the ignition. As he pulled out into the lightly traveled street, he was wondering how he'd feel if *he* had an arm blown off in the line of duty and the assigned case investigator had never bothered to talk to him.

SLOUCHED IN the front seat of a stolen Ford Ranger pickup, Danny and J. J. Queen watched Wolfe go. In the passenger seat, J.J., his red-rimmed eyes brightening with eagerness, said, "Hold back for a while. Don't get right in behind him."

Danny snapped, "You think I'm fuckin' stupid?" He turned on the ignition but left the four-speed transmission in neutral. Like his brother, he was wearing dirty flannels and grease-stained jeans. He'd had only a little less beer to drink.

Thor's portable cellular phone was on the floor by J.J.'s feet. Thor had called them early that morning and set up a meeting in the Foodland parking lot, on the north side where there weren't many cars. He'd handed them the cellular and said, "I still don't trust this fuckin' new guy." Thor described Johnny and told them where the motel was, and the room number. "Just follow him," he'd instructed, "and if he does anything fishy, give me a call."

They'd been here for hours now, and had gone through three six-packs of Old Milwaukee. Danny hated the stuff, but it was on sale and J.J. swore it was exactly the same as their favorite brand. As if, Danny thought, J.J. could tell even the expensive European imports from dog piss after the first three or four.

J.J. had insisted on taking the right front seat. Alongside him, wedged down low between the seat and the pickup door, was the 870 pump shotgun they'd taken from the DEA agents' car. The Armorer had scrupulously ground off the serial numbers and cut the barrel down flush with the tube magazine that extended in front of the pump handle. He had removed the regular wooden buttstock entirely and replaced it with a black rubber pistol grip. It was loaded with five rounds of buckshot, double-ought. Each pull of the trigger would send out nine pellets that looked like lead ball bearings, each nearly the diameter of a .357 Magnum bullet and traveling at about the same velocity. The ammo, like the shotgun, was Remington brand.

"If he turns out to be a ZOG, it's my turn," J.J. had told him adamantly. "You already got Aryan Warrior. Now me. That little gook wasn't so fast an' sneaky that night, I woulda got him then. We'd be the only Aryan Warriors in the country who was brothers, prob'ly."

Danny let the white sedan get a block ahead, then rolled the pickup out of the parking lot after it. The stolen truck was four or five years old, but it had been used hard. Its red paint had already gone dull. But it had a big engine, and was grubby looking enough that no one would notice it twice. That's why he'd hotwired it from the Long-Term parking lot at Spokane International Airport, where he hoped it wouldn't be missed until its owner had flown back to reclaim it. It would have been dismantled in a chop shop by then, and Danny and J.J. would have a little more beer money to split. Pickings had been lean lately. Will was nervous, and tightfisted.

Will seemed to be increasingly unpredictable. Danny could understand why he didn't want to go after Harold. After all, if Harold *had* squealed, they all would have been rounded up by now. Besides, it occurred to Danny that if Will would order Harold killed when he got hurt and vulnerable, wouldn't the rest of them kind of wonder what was up? Maybe even question whether Will should still be in charge instead of, oh, maybe Thor?

But Danny couldn't figure out why Will wasn't running more jobs, taking off more dopers. They could all use the money. Will said they might have to go to ground anytime and that the balloon might go up, so he would hold on to the money for a while to take care of all of them. Danny had to admit it made sense, but he was still chafing at the bit.

Up ahead, Johnny in the white Dodge was turning onto the interstate toward Spokane and the Washington State line.

BOB MONTPLAISIR was in his small second-floor apartment in a middle-class complex in Northbrook, Illinois, packing. As always, he was scrupulous about managing his time. He was only about half an hour from O'Hare in Chicago if he took the regular route and didn't risk a traffic tie-up on the expressway.

Beneath his black turtleneck, the stocky man was wearing a Point Blank bulletproof vest, a hybrid of two aramids called Kevlar and SpectraShield. It was hot with the vest on in the apartment, and sweat was breaking out on the pale skin of his forehead below the receding line of dark hair. But Montplaisir didn't mind. It was good to be armored, to feel that your loins were girded for battle.

He opened the long aluminum case, exposing top and bottom layers of rubbery foam shaped like the inside of an egg carton. He walked to the gun cabinet and delicately lifted out a Savage model 110 .308 rifle. The bolt handle protruded from the left side. Montplaisir was left-handed, and the Savage was one of the few rifles that was made in a southpaw model.

But that wasn't the only reason he'd chosen it for Code Zero work. It was one of a baker's dozen of guns he and his raid team had confiscated one night when they'd hit a crack house on the South Side of Chicago. By the time the guns were turned in to the evidence room, they were down to an even dozen and the Savage was in the trunk of his assigned car.

The Savage was a superbly accurate rifle. His would put three shots within an inch of each other at a hundred yards with the kind of ammo that was in the flat red-and-white box he threw into the suitcase. Federal Match 168-grain boat-tail hollow-point. It had been DEA issue for .308s ever since FBI SWAT tests showed it the most accurate cartridge made.

U.S. government rifles, police and military, were virtually all Remingtons. A Savage wouldn't be tied to the DEA if he left it behind on a Code Zero op, and the serial number couldn't be traced anyway.

He stripped the bolt mechanism out and put it in a chamois pouch, laying that and the rifle reverently into the cushioned case next to the twenty rounds of ammo.

Next came the shotgun. It was an Italian Benelli Super 90, black and deadly. Montplaisir thought the old-fashioned pump guns the DEA issued were obsolete junk. The Benelli was semiautomatic. Nothing to manipulate, just eight blasts of 12-gauge buckshot as fast as you could pull the trigger. It was better than a machine gun for close, fast mayhem. Like the Savage sniper rifle, it was untraceable.

Turning toward the floor safe that held his handguns, he thought of Wolfe. The director had said he'd be working with him again. Wolfe carried a Glock, but what the hell, what did Harry Wolfe know about guns? Sure, the guy was cool under pressure and he was a hell of a good shot, but Wolfe just didn't seem to have the feel of a fine weapon. He wondered if Wolfe still carried all department-approved or department-issued guns. Montplaisir shook his head and smirked. Company man, pogue, ass-kisser. Why else would Wolfe have been promoted to head of agent-involved shooting investigation for Centac?

As he withdrew his custom shoulder holster from the gun safe and tossed it toward the suitcase on the floor, Montplaisir thought about Wolfe bittersweetly. When they did the first Code Zero op, the one that was triggered by the death of the former director, Wolfe had been good to work with. On that final day, when coordination literally to the fraction of a second had meant so much, it was good to know that a cool head like Harry was behind the other sniper rifle when the two high-powered weapons had to go off together like the single tick of a clock. And it had worked. Montplaisir indulged himself in a grin. South American television had recorded the deaths, the heads exploding in balloonlike clouds of crimson mist. The other drug cartel leaders must still have nightmares about it.

Montplaisir checked the action of the dark blue Ruger Mark I target pistol, then checked the magazine with its nine lead-tipped standard velocity rounds. It was important that a gun with an integral silencer have subsonic ammunition. If the bullet went much faster than a thousand feet per second, it broke the sound barrier with a crack that violated the whole concept of using a sound suppressor. This gun when he'd tested it sounded like an air pistol or BB gun. A *thwip* sound you couldn't hear in the next room, and the muted metallic noise of the action racking itself between shots.

Montplaisir loaded the gun, racking the first of the nine rounds into the firing chamber and pushing up the thumb bolt that locked the gun on Safe. He checked to make sure the retrofit bolt, the one DEA armorers put on instead of the Ruger company, was in the Off position. That second bolt stud would, when pushed up, lock the operating bolt in place so there wouldn't even be the click-clack of the mechanism cycling semiautomatically. He was going to be carrying this one, and he wanted it ready for speed.

The gun could have taken a tenth round, but he left it at nine shots. He had learned that when you pushed things to the limit, they often went over the limit, and if you stayed about ten percent down from what you could theoretically get away with, you would in fact get away with it in real life. He walked over to the suitcase and inserted the silenced Ruger pistol into the pouch of the shoulder holster that would hold the gun under the left armpit, where his nondominant right hand could reach it easily.

Don't push that last ten percent, he thought. Christ, he'd learned that the hard way. As he walked back to the cabinet for his primary fighting pistol, he thought about the one push too far that had brought him into the Code Zero team to begin with.

Bob Montplaisir had been working the Las Vegas office of DEA. He was thirty-six then, ten years with the Agency, four years before with the Dayton, Ohio, police. Dayton had been an innocent, fun job. No chance for really big money, but you could score with the police groupies, and every night was different, and what the hell. The narcs, though, were the elite of crime fighters and Montplaisir felt he was born for the elite. DEA took him in.

The training had been great. DEA always required an overseas post early on if you wanted to have any kind of career path, and Bob had chosen Mexico. That was when he'd first tasted the illicit power that his position could command.

He'd been overweight and losing his hair even then. Women didn't go for him the way he figured they should have. But in Mexico, the drug barons gave him the finest female flesh, and *mucho dinero,* and all he had to do was look the other way just a few times. Because he looked kind of sloppy and because the dopers sensed he was one of them—a self-centered hedonist who liked money and the finer things of life and realized that ideals were for children in grade school—Bob Montplaisir had been able to work himself in smoothly undercover.

He had made many buys and many arrests. He had made many more scores from the drug barons, warning them before DEA and the *Federales* came knocking on their doors. In turn, the drug lords fed him their up-and-coming opposition.

It was a pleasant and symbiotic relationship. When he was transferred to Los Angeles in due time, grateful friends in the Mexican drug cartels gave him contacts with their people in the City of Angels, and it all continued.

Then someone had tipped OPR, the Office of Professional Responsibility, DEA's internal affairs unit. Bob had been fat and happy and careless by then, actually taking calls from his drug contacts on his home phone. His wife and kids knew enough already to leave the room when he was on the phone. He didn't realize his own people—if DEA still was his own people—were tapping his line.

Then the time had come when a mere lieutenant in the Mexican-Los Angeles connection had called him on the phone to tell him that it was over, that they themselves had recorded him and that from now on things were reversed and Bob would have to pay him to keep his mouth shut. What the cartel paid Bob would now be split fifty-fifty with Ramon, the man on the phone.

Certainly, Bob had purred, not realizing that DEA's OPR was tapping the line, but things had to be discussed, negotiated. Could they meet in, say, half an hour at the lounge of the Holiday Inn at Century and La Cienega?

That had taken the OPR team, one man from Washington and one from the L.A. office, totally aback. They didn't even have time to call in. They just raced to the Holiday Inn. One stayed in the lounge while the other stood at the pay phones in the lobby, trying desperately to get the senior L.A. resident agent on the line.

He finally did. The concerned senior agent in charge told them to stay on the case and make an arrest the moment they saw anything go down, and in the meantime, he was sending two more people for backup.

But Bob hadn't showed, and Ramon hadn't showed. The DEA men waited almost until closing time. Then one agent went out in the parking lot to check around. They found nothing. Finally they went home.

Two days later, when the rental agency reported the missing car, LAPD officers found it in the hotel parking lot. The weather had been warm. As soon as they walked around the rear of the vehicle to check the license plate, they caught the smell of decomposing flesh and called robbery-homicide division.

The Los Angeles division of DEA, which monitored LAPD radio traffic and teletypes, called the headquarters in Washington, D.D. Washington had ordered the L.A. office to come down on Special Agent Robert Montplaisir. Hard.

Bob had been in bed at three in the morning when he'd gotten the call. It was from his supervisor. "You have thirty seconds to be in the hall. You may be wearing nothing more than shorts. You hands will be raised above your head."

In twenty seconds, Bob had pulled on his B.V.D.s, thanking God that he didn't have one of his Mexican cartel bimbos with him that night, and opened the door to face eight black-clad men pointing Colt submachine guns at him. He had surrendered.

There was, of course, no arrest. The bullet found in the head of the rotting corpse was .32 caliber, and no gun that would take such a cartridge was found in the exhaustive search of Montplaisir's apartment. Bob had been sufficiently frozen by fear not to contact his Mexican counterparts, and to wait for the next move. When the call had come, he had been sleeping with a bulletproof vest and an ankle holster on, and he'd had to unstrap both before coming to the door.

Nonetheless, he was advised that he was suspended on administrative leave, with pay, until the charges had been investigated.

When he walked back into his apartment that night, the TV was still on. CNN "Headline News" was talking about the director of Centac, the Central Tactical Unit of the DEA, being blown up with his family outside a church near Washington, D.C.

Fuck him, Bob had thought to himself. Too bad about his wife and kids, but he runs the outfit that's gonna screw me now, gonna make me a pariah? Let him rot in the ground. And the same for the yellow bastards that had to kill his wife and kids with him. Bob had opened a fifth of Jack Daniel's bourbon.

Then another call had come the next morning. The ticket would be waiting for him at LAX, to fly direct to Washington, D.C. DEA business. What, he wasn't on suspension anymore? Not exactly. He should just *go.*

With nothing to lose, he did.

They checked him into a mediocre hotel at the airport, and he had orders to stay there until contacted. It was about eleven when a heavyset, weary-looking black man with iron gray hair knocked on his door, flanked by two big men, one black and one white, both with SIG 9 mm pistols uncaringly displayed in their hands as they entered. The black one held a gun on Bob while the white one holstered his and gave him a quick but thorough frisk. After the two men with the pistols had checked the entire room and rooted through his baggage, the dark man with the big body had gestured with his head, and the two had left the room.

When they were alone, the black man began to speak. He was the new director of Centac, he explained, and Bob wondered what the hell that had to do with him since he was a DEA field agent, not a member of the elite inner circle of Centac.

"We've got you for murder," the big black man said coldly and flatly, "and I have a lot to do and very little time to do it in, and I have no time at all to fuck with you."

"I want a lawyer," Montplaisir said.

"Fuck you *and* your lawyer," the director growled. "What you want is a lawyer, but a lawyer can't help you now. What you need is a chance to get your shit together. Another chance. *Another chance!* Does that strike a chord with you?"

Reflex and instinct were two different things. Reflex was something you did automatically, like ask for a lawyer when you were in trouble. Instinct was listening to your guts, and Bob Montplaisir knew how to do that. He knew he had murdered Ramon, figured there must have been a security video camera in the parking lot, and they had him cold. There had to be some reason this guy was talking this shit, this intense, and he knew he had to listen.

"My ears are open," Montplaisir had said noncommittally.

"You know the director was killed yesterday."

"Yeah."

"What was your gut reaction?"

Montplaisir hesitated only a second before he said, "Anger. Rage. If they can get him, they can get me. Fear, I guess."

"What would you like to do about it?" the new director asked.

If Bob Montplaisir had been asked what he was, first he would have said a good-looking great lay, and second, a DEA agent. He knew which response the new director was appealing to.

"I'd like to get my hands on the bastards who did it," Montplaisir answered.

The black man leered at him. "Yeah, I bet you would. Tell me, Bob, you wanna rot on death row?"

"No," Montplaisir answered instantly.

"You want another chance to be DEA? To be an elite part of it? A *really* fuckin' elite part of it?"

"Of course," Montplaisir responded automatically.

The director paused for a long, dramatic moment, and let his white teeth show in a broad smile. "Have you ever heard," he asked, "of the movie called *The Dirty Dozen*?"

It had gone from there. *The Dirty Dozen* was a movie about criminals given the chance to kill on behalf of their country or die in the execution chamber. To kill scum worse than themselves. Bob Montplaisir had sensed instinctively that they had him on the Holiday Inn kill, and that this was his only way out.

When the director told him that things had gone far enough, that DEA had authorized a CIA-like Phoenix team that would kill the killers, hunt down and exterminate them like the cockroaches they were, Bob Montplaisir had felt reborn. An hour before, he had been thinking about sucking off his own pistol, and now he had a chance, and no one was even asking him to give the money back!

He had grabbed it in a heartbeat, and the next thing he knew, the first Code Zero had been underway. The hunt had been swift and certain.

Running behind the dogs that bayed the quarry, he just had to pull the trigger when the target was trying to climb the tree. Montplaisir had done little of the hunting, but he most certainly had done his share of the trigger pulling, and he suspected that Wolfe had been one of the hounds who brought the targets to bay. He knew for a fact that Harry Wolfe had been one of the executioners on that blood-tingling day in South America, when Harry manned a sniper rifle on one side of the street and Bob was behind the scope of the one on the other side, and the trail of the previous director's killers ended in a welter of blood and shattered bone fragments.

After that the director had called off the dogs of the OPR. The word was that a high-level investigation had shown that Bob Montplaisir was in no way connected with the death of Ramon Guiterrez, and had been fully reinstated, and had in fact been transferred to the newly revitalized Centac squad in Chicago, and all that was left was rumors.

Well, it was more than that. His wife, Nyleen, left him—not that he'd been around a lot or been much of a husband anyway—and once a year he flew out to Los Angeles and took Bobby and Kimberly to Disneyland and told them solemnly that soon they'd be in junior high school and they'd have to get their act together.

But Bob Montplaisir paid his alimony and child support like clockwork, as well he should have with almost two million dollars in his Swiss bank accounts, and the maintenance he paid for the wife and son and daughter of his former life merely nibbled a little bit at his annual interest income.

That was why he had been clean as a whistle, scrupulously clean, since the new director caught him with Ramon Guiterrez's blood on his hands. Being suspended and facing a total firing had been a shock to Montplaisir, a shock that startled him straight. He realized he already had all the money he would ever need, and enough money in reserve to buy all the sweet young flesh he could ever handle.

He could, in short, afford to stay straight.

Such were Bob Montplaisir's thoughts as he walked to the gun safe and pulled out two more pistols. One was a Seecamp .32 automatic, a pistol the size of a .25, tiny enough to fit in a vest pocket. He slipped it into the right hip pocket of his jeans instead. It was loaded with Winchester Silvertip hollowpoints.

Montplaisir felt warmly comfortable. The understanding in *The Dirty Dozen* had been, "If you die, you die more honorably than you were fated to, and if you live, you get all the debits wiped off your balance sheet... but of course, you *are* going to die."

But Bob hadn't died. Bob also knew that the director of Centac was now beholden to *him* and the other members of the Code Zero team. He wondered if Wolfe fully appreciated that. Poor by-the-code Harry Wolfe.

Bob had gotten a comfortable assignment in the Midwest after he returned from the final South American stage of the first Code Zero. He was well aware that he was a murderer with legal sanction... and that the director of Centac was guilty of murder by contract. Bob was comfortable with that as a balance of power, of mutually assured destruction.

Besides, there was the other thing.

The director had opened a new world to Bob Montplaisir. Or, if he didn't open it, at least held open the door.

Bob had never killed a man before that night in the Holiday Inn parking lot on Century Boulevard. He had somehow sensed the night would come, though, and for that reason he had begun to stockpile untraceable guns he had taken from the suspects he'd put under arrest.

It had been dark in the parking lot, and medium late, and jets from nearby LAX were flying overhead. He'd met the blackmailer of the telephone, whose full name he didn't know until later, and he had looked around and seen that the man was alone and had told him, "Get into the back of your Grand Prix. Get all the way down on the seat where no one can see you. I'll drive."

The dark man had grinned and obeyed. He was used to working with rental cars and handing the keys around. He had unlocked the driver's door of the two-door coupe, opened it and handed the keys—still with the plastic rental agency ring attached—when he bent forward and pushed the front seat up so he could climb in the back.

That was when Bob took the rusty Colt .32 automatic he had confiscated from a spaced-out informant a year before and put it behind the base of the man's skull and pulled the trigger.

Bob had looked around for a second, found the ejected shell casing and stuffed it in his pocket. He had dragged the man to the back of the car, opened the trunk and quickly scooped him inside. Then he locked the car and left, walking the short distance to Sepulveda, where he'd parked his own car facing west. The gun had wound up in the bay off Long Beach, in pieces, and the spent casing had gone down the sewer.

During the killing, a jolt had run through his body, like a diffuse current of pleasure... and now, years later, he was an ordained killer for the United States government.

Montplaisir smiled as he took his primary carry gun out of the safe, then closed the door, dropped the lever and spun the lock. The gun he had retrieved was a SIG-Sauer P-220, its surface gleaming white with an electroless nickel finish. He carefully loaded the pistol with eight rounds of .45-caliber MagSafe ammunition, then slipped the pistol into the part of the shoulder holster that would hold the .45 under his right arm. The shoulder rig was complete.

Montplaisir lifted the heavy leather harness and slipped his arms through it, smoothing out the flat straps that went over his shoulders and across his back. Under his left arm hung the silenced Ruger .22, and under the right, the SIG .45 with the extralethal bullets.

Montplaisir looked at himself in the mirror and found himself good, and deadly. Hell, he looked like James Bond! Wolfe was probably out there with his stupid Glock, and maybe a Remington 870 pump shotgun. Company man. Stupid.

He glanced at his watch. He had more than an hour before he started to the airport. He'd arrive in Spokane by midnight their time there, ten o'clock his time.

Montplaisir grinned. He wondered what awful thing a tight-ass, by-the-book agent like Harry Wolfe could have done that would get him into the Dirty Half Dozen to make him a Code Zero man in the first place.

It pleased him that Wolfe was apparently in over his head and needed backup. No one could provide that backup better than Bob Montplaisir. He grinned into the mirror, enormously satisfied with himself.

The second chance, like the second marriage, was often the strongest. So it was with him. Bob Montplaisir had all the money he'd ever need, and he was too smart to take drugs, and sex was something he could easily afford. Doing police work well was satisfying, but hell, half a million people in the country at any given time were certified to do that.

Montplaisir salivated. He was about to do what only he and a tiny handful of his peers were authorized to do by the United States of America. It was something he loved for its obscene power.

He was authorized to kill, and he was being sent out to do it.

The only thing that disturbed his pleasure was the thought, What did Harry Wolfe do to deserve this? What did Harry Wolfe do to be like me?

"I GOTTA TAKE A PISS," J.J. told Danny Queen moments before Harry Wolfe took his final turn into a parking lot in Spokane, Washington.

"Quit bein' a dumb fuck," Danny mumbled angrily. "Keep lookin' straight ahead. Don't let him see ya' lookin' at him. We gotta go down a block or so, make sure he stays where he is."

They went a block up and stopped at a light. "Don't look over your shoulder, man," J.J. blurted, "just check in your rearview. Where'd he go?"

Danny was incensed. God, where did he get this stupid drunk for a brother? "Into that fuckin' lot, dipshit, that's where he went! Don't tell me, don't look over my fuckin' shoulder, man! Just remember who's an Aryan Warrior and who *ain't,* man!"

The light changed, and Danny pulled into the next parking lot. He looked around.

J.J. said, "You don't know what the fuck this place is, either, do you, man?"

Danny looked at him, his eyes narrowed in fury. "Don't mess with me, man! Just call Thor. Tell him where the hell we are. Let him look it up, he's supposed to be so fuckin' smart."

USUALLY WOLFE didn't carry his leather-bound ID case, which looked like a flat wallet, when he was working undercover. But he was about to enter a police bastion where he wasn't a regular soldier and needed ID. Wolfe flashed the leather wallet with the dual Centac/DEA identification. That got him in the door of Spokane's DEA office and all the way to the inner sanctum of the assistant special agent in charge. Wolfe knew the guy. They'd met the night he and Carmelita had turned in their guns for evidence and been issued new ones.

The man sat alone behind his desk. Harry tried to break the ice by saying, "Any news on when my partner and I get our guns back, so we can return yours?"

The ASAC grimaced. "Least of my concerns. All I can tell you is, not yet. Look, you know what you're here for. You ready?"

"If I wasn't," said Wolfe, "I wouldn't be here."

The ASAC reached forward and hit his intercom. "Sally," he said, "tell Agent Komeito that I'd like him to come into my office, please."

The ASAC's office was a rectangle. Harry had come in from the standard entry door, opening from the reception area. The door that opened now was to the far right...the direction where the inner sanctum of the special agent in charge, or resident agent in charge, was located.

That meant that the agent he was going to meet was already in the inner sanctum. Wolfe had spent some time working internal affairs and was familiar enough with charges against accused agents to know that they only got in that far when their own bosses figured they were in the right. He caught the angry glare in the ASAC's eye. He felt very much the outsider here.

The door swung all the way open, and a compact man walked through. He was shorter than Wolfe, with straight glossy black hair combed back from the forehead in a widow's peak. Slimmer than Wolfe, too. The man stood erect. He was wearing a blue sweat suit with white stripes down the sides of the arms and legs.

The sleeve of the right arm was truncated at the elbow. Beneath it was a five-inch stub wrapped in heavy white bandaging.

The man behind the desk stood up at the same time Harry did. "Agent Wolfe," he said, "I'd like you to meet Ichiro Komeito."

The one-armed man's eyes were impassive. He pointedly extended his left hand. Wolfe automatically reciprocated with his own left hand.

They shook. Wolfe was surprised at the iron strength in the smaller man's grip. Komeito didn't let go.

"It's automatic for you to respond with your left hand," said Komeito with only a slight smirk of sarcasm on his face. "You didn't miss a beat. I guess you've shaken hands with crippled agents before. Crippled *former* agents," he finished acidly.

Wolfe held the firm handshake. "Both," he said flatly. "Guys who got hurt and stayed, guys who got hurt and left."

The hands separated. Komeito said, "I guess you do this a lot. I suppose I was asking too much to hope that my case would be investigated by someone who gave a shit enough that they'd talk to *me* about it. But it's nice to know that some of the people you investigated who had their arms shot off—I guess there must be a lot of them, huh?—stayed on the job. See, my boss here says I'm out of the picture."

The assistant special agent in charge began to stand. "Wolfe," he began, "I have been trying to tell him about permanent disability retirement, and he won't listen."

Komeito sneered at him. "Oh, Agent Wolfe, he's wrong. I listen. I just don't accept what I'm hearing. He took my guns away, said I'm going to be mustered out. Said Washington would send an agent who does this all the time to evaluate my case. That agent is you. But you know, Wolfe, I'd have felt a whole lot better about that if you had, just once, tried to just fucking talk to me!"

"Goddammit," snapped the ASAC, all the way upright now behind his desk, "I will not stand for this kind of insubordination!"

The one-armed man fixed him with an icy glare. He said, slowly and clearly, "Get fucked, sir."

The ASAC gasped. "You little prick," he growled. "You thought you were out? Let me just tell you how far out you are! You're—"

He suddenly stopped talking. He realized that Harry Wolfe was staring him straight in the eye, his mouth tight.

"What the hell is your problem?" the ASAC snapped at Wolfe. "This man, he—"

The ASAC stopped talking again. Wolfe had just raised his hand, palm forward, in the direction of the assistant special agent in charge. It was the international sign language gesture that meant, *stop.*

Harry Wolfe said softly, "Shut up."

The assistant office director began to sputter. "How dare you!"

Wolfe said, slowly and coldly, "Agent Komeito is right. Get fucked. We're leaving now."

Wolfe gestured to the one-armed man. Ichiro Komeito paused only long enough to flash a surprised but triumphant smile at his former boss. The man behind the desk realized it was not wise to speak anymore. The door to his office closed silently behind Harry Wolfe and Ichiro Komeito.

"Bastards," the assistant special agent in charge of the office breathed a moment later. "Stupid bastards!"

He reached down to his intercom and punched the button for his secretary. When she responded, he told her, "Get me the director of Centac! And I mean, do it now!"

It was a request he would regret for the rest of his career.

THEY SAW WOLFE PARK and go into an official-looking building on a busy Spokane street. J.J. dialed Thor's home number, and the Team's squad leader picked up on the second ring.

"Yeah?"

"Uh, Thor? J.J., man. Listen, he's in like a federal building in Spokane. We're outside, the other side of the parkin' lot." He read off the address.

"Hang on a minute," said Thor. He reached for a phone book. If this guy was a cop, it was probably DEA or Centac. He looked under the U.S. government listings. There was nothing under Centac. He tried Drug Enforcement Administration.

Bingo.

"DEA," Thor said tensely into the phone. "That's the address for the fuckin' DEA!"

"Hey," answered J.J., "it's a big buildin'. Maybe he's gotta take care of some Social Security or somethin'."

On the other end of the phone, Thor felt his face tighten. Where had Will found these idiots?

"Yeah," he growled, "an' maybe he won the fuckin' lottery and he's come to collect from the Treasury Department. Look, I'm gonna call Will. Stay right on him."

"Gotcha," said J.J. "We'll—hey, wait a minute. He's comin' out. He's got a guy with him. Oh, Jesus. Oh, Christ! Oh, *fuck!*"

Thor snapped, "What is it?"

"The guy with him's a gook," said J.J. excitedly. "Holy shit! The gook's only got one hand. I recognize him from the papers. It's the gook from that night! From the shootin'! DEA or whatever the hell it is!"

Thor's facial muscles were so tight he looked as if he was wearing a mask. His hand crushed against the telephone receiver full force.

"He's a fuckin' narc," Thor growled. "I knew there was something about him. Goddammit!"

"They're gettin' in his car, Thor. Whaddaya want us to do?"

Thor's fury made the decision for them. "Waste 'em!"

J.J. squealed, "Here?"

"No," Thor grated, "follow 'em. Get them someplace you won't have too many witnesses. Blow their heads off and get the fuck out of there. Hang on to the cellular. I'm going to mobilize Will and the rest. I'll be back in touch."

"You got it," J.J. blurted excitedly, but Thor had hung up.

The white Dodge was already moving into traffic. "Thor says to do 'em," he told his brother excitedly. "Let's follow 'em. Thor says blow their brains out, just do it someplace quiet without too many witnesses." J.J. paused. "Goddammit," he muttered.

"What's the matter? You said you wanted to off some ZOGs."

"Yeah," J.J. answered, looking down ruefully at the pile of beer cans that littered the floor of the pickup, "but I gotta take a wicked piss."

AT THE WHEEL of the Dodge, Wolfe said softly, "You want to just drive around, maybe out by a lake or someplace quiet, and talk?"

"Sounds good," Ichiro said sullenly. "Follow this street to the end and take a left. We'll get on the highway, maybe go out by Fernan Lake."

Wolfe nodded agreement. "I feel bad about not having contacted you sooner," he said. "I thought you'd given everything to the on-scene investigators, and I figured you'd want to be alone for a while." It was, Harry knew, a lame excuse.

"I didn't tell them everything," Ichiro Komeito said, looking out the window. "I didn't tell them what it was like to hide like a dog in the underbrush, trying to pinch shut the artery in my arm so I wouldn't bleed to death. Thinking they were going to hunt me down and put a gun to my head and pull the trigger. I don't even remember how I got to the Blazer to call in on the radio after they were gone. I remember the first thing I looked for was a gun. Do you know what 'helpless' means, Wolfe?"

"Yes," Harry answered simply. He remembered the day in Miami when he had emptied his revolver, not knowing the cop-killer he faced was wearing a bulletproof vest... watching the man's finger tighten on the trigger as Harry started to drop his useless, empty gun... the sense of merciful relief when he saw the red blossom of the wound bloom in the gunman's throat when the other agent shot him a split second before he could blow Harry's brains out.

"Yes," he said again. "I know what helpless means."

"Oh," said the other man archly, "then you know what it's like to wake up in the hospital with half an arm and to have your girlfriend come in to visit and tell you, by the way, that the Agency came to your house and said they didn't need a warrant, then confiscated your guns just in case you might decide to eat your pistol."

"They thought you were depressed enough to be suicidal, I guess," Wolfe replied automatically. God, he thought, now I'm parroting their cheap excuses. "That doesn't mean they were right to do it," he added.

Komeito fixed him with his eyes. "Did you notice," he asked Wolfe, "that my given name is as Japanese as my surname? You don't see that much with Americans of Japanese descent. They usually keep the last name and give the kids born in this country a generic Anglo-sounding first name. My father named me in the Japanese tradition. He's a karate instructor. We have, my whole family, a strong sense of *budo,* the warrior code, the warrior spirit. It was *budo* that kept me going that night. Kept me alive."

"You did well," Harry interjected. "You got one of them."

Komeito almost spit. "Yeah, right. *One* of them."

"They said you were trying to fight the rest with your good hand till you realized the bullet had put your gun out of commission."

"Yeah," the agent said bitterly. "Lot of good it did me. I swore that night I'd never do a job with only one gun on again. I figured the artillery in the backseat was all we'd need. We never thought that they'd have a scout team coming in on us. But that doesn't matter for me now, does it? Carrying two guns?"

"Why not?"

"You know how many I've got on now, Wolfe? None! The Agency took 'em away, remember? I asked the ASAC to issue me another pistol to replace my SIG that got blown up. Know what he told me? 'You're off active duty till we process your retirement, Ichi. Don't worry, Ichi. We'll take care of you, Ichi. You won't need a gun anymore, Ichi.' Then he gives me the same bullshit about the shrink thinks I might be depressed enough to commit suicide. Shit, if he believed that, why didn't they send someone to be with me? Okay if I go home and open a vein with a kitchen knife or take some pills, just don't go killing yourself with a Centac or DEA gun. The family might sue the Agency, huh? Asshole told me, 'Hey, Ichi, the shrink said you were feelin' so down, you might commit hara-kiri.' Then he gives me this little nervous laugh. Didn't even pronounce it right. He said it like Harry Carry."

Wolfe knew it was good for the angry, mangled agent to vent. "Didn't even know hara-kiri from seppuku, huh?"

Komeito looked at him in surprise. "You're a *budoka,* huh? What arts you in?"

"None anymore," said Wolfe. "Isshin-ryu karate and shotokan for a while, a little kendo."

"My dad taught me goju-ryu," Komeito said wistfully. "I haven't kept up with it like I should. Maybe after Centac dumps me, I can get a job teaching karate to cripples."

Wolfe glanced at the blunt stump that ended just below the agent's elbow. "You'll have one hell of a focused right reverse punch," he observed.

There was a pause, and then Komeito laughed out loud. "Wolfe," he said, his voice free of tension for the first time since they met, "anybody ever tell you, you got a sick sense of humor?"

"Yes," Wolfe answered with his own smile. The ice was broken now.

"So where do I go from here?" Komeito asked quietly. "I don't suppose there's any way to change the policy? They said I'm fully disabled, so therefore I'm out, a hundred percent pension, thanks for giving your right arm for us, *sayonara.* That's it?"

"It usually is," Wolfe admitted. "But remember, even though you started with DEA, you're still Centac now. Centac does a lot more Intelligence analysis work, like CIA. There are things you could be doing for us that would keep you out of the field but still on the job. It would have to be the director's decision. Let me talk to him."

"What would be the chances of me getting back on this case, Wolfe? Finding the men who did this to me? Who killed my partners?"

"Something between slim and none," Wolfe said straightforwardly. "You know that. If the guys go down, their families will say you did it for revenge. Puts you and the Agency both in a bad civil liability posture."

"Bullshit," said Ichi. "What about the Hispanic agent, the woman that was kidnapped after the Michigan massacre? Centac got her out, put her right back on the case soon as she was out of the hospital, and she got both the bastards that done it to them. What was her name, Carmella something."

Wolfe forced himself to stay expressionless in face and voice as he said, "Carmelita Morales. I know the case. That was different for a couple of reasons. The first guy she shot had just murdered a lawyer, and he was the object of a nationwide manhunt. No jury in the country would have found against her. We—she got the second one in Venezuela. Criminals in Venezuela don't have any recourse in civil law for injuries they suffer. Besides, it was a public-relations coup at a time when DEA and Centac both needed a good morale builder. What I'm saying is that's an exception to the rule. Nothing like that ever happened in the history of the Agency before, and nothing like it probably ever will again."

"Yeah, but—Wait a minute! That's the exit there! Shit!"

"No problem," Wolfe answered coolly. A quick look at the three rearview mirrors showed that the traffic was way behind him. Harry executed a "one-eighty," the evasive driving movement that snaps the steering wheel halfway through a full revolution and then immediately back. Within a few feet of forward movement, the Dodge crossed from the center lane to the inside and then into the exit lane, its tires squealing in protest. Wolfe jabbed the brakes rapidly to slow the car enough to make the curve of the exit ramp.

"Thank God for seat belts," Komeito said dryly.

Wolfe glanced one more time in the rearview. Several cars behind, he saw a faded red Ford pickup truck lurch into the exit lane from the centerline of the highway, nearly overturning when it went over the median strip. The pickup righted itself as behind it angry motorists blared their horns.

Komeito started to turn toward the sound. "Don't look over your shoulder," snapped Wolfe. "Use your side mirror."

They both tried to be nonchalant, not giving off the body language of alert, as they scanned the rearviews.

"You know a couple of hillbilly types, scraggy beards?"

"Negative," said Komeito.

"Could they have been there the night of the shooting?"

"Damned if I know," Komeito answered. "All I saw was muzzle-flashes."

The truck's movement pattern was consistent with someone following them. There was no radio, no cellular phone in the rented Dodge. Wolfe knew the two of them were alone, and the one-armed agent had no weapon.

Wolfe asked, "You familiar with the Glock 17?"

"Enough to work it, I guess."

Wolfe slowly drew the pistol from behind his right hip, keeping it low and out of sight as he slid it across the seat. "It's got the plus-two magazine extender on it. Twenty rounds total, 9 mm. No safety catch, it just shoots like a revolver. Keep your finger out of the trigger guard till you're ready to fire. It's got a lot easier trigger than the SIG you're used to."

Komeito asked, "What about you?"

"I've got a backup on my ankle," Wolfe said.

The one-armed agent glanced into the side-view mirror. The exit ramp had taken them almost immediately onto a narrow, two-lane road. A beautiful lake, wide and blue, spread off to their right. "So," Komeito asked, "what's the game plan?"

Wolfe answered, "Do you remember the FBI firefight in Miami?"

14

There probably wasn't a cop in the country, and certainly there was not a single Federal agent, who didn't know the details of the April 11, 1986, gun battle. It had been made into a reasonably authentic TV movie, and the FBI had done its own dramatic video recreation, which included interviews with survivors. FBI agents had been involved in many shootings in Miami, but there was only one FBI Miami firefight.

A rolling stakeout of more than two dozen agents had been put in the field by the FBI's two-hundred-man Miami office after a pair of gunmen who used assault weapons and paramilitary tactics to rob banks and armored cars. Their pattern of violence was escalating. They had gone from robbing their victims to gratuitously murdering them. The Bureau knew it was dealing with two white males in their thirties, possibly members of an organized right-wing hate group.

On the eleventh, an unmarked car with two FBI SWAT men assigned to the project, Ben Grogan and Jerry Dove, spotted a black Chevrolet Monte Carlo. The car and its license plates matched those of a target shooter who had been befriended by the two suspects at a lonely public shooting area in the Everglades, and then shot down and left for dead while they stole his car and his guns. Grogan broadcast the description of the vehicle excitedly.

They were on the South Dixie Highway on the outskirts of the city, near a heavily traveled Burger King and shopping mall type thoroughfare. As the fugitive vehicle turned down a side street, the agents broadcast for assistance.

There were some fourteen FBI men on the assignment. Not all of them got there in time. The net had been cast too wide. Six agents, including the ones with the submachine guns, never made it.

But another six did. The car with big Edmundo Mireles and suave, graying John Hanlon was soon behind Grogan and Dove. Next in the deadly prefuneral cortege was Richard Manauzzi, alone in his unmarked car. Expecting trouble, both Manauzzi and Hanlon drew their service revolvers, one placing the gun in his lap and the other under his thigh for quick access.

Agents Ron Risner, another SWAT man, and Gil Aurrantia were in a fourth FBI car racing to assist. Coming in from the opposite direction, alone in his Oldsmobile, was the supervisor of the operation, Gordon McNeill.

McNeill passed the Monte Carlo to connoiter it. The driver just glared at him coldly. It was, McNeill would remember later in his hospital bed, the purposeful stare of a man on a mission. McNeill saw the man next to the driver shove a long, banana-shaped cartridge clip into an automatic rifle. Barking a warning into his microphone, McNeill slammed his car into a U-turn and joined the ominous convoy.

In the lead car, Grogan, who had been head of the FBI/Miami SWAT team, said excitedly into the microphone, "Felony car stop! Let's do it!"

Grogan and Dove passed the Monte Carlo, then pulled in front of it and jammed on the brakes. Police pursuit drivers called it "bulldogging." McNeill swung out and up, alongside the fugitive black coupe to keep it from passing the lead FBI car through the open lane on the left. Manauzzi closed in from the rear, completing a three-car box-in of the Monte Carlo.

McNeill rammed the robber-killers' car from the side. Manauzzi rammed it from the back.

Inside the Monte Carlo, the fight was on. Edward Matix, at the wheel, and Mike Platt, holding the assault rifle, had met in the Army at a ranger school. They had known the day would come when they would face a challenge more formidable than helpless, unarmed victims begging for their lives. They had been firing a thousand rounds a week in combat practice out in the swamps.

Matix fought back savagely, ramming the long-nosed coupe back into the Olds, then cutting right toward the one open avenue. There was no sidewalk there, just sandy road shoulder, and the furiously churning wheels of the black Chevy spewed up a wall of dust like a sandstorm. He rammed Manauzzi's vehicle, sending the agent's revolver flying into the backseat and springing open the driver's door. Manauzzi thought his only gun was gone onto the roadway.

Out of the cloud of dust came the Monte Carlo, fishtailing, racing desperately in the other direction. McNeill slammed his Oldsmobile into a racing drift and followed, but Manauzzi got there first, smashing his car into the left door of the fleeing coupe and driving it up onto the sidewalk until it crashed against a tree, coming to rest at last with Manauzzi's car locked against it in tandem.

It was then that Michael Platt came up shooting.

Flame roared from the muzzle of his Ruger Mini-14 assault rifle again and again as he fired across his partner from the right front seat, blinding and deafening Matix. Hit in the shoulder and chest and believing he had lost his gun, Manauzzi rolled out his left door, out of the line of fire.

And then McNeill was there, braking his Olds to a screaming stop behind the Monte Carlo, blocking it. He bailed out and ran around the other agent's car, drawing his snub-nosed .357 Magnum.

From across the hood of Manauzzi's car, McNeill opened fire, and Platt shot back. One of the senior agent's bullets hammered into the chest of the driver, Matix, but a high-velocity bullet from Platt's rifle tore McNeill's gun hand apart in a welter of blood and bone fragments. McNeill managed to empty the .357 before he ducked behind the car to reload.

Hanlon and Mireles had now joined the fight. The big Hispanic was the only one of the agents with a long gun where he could reach it, and he grabbed a Remington 870 pump shotgun as he raced to help McNeill, who was trying to reload. Hanlon's gun had gone flying from the seat during the violent movements of the pullover attempt. He grabbed his 5-shot Chief Special .38 from his ankle holster. Seeing Grogan apparently alone by his Buick, he sprinted toward him to back him up.

Mireles was bringing his shotgun up when the .223 slug caught him in the arm with a sledgehammer blow that flung him flat on his back. He looked down at the mangled arm and knew he would never use it again.

Near him, McNeill tried to pull out of the way as he struggled desperately to reload his revolver. Blood and bone chips fell from his hand into the gun, jamming it. And then Platt loomed over the roof of the car with the assault rifle in his hand. There was time for McNeill to see the killer grin before the high-speed bullet slammed into his neck and ranged down into his liver. McNeill collapsed, paralyzed.

The firing was now fast and furious. Matix had crawled out of the car and opened fire with a sawed-off shotgun that had an extended magazine. Platt had grabbed spare ammo clips and was firing his rifle as fast as he could pull the trigger, each jerk of his finger spitting out another deadly .223-caliber M-16 bullet.

Dove, on the other side of the Buick, emptied his 15-shot Smith & Wesson 9 mm rapidly. One of the bullets ripped through the rifleman's arm and into his chest, cutting the pulmonary artery. Instead of falling down, though, the raging killer returned another fusillade of fire. Dove reloaded his empty gun, then ducked through the front seat of the Buick and emerged on the left side.

Across the street, Risner and Aurrantia had come to a stop. From his vantage point, Risner could see what the other agents could not: as Matix distracted the ones by the Buick with the shotgun, Platt was making an end run around behind the black sedan.

"Look out," Risner screamed. "He's coming behind you!" But in the excitement and the din of the gunfire, no one could hear him.

Hanlon fired all five shots at the running gunman, but his snub-nosed .38 was a last-ditch, close-range weapon, and the bullets missed. As he scrunched down behind the Buick to reload, one of Platt's bullets shattered his arm and sent him rolling. His gun fell to the sidewalk, a cartridge inserted halfway in the cylinder.

No one heard Risner's warning, and the agent couldn't fire from where he was without hitting his own men. Platt rounded the trunk of the car and opened fire, blood pouring from his own wounded chest onto the trunk of the black Buick. He shot Hanlon between the legs, the bullet entering beside the privates and exploding deep in the agonized agent's belly.

Grogan and McNeill turned to face the threat from behind, but the rifle was already bucking in the killer's hands. Grogan cried "Oh, my God," as the bullets tore his life away. Platt shot young Agent Dove in the head and chest, and he fell without a word alongside Grogan, partners in death as in life. Platt fired a coup de grace into the dead agent to make sure.

From across the street, Risner and Aurrantia emptied their guns, and Platt shot back. Wounded, Aurrantia ducked down into the front seat to reload, but Risner put a bullet through Platt's wrist.

The killer's arm had been hit again by a 9 mm slug, and this one finished destroying the limb. The assault rifle dropped from his dead arm.

He was next to the open driver's door of Grogan's FBI Buick. The wounded Matix had made his way to the other door of the same car. They'd dropped their primary guns, but both were still armed with long-barreled .357 Magnum revolvers in shoulder holsters under their flowing print shirts.

As Platt jumped behind the wheel, big Ed Mireles crawled to the nearest car, braced the barrel of his shotgun across its bumper, and fired one-handed. To pump the empty shell out and another one in, he had to brace the butt on the ground, then bring it back up to aim, using only his right hand.

One blast on the double-ought 12-gauge Magnum buckshot tore Platt's left foot apart. Another smashed into Matix's face, tearing his jaws and teeth asunder.

Platt pulled himself out of the car, twisting the big black revolver from his shoulder holster left-handed. He triggered three shots at Mireles and, satisfied that he had killed him, staggered back to the Buick and pulled himself behind the steering wheel.

His ruined arm pulsing in agony, his shotgun empty, Mireles saw they were going to drive over the corpses of his friends and escape. The red, killing rage of battle was upon him.

No, you bastards, Mireles thought. It's over.

The witnesses huddled behind cover in their nearby suburban homes peeked out as the gunfire lulled, and saw the huge man with the tattered arm loom up from behind a car. They saw him tug a revolver from under the windbreaker. Mireles was losing consciousness, and every step was agony. He walked like

Frankenstein's monster, slowly, stiffly, as he made his way toward the Buick with the gun at the end of his one good arm.

He began firing.

Platt jerked as the bullets hit him in the head and neck, paralyzing him. The heavy Magnum fell from his nerveless hand. Before Matix could bring up his own .357, Mireles shot him three times in smooth cadence—blam...blam...blam—in the head and neck.

Just before Eddie Mireles's knees buckled, he carefully peered through the gathering darkness of unconsciousness, sighted his gun on Platt and fired his last bullet through the cop-killer's brain.

ICHIRO KOMEITO had studied the classic firefight in training, and Wolfe had gone over it as intensively as a West Pointer analyzing the Battle of Waterloo. In less than four minutes, seven of the eight good guys had been shot, two of them killed and three injured for life.

All that had been done by two ruthless criminals who knew how to fight and how to shoot, in what had started as a car chase.

It had turned out that Platt and Matix had no drugs or booze in them, and were never involved with any organized group. They were just free-lance bandits who knew what they were doing, ready to kill and ready to die.

And now, behind the two Centac agents on the lonely lakeside road, loomed a pickup truck with two men in it, God knows how heavily armed or how stoned, and it was two against two instead of two against eight. More correctly, it was two men against one agent whose hands were tied up on a steering wheel, and another with only one hand and an unfamiliar gun to hold in it.

When Wolfe asked him if he remembered the FBI firefight in Miami, Komeito replied tightly, "Never forget. Never again, anyway. I should have learned from those guys to always have extra guns on. I should have that night in the national forest."

"There are more lessons than that," said Wolfe evenly, eyeing the pickup behind them in his mirror. "Ramming the cars in the beginning was an act of deadly force, in itself. If they could do that, they should have opened fire as soon as they came abreast of the Monte Carlo."

"But we don't know if they've got guns, or even who the hell they are," Komeito protested.

"True," said Wolfe, "which is why we aren't going to pull up alongside and open up. But if we see guns, we'll shoot first if we can. Look, these could just be a couple of drunks out running around.

"But the other thing," Wolfe continued. "Did you ever wonder why Platt did all the killing, and Matix just got off a round or two with the shotgun and didn't hit anybody? The wound McNeill put in his chest wasn't that bad. But his partner was stupid enough to open the gunfight by firing more than half a magazine from a high-powered automatic rifle right in front of his face. He must have been stunned out, half-deaf and half-blind.

"That means, if we're going to shoot, we want to be on the left so you can fire out your side instead of across me. That'll force them to shoot across each other. Hey, maybe we're paranoid and it's just a couple of good ol' boys who can't drive worth a damn."

Ichiro Komeito, his index finger extended away from the trigger and his other fingers clenched tightly around the gray plastic handle of the Glock, said tensely, "I think we're about to find out."

"I THINK THEY'RE on to us, bro," Danny Queen growled. "Keep lookin' at us in the mirror. I can see the white guy's eyes. Mr. Cool, like he don't give a fuck."

"We'll change that real quick," giggled J.J. excitedly. His bladder was about to burst. "You ready?"

"Thor said do it where there weren't no witnesses. We only had one car go by us on the other side since we got off the interstate, an' ain't nobody on our side of the road 'cept us an' them. You got a round in the chamber, safety off?"

"Yeah, yeah!"

"I ain't got a gun," Danny told his brother. "Gimme your sixgun."

J.J. frowned. "Okay," he said after a moment, pulling his Taurus .357 from his belt and handing it across the seat. "But remember, now, these fuckers are mine! You got your own Aryan Warrior. Now it's my turn."

"Okay, okay," said Danny, agitated. He shoved the gun in the front of his waistband. "Look, you ready or not?"

J.J. giggled, bouncing up and down in the seat like a little boy. His hands were sweaty on the shotgun. "Fuckin' right, I'm ready!"

"Okay, then," Danny said solemnly, downshifting. "Let's do it."

"WE'VE MADE eye contact," Wolfe said calmly. "Leave your lap belt on and slip out of the chest belt so you can move." In a fluid, practiced motion, Wolfe shrugged the chest restraint behind his back. It took Komeito a moment to maneuver the belt with the tender stump of his arm. He didn't want to raise the pistol or let go of it.

Wolfe touched the buttons on his armrest and brought all four windows down as far as they'd go. The glass wouldn't stop a bullet, but it could make *them* miss, firing from the inside out. The open windows would vent the sound if they did have to fire from the front seat, and keep them from going deaf afterward. Besides, they didn't need flying glass in their eyes, and the safety glass down in the door frame gave the doors a laminar effect that would stop pistol bullets or buckshot pellets better.

The narrow road that ran alongside Fernan Lake grew straight for a moment. Suddenly the red Ford slewed out to the left and raced forward, coming up hard and fast along Wolfe's left side.

Harry forced himself to keep the pace even. He poised his left foot above the brake and locked his hands tight on the steering wheel at nine and three o'clock as he kept an even pace with his right foot on the accelerator.

Wolfe glanced left.

He saw the ugly blue muzzle of the sawed-off shotgun come up.

Wolfe pulled his right foot off the gas pedal and rammed his left foot down hard on the brake. At that moment, the shotgun fired. Even in the bright daylight, the burning gunpowder at the muzzle of the powerful, stubby weapon created a huge orange fireball.

The blast of the shotgun that close was like a grenade. The pickup was less than five feet to the left when the shotgun went off. But Wolfe had suddenly decelerated, falling back from behind the blast as the gun went off, and the swarm of buckshot pellets aimed through the window went too far forward.

Even over the blast Wolfe could hear the ringing sound in from of him, of lead hitting steel, could see the grooves gouged across the hood of the car from left to right as two or three of the pellets skidded across the front of the car and flew harmlessly out over the lake.

Wolfe's fast braking forced the pickup to race ahead. Wolfe cut left, into the opposite lane, the wrong side of the road, straight behind the truck. The man in the truck's front seat could fire to four o'clock, Wolfe knew, but he couldn't fire to six o'clock without leaning out the window and losing balance. Wolfe reflexively took the six-o'clock position.

Harry stomped on the accelerator. "Brace yourself," he yelled to Ichiro Komeito as the car surged forward and collided with the rear bumper of the truck. Glass tinkled as the headlights disintegrated in the front of the white Dodge.

Then there was a mechanical whine and roar as the truck accelerated too. Amazingly it pulled forward, away from the Dodge. Wolfe realized the thing must have one hell of an engine. The transmission of the truck must have still been in third gear; Wolfe could hear the engine whining at redline.

Wolfe's car was straight in line now behind the red pickup. He saw the man in the right front twist, lean out, aim back. Wolfe jerked the steering wheel to the left. The orange fire flared again at the muzzle of the gun, and Wolfe heard through the open windows the singing sound of the pellets ricocheting from the pavement behind them.

He was now to the left rear of the truck. He saw the driver's left arm snake out, a blue police-style service revolver in the hand. The man just held the gun straight back behind him, the muzzle upside down, and Wolfe knew he was going to shoot. He swung the car right again, back into the protection of the six-o'clock position just behind the truck, even as the man pulled the trigger.

The shots sounded soft and distant, drowned out by the wind howling through the open windows, but Wolfe saw the pinecone-shaped orange muzzle-flashes and heard the dull *chong* as one of the bullets ripped into the bodywork of the car.

The truck veered a bit to the right. The driver was trying to get a better angle to shoot. He had forgotten about giving his partner a good firing angle.

There would never be a better time.

Wolfe barked, "Ready!" He did another one-eighty, snapping into the left lane with sickening G-force and righting the vehicle straight again. They were now at seven o'clock behind the pickup, and Wolfe was gunning the accelerator to maximum speed. He was grateful there was no vehicle in the oncoming lane he now occupied.

The Dodge drew abreast of the Ford pickup. In the cab of the truck, Wolfe could see that the man with the sawed-off shotgun was twisting around, getting ready to shoot out the left window. The driver had one arm out the window, holding the blue-steel revolver.

On the right side of the seat he sat on, Wolfe saw Ichiro Komeito start to lean out the window, extending the pistol awkwardly in his one good hand.

"No," Wolfe snapped. "Not yet!"

The agent cried, "What?"

Wolfe exploded, "Dammit, pull in. Now!"

Komeito obeyed Wolfe's command just as the driver of the Ford raised the pistol, trying to come level with them. Wolfe could see the hollow-nosed bullets in the chambers of the revolver.

Harry Wolfe, his car now parallel with the pickup, cut hard right. The Dodge met the pickup with a spray of sparks and the unearthly, unnatural grinding sound of steel on steel. Wolfe could almost feel the incisive impact as something soft was caught between the two auto bodies. There was a muffled thud as the Magnum went off, its bullet going harmlessly into the pavement, as the roof of the sedan at the rear window met the truck just below its higher driver's window, severing the arm of Danny Queen. There was another shotgun blast, but nothing hit Wolfe's car.

The truck jerked out to the side.

Wolfe shouted, "Now!"

Ichiro Komeito opened fire.

DANNY QUEEN CURSED when his brother's shot missed. J.J. fired just as the Dodge they'd pulled abreast of had suddenly decelerated, and the shotgun blast had gone too far forward.

J.J. felt a cold chill as he pumped the shotgun to chamber the second round. This bastard had anticipated. He'd made him miss.

Then the white car was behind him, and J.J. felt his body jerk as the bumper of the sedan rammed the back of the stolen Ford pickup. He leaned out and forward, trying to get the shot, and just as he jerked on the trigger, the white car seemed to dance out of range. J.J. saw a whitish puff as the lead pellets hit the pavement, harmlessly ricocheting away behind the car.

The next thing J.J. knew, he heard a shot from his brother's side. He had the revolver just stuck out the window, holding it upside down, shooting backward. He did it again.

"Stop it," J.J. screamed. "They're mine! I told you! They're mine!"

It was going wrong, all wrong! The white Dodge was swinging out from behind them now, coming up on the left, coming up fast.

J.J. pumped the Remington again.

The white car was next to them now. J.J. was going to fire when the white car lurched suddenly toward them, slamming into the truck with a shower of sparks, and the impact threw J.J. back against the door on his side. He felt the pain of a rib breaking as it was squashed against the armrest.

J.J. ignored it. Aryan Warrior, he thought. Aryan Warrior!

Beside him, Danny cried out, a wordless wail. "Aaaahhh!"

He saw his brother's left arm come up from reflex.

There was no gun there.

There was no *hand*.

There was only the stump of the wrist, and dark red blood gouting out, pulsing in a thick heavy stream.

The car was next to them now, the bearded Aryan at the wheel and the gook on J.J.'s side of the car, coming up with an ugly black pistol. The Aryan had done this.

Betrayer!

J.J. shoved his gun toward the target and jerked the trigger again.

Danny screamed once more. "Aaaahhh!"

The muzzle blast had gone off right in Danny's face. The orange fireball of burning gunpowder had burned into his eyes as the buckshot pellets swept past him, going harmlessly over the roof of the white Dodge. The explosive blast of the shotgun had been inches from his ears. Neither man noticed, but blood began to trickle from the ears of Danny Queen. His eardrums had been ruptured.

"Aaaahhh!" Danny screamed again. But he couldn't hear his own voice, and his brother didn't hear him, either. He had tuned him out. He was pumping the shotgun to fire again.

The gook! The Aryan Betrayer! They were his now, *his!*

Then Ichiro Komeito started shooting.

It was strange. J.J. couldn't really register the sounds of shots fired, but he could hear clearly the *chong-chong-chong* of the bullets biting into the sheet metal of the Ford's left side.

Something smashed J.J. in the shoulder like a ball-peen hammer. He jerked back. There was a sudden deep burning pain, from the right front of his chest to the right back, as if someone had run a red-hot poker through his lung. Another agonizing pain impacted in his knee, and all the pains acted together in a chorus of agony that made him scream. He could hear that his brother was screaming, too.

The metal-hitting-metal sounds wouldn't stop. He heard his brother's cry stop suddenly in a choking, gagging sound, and he heard something like flesh being slapped, and Danny was thrown sideways into him.

There was another smacking sound. Something wet and fleshy slapped into J.J.'s face. He realized it was something blown out of his brother's mouth as a bullet hit him, because now Danny was slumping toward him, his eyes glazed and rolling up into his head, and blood pouring out of both his nostrils like a faucet.

No, his mind screamed. Danny can't be hurt. Besides, Danny's driving.

A new pain bit him deep in his belly, joining the others, and J.J. heard his own voice cry, "Stop! Stop!"

And then there was one more terrible steel impact, one more howling, grinding sound.

The world seemed to tilt crazily, and J.J. heard his own voice screaming as his brother's dead body fell heavily and wetly onto him, the blood pouring everywhere.

Then the truck was airborne, and the world was turning. Just before the sickening crash that made J.J. black out, he felt the force of the impact that ruptured his full bladder and tore it loose from the ureters. The pain was like nothing he could ever have imagined.

After that, there was silent darkness.

THE SHOTS CAME FASTER than Wolfe had anticipated. His first thought was, The kid's shooting too fast, he's going to miss them all. But when he glanced to the side after he slammed against the Ford and amputated the revolver man's arm, he saw the holes appearing in the car door and in the driver's face and saw the man on the other side take the hits. The bullets seemed to appear as dark dots on his flannel shirt, sucking the fabric inward, then the fabric came back out again under the pressure of the spurting blood.

He rammed the car once more, and the truck suddenly disappeared behind him. Wolfe fought to keep control of his car. In the rearview mirror he could see the pickup arcing over the edge, down toward the water and the beach below.

Wolfe stopped the white sedan as soon as he could. He glanced over to his right, and saw that the slide was locked back empty on his Glock pistol in the other agent's hand.

"I'm empty," Komeito said, and his voice was tense more from excitement than fear.

Wolfe's ears were ringing from the gunshots, even though the windows had been open. "Here," he said, pulling his spare 19-shot magazine from the pouch behind his left hip and holding it across the seat to the other agent.

He turned to look over his shoulder as Komeito reached over for the cartridge clip from his hand. Behind him there was only a cloud of dust on the side of the road where the truck had gone over and down, toward the lake and maybe into it.

The magazine was plucked from Harry's hand. He glanced over. Komeito had already used the tip of his middle finger to press the magazine release button left-handed and dump the empty clip. He saw Ichi put the empty gun down between his thighs, the muzzle toward the floor of the car and the butt up. He jammed the plastic magazine into the butt of the gun until he felt it click into place, then he twisted his left wrist and picked the gun up, rotating it into a firing position. He had to fumble for a second before he realized that the tip of his left index finger could trip the slide release.

As the slide slammed forward, reloading the gun, Wolfe realized that the snub-nosed custom .357 Magnum revolver was in his right hand. He didn't recall reaching down for it.

They both held fully loaded guns in their hands now. Harry said softly, "You okay?"

"Never better," said Ichiro Komeito with an edge in his voice. "*Never* better."

Wolfe guided the car forward, then turned back the way they had come, until they reached the point where the tire tracks had gone over the edge of the low cliff. They got out of the car, their guns in their hands.

The truck was fifteen feet below them beneath a rocky outcropping, its front end in the water up to the windshield, which had been blown out by the impact. Wolfe could see that the shore was steep. It wasn't just a lake. It was what Scotsmen called a tarn, a mountain lake, a pocket of water forged between two steep cliffs. It dropped off rapidly into incredible depths.

Harry and Komeito could see that the vehicle was almost imperceptibly quivering. It was right on the edge of going all the way under. Their pistols extended in front of them, the Centac agents descended the sand-covered rocks of the slope to where the truck lay.

J. J. Queen was half in, half out of the upside-down pickup. His eyes were closed. The corpse of Danny Queen was curled up in a fetal position between him and the other side door. The wounds in his face and head and neck were obvious. He had been dead before the truck hit the water.

They pulled J.J. out of the truck and up onto the sandy beach. They felt the truck inch forward as they took his stabilizing weight away.

J.J.'s eyelids fluttered, then held open. His eyes rolled around for a moment before they fixed on the face of Harry Wolfe hovering above him.

"Oh, God," J.J. whispered. "Oh, God..."

Wolfe ran his eyes over the man in front of him. J.J.'s left arm was bent at a crazy angle. Blood soaked his shoulder and the ragged hole where the bullet had entered. There was another hole in his right chest, and as J.J. fought to breathe, Wolfe could hear the telltale slurping sounds of tension pneumothorax, the sucking chest wound. There was a bullet hole in one knee. The man's jeans were dark and wet: he had urinated and defecated in his pants the moment of impact, but it had been too late to relieve the pressure of the full bladder that had ruptured during the crash, exploding the insides of his lower abdomen. Wolfe realized the man was probably dying and that he couldn't tell how long it would take for that to happen.

Harry slipped his revolver back into his ankle holster, then knelt next to the fallen man. He ran his hands over him. J.J. had no weapons left on his person.

"Ichi," said Wolfe softly, addressing the other Centac man by his nickname for the first time, "I need the medical kit that's in my leather case in the backseat."

"Okay, Harry," said Komeito in the same hushed tone of voice. The danger they had been through had forged them into friends.

When Ichi was gone, J.J. said, "I can't move my legs, man. It hurts. Oh, God, it hurts..."

"I know," Wolfe said gently. "But I have to ask you some things."

"Fuck you," J.J. gasped in agony. "Fuck you, man!"

Wolfe thought about saying, "No, fuck *you,*" but he kept silent. He didn't want to antagonize the man he was about to inject with truth serum.

Komeito was back at his side now. He held out the attaché case that had been in Wolfe's backseat. The Glock was in his waistband.

"Thanks," said Harry. He withdrew the narrow, foot-long leatherette case that looked like a huge eyeglass container. "Ichi," he said, "the rest of this has to go back in the car now."

The other agent looked at him. "Don't give me that shit, man! *I* put these guys down. I ain't your gofer!"

Wolfe returned the stare. "Do it," he said flatly. "If you want to ever be an agent again, I'm telling you Ichi, do it. And stay by the car for a minute."

Komeito hesitated for an instant. Then he snatched the attaché case from Wolfe, turned on his heel and started to struggle back up the incline.

Wolfe opened the case. He quickly fixed the needle to the syringe, inserted the tip into the one remaining ampoule of Amytal and filled it. Then he grabbed J. J. Queen's arm, inserted the needle into the brachial artery expertly and emptied the syringe.

It usually took a while for truth serum to take effect. But J. J. Queen was weak and drunk to begin with, and his body was shattered and dying, and the medicine took hold far sooner.

Ichi Komeito was already back when Wolfe began the questioning of the dying man.

"What's your name?"

"J. J. Queen. John James Queen."

"Who's the other guy in the car?"

"Danny. My brother. Oh, Jesus, is Danny okay?"

"Danny's not in pain or anything, J.J. I need to ask you some stuff, okay?"

"Okay. Ow. Oh, God, it hurts..."

"It's cool, J.J.," Wolfe said soothingly. "Tell me the truth, and in a minute, I'll give you a shot, make the pain go away."

"Yeah. Gimme the shot, man."

"Not yet, J.J. Tell me the truth, were you there when they shot the agents in the national forest?"

J.J. giggled through his pain. "Fuck, man, was I *there?* Danny killed the pig, man. Killed the ZOGger. I was up on the hill shootin' it out with two of 'em, man. The nigger and the gook. But it was Rhino blew away them two, man. Ow. Uuunh! Jesus!"

"Never mind the pain, J.J. I told you, I'll give you a shot for that. Who killed Passeretti? The agent with the Jeep station wagon?"

J.J.'s eyes were glazing over. His voice began to match. "The Armorer and Thor said they shot him, but it was Danny. My brother, Danny, man! He killed that ZOG motherfucker! Them other ones just shot him and didn't kill him, or shot him after he was dead. The Armorer and Thor—they're chicken-shit, man. Danny Queen done *that* pig, man!"

"You were down by the Jeep, then?"

"No, man, I was up on the hill! I didn't get the nigger or the gook, but I tried, man. I tried! Aaaahhh!"

"Easy, J.J., easy," Wolfe said in his softest voice. "I told you, I'll give you a shot in a minute, make the pain stop."

"Gimme it now, man! Gimme it now! Aaahhh..."

"Who sent you out, man?" Wolfe's voice was solicitous. "Was it the Team?"

"Yeah, yeah, 'course. Help me, man! It's like my guts are burnin'!"

"I'll help you in a minute," Wolfe said placatingly. "You were sent by somebody, right?"

"Yeah," J.J. blurted. "Will. Will Pelham. Will's gonna save the white race from the mongrels, man! Gonna be President one day, man!"

"Where," Wolfe asked gently, "is Will now?"

"In the hills," said J.J. "In the hills. Away from our citadel. Can't let 'em find us. Can't let Jew-nigger-Commies from ZOG find us...."

"The citadel," Wolfe said encouragingly. "Where's the citadel, J.J.?"

"Can't tell ya..."

"Come on. I'll get Will for you. I'll bring him here, to help you."

"No," croaked J.J. "No! Can't tell. Can't tell!"

What kind of fanatics are these? Wolfe thought. The Medellín cartel's enforcers gave up their info for this drug. The Cali cartel gave it up. What does this 'Will' do to keep them from saying it, even when they're in extremis and dying, and they've got the truth serum in them?

"Where is Will, J.J.?" Wolfe's voice had become sharp and harsh, the command voice he would use on a dog. It was what he'd been told to do with an uncooperative suspect under the drug.

"No," wailed J.J., "No! Will's like God, man. Will *is* God, man! I ain't gonna be the one rats him out, man!"

It was going nowhere. Wolfe changed the subject.

"You tried to kill us today. Why?"

"ZOG, man," bleated J.J. "White Dodge. ZOG! Gonna fuck us! We gotta fuck 'em first, man! Make Aryan Warrior, man..."

The voice trailed off, and Wolfe realized that he had learned nothing he hadn't already known and that there was nothing more to be gained by pursuing this line of questioning.

Ichiro Komeito was standing behind him, staring over his shoulder. Wolfe turned. "Ichi," he said, "I need you to get back up on the road, flag down a car."

"Get fucked, Harry," Ichi sneered back. "You're crazy. There hasn't been a car by here since it happened.

Wolfe glared at him. "I have to do something now," Wolfe said, finally and simply. "I want you to still have your pension. I want you to still have a chance to be Centac. And I *need* you to get up on the hill, okay?"

There was a long pause. Then Ichiro Komeito returned Wolfe's stare and said, "Okay. I'll go up the hill. And I'm going to hold you to what you said."

"I think you should," Wolfe replied, and Ichi waited a moment before he turned and walked back up to where the white Dodge was parked.

As soon as Ichi turned away, Wolfe did what he had to do. He opened the long case with its full-length miniature piano hinge and withdrew an ampoule of dark brown fluid. It was the stuff that CIA had given him.

Wolfe punched the tip of the needle through the ampoule, then drew back the double finger-loops of the syringe, creating a suction effect. In a moment the syringe was full of the deadly brown liquid.

The first game plan, the truth serum, hadn't worked. The second plan would. Wolfe looked down at the inside of J. J. Queen's blood-soaked elbow. He thought, cruelly, that AIDS would not be a concern for this particular patient.

As Wolfe took J. J. Queen's arm into his left hand, he felt the man convulse, then twitch again.

There was a raspy *ch-ch-ch* sound in the fallen man's throat. Wolfe recognized it instantly. He had heard the death rattle before.

Wolfe heard Ichi yell "Look out!"

The weight of the precariously balanced truck had finally won the battle of gravity. The crumpled upside-down Ford pickup was sliding forward into the lake. Slowly at first, then faster. The open windows helped the water rush in. The truck, and Danny Queen's corpse, disappeared in a few seconds under the dark surface of Fernan Lake.

Wolfe saw it go under with a few giant bubbles. He turned to J. J. Queen again.

J.J.'s eyes fluttered at the lids. The eyeballs seemed to roll up. The eyelids closed, and then they slowly drew open again, and when they did, there was mostly white showing. The brown irises were turned up halfway out of sight.

In the center of those irises, the pupils of the eyes had turned from small dark dots of the normal, living human eye looking into daylight to wide-open black holes. "Fixed and dilated pupils." That's what Wolfe had been taught in the emergency trauma medical class.

He looked down, close. There was no movement. Wolfe touched his finger to the mandibular notch at the back of J. J. Queen's jaw, where the carotid artery would give the strongest pulse beat to the fingertip of someone outside that particular body.

Nothing.

Harry Wolfe realized that the filled syringe of CIA poison in his hand was superfluous now. J. J. Queen was already dead, as dead as his brother.

Wolfe stood up, away from the corpse. He heard the bubbling sound of the truck going under the water all the way, beginning its final descent to the bottom.

"Holy shit," he heard Ichiro Komeito breathe softly behind him.

The metal case, a foot long and piano hinged and covered with leatherette, lay by his foot. Wolfe reached down and picked it up. He realized now why CIA had made the carrying case this way, and how important it was to have a case he had originally considered too big for the instrument and its four ampoules, the two of Amytal and the two of "the other stuff."

Three of the four ampoules were gone now. Two of the truth serum had been used up, on Harold Howe and J. J. Queen. The third, the first of the two lethal ones, had been sucked up into the syringe.

A syringe case usually carries its burden the way a trap-shooter's case carries his shotgun: broken down in parts. The CIA death master who had crafted this system had obviously been thinking ahead, and that explained the extralong case: it could contain a fully assembled, fully charged syringe, and its steel walls kept it from nailing the owner accidentally if he fell on it.

The hypodermic was already charged with the killer fluid. Wolfe set it gently into the case and closed the lid. There was no place to put it. He shoved the whole steel-lined case into his left hip pocket.

Ichi Komeito was staring at him in horrified fascination.

He said slowly to Wolfe, "You weren't just here to investigate, were you? You were here to take care of it."

Wolfe suddenly felt too tired to lie. "Yeah," he said, "but you took care of it first. Remember what we talked about in the car? You wanted revenge, you wanted your *budo* and your *bushido,* your warrior honor. Well, Ichi, you got it. Happy?"

Komeito shook his head slowly. "I'm not sure."

Wolfe snapped, "What do you want, for Christ's sake? They did you. You did them. You did, you know. Have you accepted that yet?"

Komeito looked him in the eye. "Yeah. Yeah, I guess I have."

In the distance, they could hear sirens. Komeito said, "We didn't run across much traffic, but we went by some houses and mobile homes when the shooting started. I guess somebody called the cops."

"Yeah," sighed Wolfe, "I guess somebody did. Tell you what. You did the shooting, you make the report."

"Bull *shit,* Wolfe," the Asian agent responded. "How the hell am I going to explain this?"

"Tell them the truth," Wolfe retorted instantly. "The truth works great. If nothing else, it hasn't been overworked in court yet. Tell them you were with the lead agent investigating your shooting for Centac, and the shit hit the fan, and—dammit, just tell them the truth."

"You want me to mention the needle?"

"No," Wolfe said, "that's the one part of the whole thing I'd just as soon you left out."

"Why me?" Komeito asked. "You were here. You were driving the car. Why can't you stay here, explain what happened?"

"Because," Wolfe said edgily, "my partner doesn't know where I am. Because we've got to find out about the rest of this crew of scumbags that blew your arm off and left your two buddies for worm chow, remember? Dammit, I'm here to make it as right as we can, what happened to you, okay? And the job ain't over yet, *okay?*"

Komeito took an involuntary step backward. "Sure," he said, "that's cool. But they're going to wonder why the other guy with me, if I'm going to tell the truth like you say, doesn't happen to be here."

"I'll deal with that," said Wolfe. "It's real simple. When the regular cops get here, tell them we got into a shoot-out, and don't go into any details. These dead guys probably have family someplace, and the family's going to sue you for violating their right to life, liberty and the pursuit of killing cops. Tell them you were with me, what the hell. They already know I'm out here assigned to this case."

"What about the gun, Harry? I shot them with your gun."

"It isn't mine," Wolfe replied. "That's a DEA Glock, out of the Spokane office. They issued it to me after they took mine in evidence when I shot Harold Howe. It's the gun they probably should have issued you as soon as you got out of the hospital. Now it's where it belongs. They'll take it back, of course, because you'd been in a shooting with it. But now they'll know that a senior OPR inspector out of D.C. headquarters trusted you to hold his gun for him, and use it, and it worked. Use my name, Ichi. I'll back you up."

The sirens were drawing closer. Wolfe had his .357 snubnose in his ankle holster, and he figured that would get him through the night. After all, reinforcements were coming in at midnight, with more guns.

"Gotta go," Wolfe said. "My partner's waiting for me in a motel in Coeur d'Alene. She doesn't know our cover's been blown. I have to get back there. I hope you understand."

Ichiro Komeito had only one hand to reach out with. He extended his left hand, and Wolfe automatically did the same. Their palms met, and it seemed awkward for a second. Each man squeezed hard. It was a sign of friendship, of brotherhood, of a death battle fought together.

And then Wolfe was going up the hill toward the Dodge. The sirens were coming closer, but they both knew Wolfe would be in the car soon enough to pass the police cars coming in, while he was going the opposite way.

The truck under the lake didn't even bubble anymore. Neither agent had ever noticed that there was a cellular phone wedged under the dashboard, and therefore, neither man knew that the message had gone out to the Team that "Johnny" was an undercover officer from the central tactical unit of the United States Drug Enforcement Administration.

WOLFE FOUND HIS WAY back easily. He felt a sense of relief as he pulled into the parking lot of the cheap motel. He came to the door, rapped once, paused, rapped his knuckle on the door again and, knowing that his secret knock had identified him, inserted his key into the door lock.

He started to reach for the only gun he had left, the one in his ankle holster, and then he caught himself. God, you *are* getting paranoid, he said to himself. He brought his hand back up, empty.

Wolfe was just inside the door when the familiar gaunt figure he recognized to be the Armorer stood out from behind the low bureau and the TV set, holding a big pistol with a heavy-tubed silencer sticking out from the end. The silenced gun was pointed at Wolfe's throat.

"Gotcha," the Armorer muttered triumphantly from behind the silenced pistol. "Gotcha now, you ZOG rat! Just come on in and finish closin' that door behind you."

Harry Wolfe, caught and knowing it, said to himself a word of the kind he didn't usually say out loud. Shit!

15

Carmelita Morales had learned that sometimes she had to go long periods without sleep, on short notice, and she made a point of storing up as much rest as she could during downtime. If Harry was going to do the post-shooting trauma intervention with the survivor of the national forest shooting, she could get in a few winks in the motel room.

She was dozing there when they came for her.

There was no warning before the crash that tore the door off its hinges. Rhino was through the door first, looking like a malignant Gary Larson cartoon with his thick spectacles dwarfed by the beefy face and the huge body. She instantly recognized the gun that was in his hand, pointed at her. It was a DEA-issue Colt submachine gun, the special one made for hitting clandestine drug labs with the flash-and-sound suppressor. She had no doubt it was set on full automatic, nor that it was the one taken from the Centac shoot-out.

Behind him the broad shoulders of Thor filled the doorway, the silvery Walther pistol tiny in his hands, the acne making his face look like a red devil mask. Bringing up the rear was the cadaverous figure of the Armorer, his unwashed face contorted with hatred. In his hand was a pistol with a large silencer on the end.

She knew they had her cold. The 4516 pistol was only a few feet away on the dresser, but she knew they'd blast her to doll rags if she reached. The little .38 was still in the belly band under her sweats. If she could buy some time...

The Armorer scooped the 4516. "He left his piece with you, huh, Chiquita? Lot a good it done ya." He shoved it into the back of his waistband.

Thor put his gun in his pocket and grabbed Carmelita roughly, spinning her around and locking his hands over her upper arms with crushing force. He dug his thumbs into her brachial nerves cruelly. Damn, thought Carmelita. He knows his pressure points. That means he's not just strong, he's trained.

She tried to stay in character and play the helpless little girl. "You're hurting me," she squeaked. Thor snorted in amusement, but he lightened up a little.

Rhino handed the submachine gun to the Armorer and searched Carmelita roughly, pawing her breasts and backside and crotch. He almost missed the bulge below the navel. Then he did a double take and pulled out the waistband of the sweatpants.

Rhino whistled softly. "Check it out, man. Little .38, light as a feather." His piggy eyes narrowed behind the Coke-bottle glasses. "Smart bitch, ain't ya? Gonna shoot us all in the back, second we turned our backs on ya, weren't ya? You know what? I hate smart bitches."

"Gimme that gun," Thor said, gesturing toward the 4516. "You won't need but the one for what you gotta do." The Armorer grudgingly gave him the pistol, and Thor shoved it into his belt at the small of his back.

Helpless. Kidnapped. Not again. Carmelita tried to tune the men out, tried to fight the waves of panic. She remembered the terror of the last time, the helpless dizziness and darkness of the head injury. Not again, *Dios mio,* not again.

She heard the Armorer cackle, hefting the little .38 before he handed it back to Rhino, who stuffed it in the hip pocket. "Another one for the arsenal," the Armorer snickered. "Hey, Chiquita, what is it that makes me think you ain't just a dumb little chick, just got off the banana boat? What is it makes me think you *and* your lying rat boyfriend are ZOG?"

Carmelita forced herself to whimper. "I don't know what you mean. Please, don't hurt me. Johnny'll go crazy if you hurt me."

All three of them laughed out loud. "Ha," Rhino brayed. "Johnny ain't gonna be doin' a whole lotta nothin' no more."

Carmelita said softly, "What are you going to do to me?"

Thor sneered, "I ain't gonna do nothin'. I don't fuck ugly colored pigs like you. But Will has plans for you, Chiquita. Will likes his brown meat. He says only thing you greaser bitches are good for is fuckin' an' cleanin' house. An' we don't need no cleanin' done right now."

"Yeah," blurted Rhino. "You're gonna get a banana, Chiquita! Maybe after Will gets done with ya, you're gonna get a whole lotta bananas." He laughed uproariously at his own joke.

"Let's get goin'," Thor said in a hard voice. He looked at the Armorer and commanded, "Get out the handcuffs."

Carmelita calculated. If they got lax now for one moment... if she could get to a gun and if they dropped their guard, she could take out the three of them.

No good. The iron grasp of Thor on her arms did not relent, and Rhino cautiously covered her with the submachine gun as the Armorer set down his own gun, an ugly one she couldn't recognize, with a silencer. It was out of her reach.

It offended her professionally to see a man covering a prisoner at that angle. If he fired, the bullets would go through her and into the guy's own partner. That gave her small satisfaction. There was no opening to fight. Carmelita did not resist as the thin man twisted her hands painfully behind her and clamped on the handcuffs. If her wrists hadn't been so small, the cuffs would have cut off her circulation, they were on so tight.

"Let's go," said Thor to Rhino. He turned to the Armorer and said, "J.J. and Danny probably got him, but we can't take chances. If he does show up, don't fuck with him. Empty the clip."

"Believe it," grunted Rhino. "We seen the fucker fight."

"No problem," the Armorer said, drawing himself up straight. "Don't forget I'm the only guy on the Team who's beat him once already."

HARRY LOOKED DOWN the muzzle of the can-shaped silencer in the Armorer's hand, and did as he was told. He pulled the door slowly shut behind him and felt it lock. It took a moment. Only when it was too late, when he was already opening the door, had he realized it had been knocked loose off its hinges.

The Armorer knew in a part of his mind that this man was dangerous, that he should just do what Thor had said and fire all eight .45 slugs into him now.

But pride and hatred drove him. This Johnny had made a fool of him, mocked him. Now he, Walter "the Armorer"

Leonard, needed to rebuild his ego. He needed to bring this guy down a few pegs before he killed him.

He also knew enough not to go near him after what had happened on the street in Spokane. But he had it all figured out.

Taking a two-handed hold and leveling the silenced automatic on Wolfe's belly, he said, "Okay. Real slow. Get undressed. Any guns you got, take 'em out two fingers, real easy. This baby's got eight slugs in it, and nobody's gonna hear it go off outside this room."

Slowly Wolfe slid his jacket off. The Armorer saw the empty holster. "Where's yer gun?"

"I left it with your friends," Wolfe said calmly. It was the truth, sort of.

"J.J. and Danny? Where are they?"

"At the lake," Wolfe answered.

The Armorer's eyes narrowed. "You son of a bitch," he breathed. "You got 'em, didn't ya?"

Wolfe just shrugged.

"I knew it." The Armorer leered. "Punks. Drunks. Danny wasn't no Aryan Warrior. He got lucky. Caught the pig with his back turned. Shot him in the back. Yella fuck."

What the hell, Wolfe thought. "Funny," he said. "They told me somebody emptied a MAC into the same kid's back. Which brave Aryan Warrior would that have been, Walter?"

The Armorer gasped. "You calling me a coward, you ZOG fucker? I'll show you who's a coward! I'm gonna shoot *you* in the front, Johnny Big Shit! Johnny ZOG! I'm gonna shoot you about eight times in the front. Maybe I'll start with your balls. How'd you like that?"

He was trembling with the same nervousness Wolfe had seen at the match. Wolfe knew he'd have to move soon. The .357 was on his ankle, and if he reached for it, he'd get a slug through the top of his head. Throw himself back? No. The Armorer would start hosing the gun, and at least one of the bullets would get him before he could access the ankle rig. It would have to be hands, and he'd have to get the man distracted first. It shouldn't be too hard. He'd already forgotten that Wolfe had stopped undressing when he took the jacket off and started talking.

Wolfe asked, "Where's my woman?"

The Armorer sneered, "She's with Will by now. He likes that brown meat. Figures that's all them beaner gals are much good for, Johnny. He's gonna screw her good like a real white man does, then maybe the rest of us'll take some turns. An' when we get done, she's gonna wind up like you."

"Where's that?" asked Wolfe in the same flat tone of voice. "Your little hideout, where all the racists get together and tell each other they're superior?"

The Armorer laughed. "Shit, I can tell you, can't I? You can't do nothin' about it. You're gonna be dead pretty quick, and I'm gonna be an Aryan Warrior. You know what I'm gonna do after you die, Mr. ZOG?

"After I blow your balls off and your brains out, I'm goin' up to the falls. Pretty place at night, like now. Lotsa noise from the waterfall. Can't hear nobody scream. Nobody bothers ya."

Wolfe said, "The Post Falls, huh?"

"Yeah," said the Armorer exultantly, "an' you won't be there to see what we do to her. Reason is, you son of a whore, it's time for you to die."

Wolfe figured they were about six feet apart, chest to chest. He knew he could close four times that distance in a second and a half. Police trainers called it "reactionary gap."

He had to get the man distracted, buy himself some time. Wolfe remembered that the man seemed to live for guns and shooting. It was the only thing he was good at. If Wolfe could appeal to his ego...

"At least," Wolfe said, "I won't get shot with a cheap piece of shit gun."

"Yeah." The Armorer grinned, his hand tightening on the pistol. "Heckler & Koch, P9S, .45. I did the silencer myself."

"Good gun," Wolfe acknowledged.

"Fuckin' right!"

"Accurate as hell," said Harry.

"Reliable. It don't jam, Mr. ZOG."

"Great trigger."

"Match grade!"

"Quick takedown," said Wolfe.

"That don't mean shi—"

Wolfe moved.

Pivoting off midline as he launched himself forward, he slapped the back of the Armorer's right hand with his own left palm, and at the same time Harry's right hand came palm down on the top of the pistol. There was a *chuff* sound as the gun went off, the silencer muffling the blast, and Wolfe could hear a ringing noise as the bullet went through the wall and hit a pipe or something in the bathroom. The recoiling slide tore at Wolfe's hand, but his hold was strong.

If Wolfe remembered the mechanism of the H&K correctly, then there should be a fieldstripping latch inside the trigger guard of the plastic-framed pistol. His little finger probed and found the little fieldstripping latch. He applied pressure and jerked his hand backward as the Armorer struggled wildly to maintain control of the weapon.

The barrel and slide assembly, with the silencer still attached to the end, came free in Wolfe's hand. He let go of the Armorer's wrist. The man shoved the now-useless frame of the pistol into Wolfe's midsection and, with a look of triumph in his eyes, pulled the trigger three times fast.

Click, click, click.

The expression of victory on Walter Leonard's face turned to horror as he realized the gun had been torn apart in his hands and that Wolfe was raising the heavy chunk of metal high over his head.

Wolfe's hand descended.

The frame of an H&K P9S pistol is largely light plastic, but the barrel and slide are more than a pound of solid steel, and the silencer added another pound. It was heavier than a blackjack, and sharper edged. It struck Walter Leonard across the forehead, ripping open the skin and sending a rush of blood into his eyes, blinding him. The Armorer cried out in agony, trying to pull away, but the blows kept coming.

Wolfe knew how to fight with a short stick. This was the same length but heavier, sharper, deadlier. Wolfe whipped the full force of his body into the figure-eight pattern of blows across the head.

The Armorer raised his hands protectively, and Wolfe hammered down through them, breaking the wrists and cracking one elbow with the clubbed half gun. With a whimpering sound, the Armorer was down, and Wolfe on top of him, still savagely whipping the makeshift club into his skull.

The Armorer couldn't roll his head with the blows anymore. The floor held his head firm against the crushing force of the blows. The sound of the skull caving in was audible.

But Wolfe did not stop. They had Carmelita. He remembered the horror she had gone through before, and thought of the terror she must be going through now, and this man was part of the reason.

The roaring adrenaline made things seem as if everything was shadowed in a fine red haze. He saw the blood spray as his makeshift club came down and crunched into the man's head again and again and again.

Then, it didn't crunch anymore. There was a wet, sucking sound at the last blow.

Wolfe stopped. Gasping for breath, he stood.

The blood-soaked man with the ruined face who sprawled on the floor was not exactly breathing. The chest seemed to be struggling raggedly to fill itself, but there was a rattling in the throat that sounded like J.J. when he was dying. Wolfe looked down at the thing in his hand. It was clotted with blood and hair and bits of skin, and the silencer was bent almost into an L shape. He tossed it to the floor.

Reflexively he reached to his ankle and drew his gun. It felt sticky from the blood on his hand. He leveled it at the man on the floor.

Walter Leonard's chest heaved once more. His eyes were open, and even under the sheen of blood, Wolfe could see that the pupils had rolled up into the head.

He wouldn't need the gun, and he put his revolver back in the ankle holster. He wished he still had his Glock. He wished the dying man's gun hadn't been ruined. He would have use for a good, silenced pistol pretty soon.

First he had to finish up here. He withdrew the long syringe kit from his pocket and opened the velvet-covered metal case. He took the deadly thing out in his hands.

There was no more noise from the husk on the floor.

Wolfe bent down and pressed under the mandibular notch where the jaw met the neck. He felt Walter Leonard's carotid pulse.

It was weak.

Then it fluttered.

Then it stopped.

Time to move. Time to see if there were any more guns here he could use, wash off the blood and throw on some clothes that weren't soaked with gore, pack the still-full syringe away yet again and get to the falls.

Time to finish this nightmare.

THE MOON WAS FULL, and the night air was clear and chilly. Near the falls, it was also wet.

Alone in the back of the van, with Thor and the little gray-haired man up front and Rhino in the second seat back, Carmelita had time and darkness to work with. The van was rolling at medium speed.

Martial arts had made her agile. Slowly she worked the hands that were cuffed behind her down past her buttocks. She lifted her legs and slowly, silently, brought the cuffed hands under her feet and up in front of her body.

She reached to her hair. Ever since she'd learned the handcuff trick, she'd worn a specially modified bobby pin, its end flat and sharp. She did the thing she had to do with the handcuffs. Still with agonizing slowness, to keep the silence.

The bracelet on the right wrist sprang free. Then the left. She was loose.

Carmelita assessed her position. She had no weapons accessible, except the handcuffs. She could try to smash Rhino in the head with them or strangle him, but the man was huge. He had a thick bull neck that she knew from experience would quickly slow down that kind of attack, and the silenced Colt submachine gun was still in his lap.

The puny guy with the grayish white hair probably had a gun. Was this the "Will" these scumbags spoke of in such awe? He looked like a burned-out accountant who wasn't handling middle age well. But behind the wheel was Thor, with the broad shoulders, the man who reeked of anabolic steroids. He seemed to know how to fight, and she knew he'd have enormous strength. He also had at least two pistols, her .45 and his own little automatic. She hadn't seen where her .38 had gone but she guessed that Rhino had it.

Fighting was her business. Therefore, she knew her limitations. This wasn't the time.

Rape was in the air. She could smell it, could see the way the gray man looked at her. He would be first. When it happened, their guard would be down. That would be the time. Not now.

The tension made her head throb beneath where the bullet had torn a chunk out of her skull. It seemed like ages ago. The old fear came back, the terror of helplessness. But she used her remedy. Whenever she remembered the fear, she remembered what she had done to the one who had shot her in the head. All she suffered now were headaches and flashbacks and nightmares. She knew he suffered far worse, and the thought sustained her.

Carmelita felt the handcuffs. They were good ones, Peerless, regulation police cuffs. Quietly she put them back on, pressing as hard as she could on the floating jaw of each bracelet so it wouldn't go in its dog-toothed track, but instead went outside the main bracelet, held only by friction. From here, she would appear to be handcuffed, but she could pop them loose at will.

She slipped her feet up and through the linked hands, and now she appeared to be handcuffed behind her back. She rested, gathering her strength.

Carmelita knew the man with the silenced gun was waiting for Harry.

In the silence, she prayed for her partner. She could feel the weight of the heavy silver crucifix her mother had given her as it rested between her breasts.

She sensed that the van was slowing down.

THERE WERE no other guns in the motel room except the backup revolver Wolfe hadn't been able to reach until it was too late to do any good, and the Armorer's silenced H&K pistol. Wolfe at least pulled on his Second Chance vest. The Team had apparently been too stupid to search his suitcase and remove it. That, Wolfe reflected, might have been the problem all along: stupid people were the most dangerous, because you couldn't predict what they'd do.

The snub-nosed .357 Magnum was in his ankle holster, and there was a flat rubber Speed Strip with six spare rounds of Winchester Silvertip .357 ammo in his hip pocket. That, and the serrated-edge Spyderco folding knife in his right front pocket, were all he had.

He was going in against the entire Team . . . and they had Carmelita.

He could have called for backup, but the dangers were too great. First it would have taken forever to mobilize assistance. Second, and perhaps more important, the white racist groups had a history of going crazy and killing people when they were surrounded by what they called ZOG. Third it would cause aftershocks that could tear Code Zero and Centac and even DEA apart.

Wolfe hoped he had made the right decision to go it alone. That would leave him, given what he knew, up against no more than three surviving members of the Team: Rhino and Thor and the mysterious Will.

He had a gun and a knife and his skills. And one thing more—Wolfe had to remind himself that it was a weapon. The syringe, fully charged and primed with the deadly brown CIA nerve poison, lay in its closed steel container in the left hip pocket of his jeans.

Thank God for the old woman at the motel who had told the "young lovers" that they had to see the Post Falls. He knew where to go, knew the lay of the land. As he approached the dam, Wolfe killed the lights—after the ramming earlier, only the left headlamp still worked—and the engine, letting the car coast silently and ghostlike in neutral. He didn't mind muscling the steering wheel now that the power assist was shut off. It gave him something on which to work the anger off.

THEY DRAGGED CARMELITA out of the van and forced her roughly up the dirt-and-stone path toward where the falls rushed. She could feel the mist in her hair and in her face. It was fresh and cool. She tossed her mane of long black hair and held her head up defiantly.

They stopped near the edge, about a hundred yards down from the waterfall next to the hydroelectric plant. The rush of the waters in the gorge two hundred feet below was still so loud that they had to raise their voices to talk to her.

The little man with the white-gray hair came close to her. "Well, well, well," he said, eyeing her lasciviously. "And what has your boyfriend done with my people?"

"I don't know what you're talking about," Carmelita forced herself to say in a tiny voice.

The man chuckled. "I'm Will Pelham," he said in his smooth voice. "And, really, I'm a little concerned about my boys. Your Johnny, if that's what his name really is, may have done something to them."

"Johnny had to see someone. He didn't say anything about your boys. Ask these guys. They know him. They were with Johnny when he trashed the pimp."

Pelham sneered. "My boys weren't actually with your boyfriend," he admitted. "They were following him. Suddenly they went off the air, and I couldn't contact them on the cellular phone. I hope you understand my concern."

Carmelita tried to blink stupidly. "I don't get it," she said, still talking in the little-girl voice. "Why are you following my guy? Why did you do this tonight?"

"Why," Will Pelham retorted, "were you carrying a gun in your pants?"

"Johnny told me to."

Pelham laughed out loud. "Oh, you're good, you're good. You're smart for a subhuman, actually. I wonder if you could be domesticated. Do you clean house? Do you do windows?"

Carmelita figured she'd play the act out. "I do it for Johnny," she said just loud enough for him to hear.

Will Pelham threw his head back in laughter. "Oh, that's good, Chiquita. Or Consuela. Or whatever your name really is. But somehow I don't believe that. Somehow I think you and he both owe us a very substantial payback."

"What do you mean?"

"Well, well," he answered sarcastically. "What do I mean? Do I mean I want you to cook for me? That's supposed to be one of the things you little beaner bitches are good at. But you only cook beans and rice and other junk that subhumans eat. I never saw a Mexican restaurant that served meat and potatoes, the food for good white men. But you greaser girls *are* good for screwing, aren't you? Yes, yes, you are."

He was rubbing his hand on his crotch now. Carmelita didn't think he realized he was doing it.

"Yes," Will Pelham went on, "that's what you little brown girls are for. That's how your boyfriend can pay us back. How does that sound, Chiquita?"

It took every fiber of her being to keep Carmelita from responding in rage. Bide your time, she told herself. Be compliant. Let them see you naked. Let them be distracted and off guard.

Carmelita Morales made herself say, "I'll do whatever you want if you don't hurt Johnny."

It was as if her voice unleashed him.

Will Pelham began to undress. He pulled off his windbreaker. In his waistband was the stainless Walther .380, and in his side pocket, a tiny .22 pistol of the same brand, the model TPH. Will felt Germans were the model for Aryan manhood, and German guns, like German cars, were desirable. He left the little .22 in the pocket as he unbuckled his pants. He pulled out the .380 in its suede holster with the metal clip that had been hooked on his belt, and said to Thor, "Here, take care of this. We don't want our little Mexican spitfire here to get her hands on a pistol, do we?"

He turned his head to Rhino and snapped, "Rhino, get into the woods and cover us. I don't trust that her boyfriend won't get by Leonard."

Rhino frowned in confusion. "How would he know we was here, Will?"

"Don't argue with me," Pelham screeched. "Get out in the woods and do it! You'll get your chance, don't worry! I've had too many subordinates fail me already."

Rhino bowed his head and shambled off into the darkness, the DEA-issue silenced submachine gun he'd taken from the dead Centac agents cradled in his arms.

Pelham turned to Thor, who was holding his own stainless-steel Walther automatic aimed at Carmelita. "Now, you, Thor. Undress. Then we'll strip her. We'll show her. Uh-huh. We'll show her." Will Pelham clawed at his own clothing to get it off his body.

Thor wasn't surprised. He had always suspected that Will was something of a fag. Well, if he needed to see a well-built white man to get himself turned on for this spic gal, Thor figured he was the guy. He kept the gun on the handcuffed girl as, with his left hand, he peeled his tank top off and threw it to the ground. Will's Walther was in his left side pocket, and the girl's chunky .45 was in the small of his back. It wasn't comfortable anyway.

Thor pulled the .45 out with his left hand and set it on a rock. Still holding the pistol on Carmelita with his right hand, he unbuckled and unzipped, and after kicking his shoes off, dropped the trousers with the other Walther .380 still in the pocket. They fell next to the .45.

Will and Thor now stood nude in the moonlight, Carmelita standing submissively between them in her shapeless gray sweats, her head meekly bowed. Carmelita glanced at the men. Will's penis stood straight out, thin and erect and angry red. Thor's organ was a flaccid mushroom above his steroid-shrunken testicles. The gun was still in his hand.

Will reached down and grasped his penis. "Hold her, Thor," he breathed. "Hold her tight against you and make her naked."

Grinning, Thor moved toward Carmelita. He grabbed her hard by the upper left arm with his left hand. He glanced down at the pistol, now pointed at the ground, as if he was wondering what to do with it.

Carmelita thought, Now.

WOLFE LEFT the car door ajar so its closing wouldn't break the silence. He was wearing Reeboks. Even so, he moved with the stealth he had learned when he studied briefly with the tokagure-ryu ninjas. Wolfe put his weight back on his rear leg as the forward foot, heel first, probed gently before him. When he was sure his weight would be supported without a branch or twig breaking, he committed his movement in that direction. It had been agonizingly slow when he had learned it, but having practiced it for years, it had become amazingly swift for him.

He left the revolver in the ankle holster. There were three of them, and if he encountered one as a lone outrider he'd have to do him silently. Wolfe slipped the Spyderco knife from the side pocket into his right hand, his thumb on the hole at the base of the blade, which would give him leverage to just flick and extend three and a half inches of wicked, serrated Japanese steel.

The power plant was far ahead. On his right was the gorge above the rushing river. His ears strained for sound.

Perhaps seventy yards ahead, he could see human figures. Two of them were white and naked, one was small and gray-clad. One of the white ones closed on the gray one.

He focused in, and too late, he felt his vision tunneling, his awareness focusing in too narrow a cone. He sensed rather than heard a sound behind him.

Instinctively Wolfe began to duck.

That was what saved him from being killed when the butt of Rhino's submachine gun crashed into his head just behind his right ear. Even so, the impact was unbelievable. Before the blackness of unconsciousness closed in on him, Wolfe felt the knife fly out of his hand.

THOR LOCKED his left hand hard on Carmelita's upper left arm as he looked down for a place to set his pistol. Suddenly he felt a surge of motion, and his left arm went taut as he was jerked off balance, and an impact like the blow of a hammer caught his left elbow. He felt the crunch of his arm breaking all the way through his body.

Thor swung the pistol up even as he was falling, and he saw the gray-clad leg flash toward his hand and felt the excruciating pain of the impact as Carmelita's kick broke his right wrist so badly that a bone fragment bit deeply into the ulnar nerve. His hand opened then, and the pistol sailed away into the night from the momentum of the kick.

Carmelita had reached over and clamped his left hand onto her arm with her own right hand, to make sure the leverage stayed, and then she had pivoted in, carrying through with a savage elbow smash. Her elbow was smaller by far than Thor's, but it was flexed, and a flexed elbow was a body weapon. Thor's muscular arm was hyperextended, like the boards the sensei had once held for Carmelita to break. She felt her strong, small elbow go through his big weakened one with the same satisfying crunch she had felt in the dojo when the boards had broken. When his silvery pistol started to swing up toward her, it had been reflex for her left leg to deliver the front snap kick that had sent Thor's gun cartwheeling into the darkness.

Now arms closed on her from behind. Spindly arms not much stronger than her own. The arms of Will Pelham.

"I've got her," she heard him cry. "Thor, I've got her!"

Will's bear hug pinned her upper arms against her, but her lower arms were free. Carmelita groped for a weapon. In the exertion of the struggle, the heavy silver crucifix her mother had given her had popped out from the top of her sweatshirt.

She clutched it in her right hand, the sharp-edged bottom of the Christ figure extending from the bottom of her hand. She looked down and saw in the moonlight that Will's hands were wrapped around each other between her breasts.

She drove the sharp bottom edge of the crucifix hard into Will's hand, twisting it, grinding it like a pharmacist grinding things to powder with his mortar and pestle. The edges of the crucifix tore into the tender flesh and nerve endings between the carpal bones on the back of Will Pelham's right hand. The chain of the crucifix broke free.

She heard him scream in her ear, scream like a woman. His hands jerked back away, and she was free. She spun into him, stabbing and slashing with the crucifix as if it were an ice pick.

The sharp edge of the icon came in a downward slash that caught Will Pelham high on the forehead and gouged down, ripping his face open from the widow's peak of his hairline to his upper lip just to the left of the nose. The skin was elastic. It stretched back, allowing the wound to gape and the blood to pour.

Carmelita followed with a lateral slash. The razor edge of the crucifix cut straight across Will's face, just above the eyebrows, all the way across. Blood poured into his eyes.

He howled like a banshee, staggering back away from the hellcat with the thing that was hurting him.

In the moonlight Carmelita could see that the wounds on his face were cruciform. As the blood flowed, he looked for all the world like a vampire who had just run into a crucifix.

Carmelita coiled to move in and finish him. But before she could launch herself forward, a huge arm with the strength of steel bands locked around her throat from behind and pulled her backward.

WOLFE WAS UNCONSCIOUS for only a couple of seconds, but that was enough for Rhino. When Harry Wolfe came back to his senses, he realized that he was facedown on the ground and something huge and heavy was grinding his left shoulder into the dirt.

Even two hundred feet above the river in the gorge, Wolfe was aware of the mist, the fine spray that came from the incredibly powerful waters that churned below. Someone had his left knee on Wolfe's left shoulder. Harry glanced to the side. From underneath, he saw the distinctive outline of a Colt submachine gun.

He thought, Carmelita!

Wolfe thrust his left arm straight forward along the ground. If he'd been standing, he would have looked like a student raising his hand.

He felt rather than heard the ripping as his own deltoid muscle tore itself apart under the terrible weight. But the thrust that he had learned from a judo sensei pulled his shoulder blade up and out, rolling the knee of the man above him.

Then Wolfe finished the move, slamming his right hand palm down on the ground in a piston movement that threw his body in a roll to his left, and he felt it destabilize the big man on top of him. Suddenly the oppressive weight was gone, and Wolfe kept going with the movement he'd started.

He saw the submachine gun in front of him, held in one strong hand, the fingers of which were now coming loose in surprise as the toppling man went to instinct, the hands opening to catch him as he fell. He wasn't sure how he did it, but Wolfe smashed the gun as hard as he could with his right palm, and suddenly the gun wasn't there anymore, just an empty hand.

Rhino had knelt next to Wolfe's head, his knee on the left shoulder. Wolfe's roll had toppled both of them. As the submachine gun flew away, Rhino went down on his side and Harry was on his own right side, his head practically in Rhino's lap.

He felt Rhino claw for his face, a streetfighter's move, designed to gouge the eyes. Wolfe tried to raise his left hand, and it wouldn't come up. The deltoid muscle was no longer attached and working.

But the right hand still worked. Wolfe's right grabbed Rhino's huge paw, tried to grab the thumb and bend it back. It didn't work. The man was too strong. Rhino instinctively closed his thumb down where it couldn't be bent backward.

Wolfe knew what to do. He closed his whole hand over Rhino's bent right thumb and crushed tight with all his power, pressing the tip of Rhino's thumb into its base joint. He heard the big man make a whimpering sound as the joint separated with a snap, breaking Rhino's thumb at the base joint.

Wolfe swung with his left hand, and a bolt of pain shot through his shoulder as his fist bounced harmlessly off the big man's belly. That was when he truly realized his left arm was gone.

Rhino countered with a clubbing right hand that skidded off Wolfe's temple. Even though the blow wasn't delivered at the right angle, there was so much power behind it that Wolfe saw stars.

He broke, rolled away, scrambled to his feet. He felt his left arm hanging down at his side, useless and burning with pain at the shoulder. Wolfe tried to reach down to his left ankle for the revolver, but Rhino was up and moving now, head down, driving into him like a bulldozer. Harry felt the breath being driven from his body as the impact slammed him backward.

Wolfe had time to think, A charging Rhino, and then he was on the ground, gasping for breath, with a crushing weight on top of him. He brought up his right knee as hard as he could, and it hit something soft, and there was a gagging, retching sound over his head.

THE MUSCULAR ARM around her throat jerked Carmelita backward. She relied instinctively on her training, turning her chin into the bent elbow of the arm, dissipating the power of the fulcrum of bone and muscle that otherwise would have crushed her larynx and broken her neck.

The weight pulled her inexorably backward. Instead of fighting, she went with it, throwing her own weight to the rear. It took Thor by surprise and threw him off balance, made him scramble with his own feet to stay upright.

While he was thinking about that, Carmelita counterattacked. She hooked her right foot behind his right heel and, feeling his leg in the cleft of her buttocks, sat straight down.

If Thor had just gone with it, there would have been only transitory pain. But he tried to resist, tightening the muscles. Now it was like the board again, the board that sensei always held rigid so Carmelita could break it cleanly. Her 135 pounds came down perpendicular on the hyperextended knee joint, and the sound of the cartilage tearing out was like that of canvas ripping.

As Thor fell backward, he let go of Carmelita, and she rolled to the side, springing upright. She saw Thor clutching at his leg. She had seen that before. What instinct made people think that holding something that was already broken would somehow make it heal?

White movement flashed on her right. It was Will, scrambling to his feet, pawing at the bloody cross on his face. She saw him blink and peer through the blood, saw his eyes narrow, saw him twist his lips in a snarl and come at her.

His legs were open. Carmelita threw a powerful front snap kick into his crotch and felt her foot crush his testicles. She saw his hands go between his legs as his mouth turned into an O with a soundless scream, and just to make sure, she pivoted for momentum and hammered a spinning back kick into his chest. She felt the ribs give way with a wet crackle as Will Pelham topped backward like a sack of laundry.

THE KNEE in the crotch didn't stop Rhino.

Wolfe felt the man's crushing weight swarming over him. Wolfe's right knee was still up and flexed. He drove his right heel down hard into the ground, positioning and rolling. Rhino toppled over, and Harry was on top. Harry kept rolling, breaking free.

He scrambled to his feet. He was still woozy from the rifle butt to the head. In his unfocused vision, he could see Rhino, his glasses still on, roll onto his hands and knees and come scuttling toward him.

Wolfe lashed out again with his right foot, a front snap kick that caught Rhino in the eyes. The spectacles shattered, and Rhino uttered a high-pitched wailing sound as the broken glass was driven into his eyes.

But still he came on relentlessly. Wolfe backed up until something stopped him; his spine was against one of the trees that dotted the plateau above the falls only a few feet to his left.

Rhino's right thumb was broken, but the rest of those fingers still worked. They grabbed at Wolfe, caught him by the calf of the left leg, and crushed down with the power of a vise.

Wolfe raised his knee, carefully chambered the kick, and drove his heel into Rhino's face full power. He felt bone break and flesh tear, but the huge man clutched with an iron grip.

Wolfe was precariously upright, his back against the tree, Rhino clutching his lower left leg. Rhino himself was on his belly. A layman would have thought the man facedown was helpless, the guy braced upright, dominant.

Wolfe was trained and he knew better. The prone Rhino had the very earth for his fulcrum, and Harry, standing, was tenuously off balance. Rhino's other hand came up now, clutching at the same left leg.

Harry felt Rhino's hand close over the hardwood grip of the revolver in Harry's ankle holster.

Wolfe piston-kicked straight down again, driving his right heel into Rhino's wrist. Nothing. He did it again. This time there was the audible sound of bone cracking.

But the hands wouldn't let go, and Rhino's big left hand still tugged at the handle of the revolver, determined now. Wolfe reached down with his right hand and grabbed Rhino's left wrist. He was amazed at the size and the hard strength of it.

Inexorably Rhino started to pull the gun from Wolfe's ankle holster, and Harry realized he couldn't stop him.

WILL PELHAM LAY on the ground, cradling his ruined genitals in his hands, blood still flowing freely from the cruciform cuts the woman had made in his face.

And, incredibly, Thorvald Van Houten was getting up again.

Carmelita heard his movement and pivoted to face him. All her training couldn't keep the cold chill of horror from going up her back.

The lips were peeled back from Thor's teeth, exposing the whiteness in the moonlight. The muscles of his face were drawn back so tight that pus oozed from some of his pimples, forced out by the muscle tension and the hyperextended skin.

His right knee and his right wrist and his left elbow were smashed, Carmelita knew. She had felt them break apart.

But the man knew that she was the enemy, and he rose, the muscles flexing wildly, rippling under the taut skin.

Somehow a combination of musculature that splintered broken bone and the wild rage to live and to kill were fueling this broken monster that now loomed up at her. The shrunken testicles had been the final proof, along with the acne on the back and the inflamed acne on the face. Steroids.

Anabolic steroids. All DEA agents were trained in what steroids did. Carmelita was no exception. She had heard of the men on this hormone performing supernatural feats of destruction, taking bullet after bullet and still coming.

DEA training had warned her of the phenomenon of "'roid rage," the steroid user going out of control, becoming a superhuman beast that a dozen bullets couldn't put down.

But she was actually seeing it for the first time.

"Bitch," the naked muscle man wheezed. Shortness of breath was another symptom of anabolic steroid abuse. "Oh, you bitch! You're mine now... mine!"

Carmelita Morales was, in her way, a professional fighter. Being a fighter meant knowing your limitations. Going against this—this *thing*—was like pounding your fists against a statue.

She followed logic. She glanced around to orient herself, saw the lump of fabric where Thor had dropped his pants and his guns and dived in that direction, even as the steroid monster lunged toward her.

WOLFE'S BACK was against the tree, and he felt his legs being pulled out from under him. His foot was still on Rhino's broken right wrist, but the muscles of the huge man's hands had not relaxed. They still clutched Harry's lower left leg, clamping so hard he could feel the circulation being shut off. Rhino's left hand was on the butt of Harry's custom .357 revolver, and even though he leaned his whole weight down behind his right hand, which was locked on Rhino's right wrist, the gun was slowly starting to come out, and Wolfe knew he couldn't stop it.

Harry remembered the syringe.

In rolling Rhino, he had torn apart his left shoulder muscle, the deltoid. He couldn't lift the arm or push it forward or extend it to the side. But the forearm and the hand and fingers still worked.

Wolfe groped with his left hand down to his hip pocket and pulled out the long, flat steel container. He thumbed it open and clawed inside. Harry felt the fully charged syringe come into his hand now.

His right hand clutched desperately on Rhino's left wrist, but it was no use. The gun was almost out of the Ken Null ankle holster. Wolfe figured Null's workmanship had saved him already because Rhino's initial, powerful sideways tug on the gun would have broken it free of any but the best holster.

Squatting down, driving his weight toward Rhino, Wolfe ignored the fiery pain in his shoulder as he swung the left arm up by its own dead weight, like a pendulum, the syringe extended. He pulled his left elbow in against his belly to give the ruined arm leverage and to stabilize the distracting pain.

The cylinder of the revolver was already out of the holster. In a moment the barrel would clear and the trigger would be pulled, and Harry would be killed with his own gun.

Wolfe thought, No!

Harry Wolfe swung the syringe over the grappling hands, touched the point of the needle just under Rhino's left ear, thrust forward and closed his hand as hard as he could to drive the plunger home.

THE HUGE, muscular, naked man drove himself forward toward Carmelita. She dived at the pile of clothing, clawing for the guns she knew had to be there.

Her hand closed on something familiar. It was the butt of the 4516 Smith & Wesson pistol. She jerked it free of the fabric that covered it, running her thumb instinctively forward to break the safety catch into the Fire position.

The red-faced thing was almost upon her.

Carmelita Morales wrapped her left hand over her right hand on the gun, thrust the weapon out at arm's length until both elbows locked and felt her index finger touch the smooth polished surface of the trigger as she reared back away from the thing that was trying to destroy her.

Thor was almost on top of her, only a few feet away. Carmelita remembered her training—"It isn't the first shot that counts, it's the first telling *hit!*"—and in the dimness she lined up the three dots of the gunsights on the center of Thorvald Van Houten's onrushing chest.

Carmelita had heard the DEA and Centac war stories about dopers on 'roid rages. It was like dealing with someone who'd just ingested angel dust. They were superhuman golems. They were unstoppable. They were the Terminator.

But they can still die, Carmelita Morales thought savagely as she pulled the trigger of the Smith & Wesson .45 automatic.

THE BROWN FLUID in the CIA syringe was supposed to kill a sleeping man in one to ten minutes, depending on whether it was injected intravenously or intramuscularly. No one from CIA had injected it directly into the human brain.

Wolfe was the first.

The tip of the needle drove easily through the soft skin under Rhino's ear and into the cranial vault through the opening below the ear canal. The deadly fluid spurted directly into the medulla oblongata.

The effect was instantaneous. Rhino's huge, powerful body went soft as a grape within two seconds, collapsing at Wolfe's feet. The feet drummed a little tattoo on the ground, the central nervous system's final protest at having been traumatized, and then there was no further movement at all.

Wolfe heard and smelled the sphincter muscles letting go, the final relaxation of death, dumping body wastes into Rhino's pants.

But, most important, the deadly crushing hands fell away.

Wolfe's first reflex was to grab the revolver Rhino had been trying to take. The gun came out easily into his hand. It felt good. If only he'd been able to risk the noise, he would have gone in like this to start, with the powerful custom-made weapon in his fist. It was as small as a hideout gun, as powerful as a state trooper's service revolver and as accurate as a target pistol. That's why he'd paid the gunsmith in Georgia all that money to craft it for him.

Wolfe reached down and touched the mandibular notch under Rhino's jaw, probing for a carotid pulse. There was none. He touched the blood-dripping eye of the man at his feet. No reaction.

Rhino was dead.

Carmelita, Wolfe thought, and turned to his right. He saw movement in the moonlight, and then there was the orange flash of a pistol, and an instant later he heard the crack of the shot.

Then Wolfe was on his feet and running, ignoring the explosive agony in his head and the burning pain in his left shoulder.

Oblivious now to any need for ninja silence—quiet tends to be pointless after pistol shots—Wolfe raced toward his partner. Toward the woman he cared about more than anyone in the world.

CARMELITA MORALES pulled the trigger back on the Smith & Wesson model 4516 pistol. The movement actuated a complex arrangement of cams and levers that drew the flat-backed hammer of the pistol back, and then released it to snap forward under the powerful pressure of the mainspring that was held on a vertical rod inside the back of the gun's handle.

The hammer smashed down, driving the firing pin forward in its channel, past the safety lock that had been pulled out of the way by the mechanism as soon as Carmelita had pulled the trigger. The tip of the firing pin struck and crushed the primer cap centered in the base of the cartridge in the firing chamber of the pistol.

Sparks burst through the tiny charge hole in the base of the cartridge case above the primer, igniting the charge of gunpowder. It did not explode. Rather, in a fraction of a microsecond, it burned fiercely, setting up pressures of more than twenty thousand pounds per square inch.

It was that pressure that propelled the bullet free of the cartridge case and down the rifled barrel. There, the rifling stabilized the projectile as the awesome force drove it through the barrel and out the muzzle into the free air, traveling now at Mach I, the speed of sound.

Mindless and soulless, the .45-caliber Remington bullet roared out of the barrel and in less than three feet of travel impacted the chest of Thorvald Van Houten.

Because Thor was charging forward, the bullet ranged down through his body. The pressure of the resistant tissue along the wound track pressed the metal outward from the inside of the bullet's hollow nose cavity, forcing the front part of the bullet to spread outward like the petals of a flowering plant.

The curved rifling inside the gun barrel had imparted a twist to the bullet, and the bullet was spinning as it went through. The edges of the spreading petals were cutting like fan blades by the time they hit the top of Thor's heart and severed the aorta.

The projectile's soft lead core had spread out and peeled back, forcing the tough copper sheath of the bullet jacket away. The jacket, shaped like a copper starfish, stopped high in the back of Thor's heart as the heavy lead core, propelled by sheer momentum, kept going, tunneling a hole through the body more than an inch in diameter, gray fragments falling away in its wake.

Now the lead core smashed into Thorvald Van Houten's spine. It split apart the vertebra it hit, then the sharp-edged lead mushroom crashed into the spinal cord.

The resistance was that of cheese, or fatty meat. The spinal cord separated easily, and everything in Van Houten's body below that point went instantly dead, like shutting off a light switch.

Finally the bullet came to a stop inside the spinal cord's canal, lodging in a fracture it had just created in the dorsal part of the vertebra. It had all happened in less than a microsecond.

Neither Thorvald Van Houten nor Carmelita Morales knew exactly what had happened. Carmelita just saw the flash of bright orange at the muzzle of the gun, and saw Thor collapse straight down at the instant of the shot, like a puppet with the strings cut.

Thor lay at her feet, literally inches away. It had been that close. The semiautomatic mechanism of the Smith & Wesson pistol had already cycled the gun, ejecting the spent shell casing and feeding in a new Remington hollowpoint, the hammer cocked and the trigger still back, ready to go.

Thor made a gasping sound, like a fish. His lower body didn't move. It was dead. He reached out with his fingers, clutching.

There was one last croaking, sucking sound as Thor tried to pull the air into his lungs. But that was pointless now. He no longer had a working heart to use that air to oxygenate his blood.

He gasped again a couple of times, and then the sound stopped. Thor's eyelids closed, then drifted up open, and the pupils beneath them were widening and darkening in death.

Carmelita thought to herself, "Forty-*five!* All *right!*"

Then two other things happened. Behind her she heard a familiar voice saying "Carmelita!" And from the corner of her eye, she sensed movement.

She turned, the cocked .45 automatic still in her hand, to see Will Pelham crawling out of his fetal position and toward the bundle of clothing that lay on the ground in the moonlight.

Carmelita still had the pistol in both hands. She locked her elbows straight out in an isosceles stance, her body coming aggressively forward at the shoulders as she yelled, "Don't move!"

The man on the ground froze. Will Pelham's hand had just started to touch the edge of the crumpled pile of cloth that was his dropped trousers.

From the darkness behind her, a form emerged, a man with one arm hanging down at his side and a shiny, short-barreled revolver in his other hand. There was blood on him.

"Carmelita," he asked. "You okay?"

It was Harry's voice, and Carmelita thought, Thank God.

AGONY AND HORROR consumed Will Pelham. The terrible pain of Carmelita's crucifix tearing across his face seemed nothing now in comparison to the pulsing agony between his legs. He tried to hold his testicles in to keep them from falling off. Carmelita had ruptured both of his testicles when she kicked him.

He felt the sickening hurt of the swelling. His guts were retching, and he almost vomited. A part of him wanted to lie there and die.

But the part that ruled him, the sociopathic brain, was still in charge.

Through the choking fog of that nauseating pain, the mind said, The others are dead. But they were stupid anyway, too stupid to advance me. I'll kill these two—the cop, and the bitch who did this to me—and I'll get away. I'll start over. But first I have to kill them.

They were mooning with each other, looking into each other's eyes. The bitch in particular had taken her eyes off him. Good. She'd be the first to die. She was the one who had done this to him.

In the darkness Will Pelham's hand probed slowly, gently into the clothing. It closed over the black plastic handle of the Walther .22 automatic inside the loose pocket of the discarded trousers.

In just a couple of seconds, he'd make his move.

WOLFE AND MORALES caught the movement. Carmelita snapped, "I said, don't move!" She trained her .45 on Will Pelham's head.

From where he lay, Pelham could see that she was staring at his face over the gunsights. *Good!* That blocked her view of his hand, the hand inside the folds of the trousers, already wrapped around the butt of the .22 pistol. He let his finger slide onto the trigger. Behind her and to the side, the other one—it had to be "Johnny," the Centac narc—was also pointing a small revolver at Will's head.

"Easy," croaked Will. His mind raced. If he was in their position, what would it take to let the man under the gun go free?

"Money," Will blurted hoarsely. "Money. Money for you. Let me go."

He saw the woman relax and sigh. "You don't have enough money, scumbag," she said.

But she saw him as weak now. God damn her, she'd pay! Will was ready to go now with the little Walther pistol that she didn't know he had. In one more second . . .

THE PAIN ENCIRCLED Harry Wolfe's head, inside the skull, and it burned down through his shoulder. His left arm hung useless at his side. The right hand held the snub .357 so tight it began to quiver. Wolfe took a deep breath.

The man on the ground seemed the last one left. He looked naked and beaten and helpless. He was about fifteen feet away on the ground.

The blood pulsed inside Wolfe's brain. He knew what that meant, as much as he wanted to ignore the pain behind his right ear. Rhino's blow had given him a concussion, a massive bruise of the brain, and now his brain was starting to swell. He could lose consciousness at any moment. Wolfe felt dizzier and dizzier.

The sights of the gun at the end of his arm blurred. He forced himself to focus on the front sight, and he did until every groove in the sight was in crystal focus. But the result was that he couldn't focus on the man, the man he knew now to be Will Pelham.

He could sense evil emanating from the nude man on the ground. Something dark and deadly and terrifying. Something more terrible than Rhino, or anything else he had faced tonight, or anything Wolfe had ever faced. Every alarm bell inside his battered body was sounding off. Danger, the gut feelings cried. Evil. Monstrous. Deadly! This thing will kill us.

Wolfe thought for a moment about the changes he had been through, the tortures of the damned that he had suffered, the guilt for killing and the guilt for murder that went beyond just killing. Something told him he could not commit murder again. He could never kill again unless he knew beyond doubt that there was no choice, no alternative, unless he knew beyond doubt that the evil had to die so that the good could live.

Over his gunsights, Wolfe caught a flicker of white movement as Will Pelham moved slightly, subtly.

The blast of the shot split the night.

The bullet took only a microsecond to leave its gun barrel and tear apart the brain of the target.

The unexpected, concussive blast of the pistol made Carmelita Morales jerk violently and reflexively pull the trigger of her own .45 automatic. The bullet struck Will Pelham in the right side of the neck, and because he was lying facedown toward her, the bullet ranged all the way down through the body, exiting his scrotum and taking with it what was left of his testicles. She saw Will's body convulse and then go still.

"Harry," she cried. "Harry!"

She turned to her side, expecting him to be down, but Wolfe was still on his feet, the little revolver extended at arm's length in front of him. A tendril of gun smoke curled upward from its barrel. Carmelita saw that he was focused on the man in front of the gun, Will Pelham, with a terrifying intensity of purpose.

"Harry," she said again. "What—"

She stopped talking as Wolfe moved slowly forward.

"There's a flashlight in my left side pants pocket," Wolfe said, his voice strangely cold and detached. "Get it. Beam him. I can't use my left arm anymore."

Carmelita remembered her DEA range training with the Smith & Wesson semiautomatic pistol. She took an instant to thumb the lever on the slide down and then up, decocking it and putting it back off Safe and ready to fire with a hard, intentional pull of the trigger. Then she reached over with her left hand, found the flashlight in Wolfe's pocket and fumbled with it until the beam was on. She directed the light at Will Pelham.

There was a big, round, black entry hole in the side of his neck where Carmelita's bullet had gone through. There was also a medium-sized hole at the bridge of his nose, between his two gaping wide-pupilled and sightless eyes, where Harry's .357 Magnum Silvertip bullet had entered.

Carmelita moved forward, flashing the light. There was an exit hole in the back of the skull, surrounded with bright gobbets of brain matter. The dark puddle of blood had already collected inside the cavity.

The shot she had heard had been Harry's. He had shot Will Pelham between the eyes. In cold blood.

She played the flashlight down the dead man's arms. His final convulsion when Wolfe's bullet had torn his brain apart had thrown aside the pile of clothing beside him.

Carmelita locked her flashlight on the pistol. It was a little stainless-steel Walther, and it was clutched in the dead hand of Will Pelham.

"My God," Carmelita whispered, barely audible over the rush of the falling water nearby. "He had the gun in his hand, and I never saw it. I never even saw it! Harry, you saved my life."

She turned toward her partner. Wolfe seemed to be looking away into the darkness of the night.

"Harry," she said, "you saved me!"

But Wolfe did not really hear her. He was wondering if she would understand if she knew the truth.

If she knew that Harry had never seen the gun in Will Pelham's hand before he shot him through the head with a .357 Magnum revolver...

EPILOGUE

It had been three in the morning when the dispatcher at Centac headquarters patched the call from Harry and Carmelita to the director's secured line at home. "How's it going?" he asked sleepily.

"It's over, sir," Wolfe said, and there was an edge of pain in his agent's voice that brought the director instantly to total wakefulness.

"You're hurt," he said.

"Yes," Wolfe answered. "Concussion, screwed-up shoulder. Carmelita's okay. We're both all right."

"Where are you?"

"Pay phone," Wolfe replied, gritting his teeth against the pain. The adrenaline and the endorphins had kept the agony at bay when he had been fighting for himself and Carmelita. Now it was hitting him full force.

"Bob Montplaisir's here," Wolfe grated. "He doesn't like coming in late. He keeps saying over and over, 'Oh, shit, I missed it.'"

The director smiled in spite of himself. "Talk to me about cleanup," he said.

"A lot," Wolfe replied. "More than we've ever had before. Sorry about that. My issue gun, and Carmelita's, are still in at DEA Spokane from the Howe shooting. We'll have to get those back later. They gave us each replacement guns that, ah, got dirty. Ichi Komeito used the Glock they gave me to put down a couple of the Team."

"I know," the director interrupted. "The state patrol and the county sheriff's office are not happy about you leaving Komeito at the scene and then disappearing. Our local DEA office is not happy that you took the gun they issued you and then reissued it to a man they had determined not fit to possess firearms."

Wolfe sighed. "Yes, sir. With all due respect, screw them, sir. Ichi saved both our lives with that Glock."

The director chuckled. "I know. I read that between the lines. It's no problem, believe me. I'll take care of it. You said you, ah, got two guns dirty."

"Yes, sir. One of the local agents lent Carmelita a privately owned, Agency-approved .45 Smith & Wesson. We have it with us."

"No sweat," the director said. "I assume you're coming back here? Bring it into my office tomorrow morning. We'll, ah, clean it for you."

"There's a little problem in my motel, sir. I asked Bob Montplaisir to take care of that. He told me, in no uncertain terms, to tell you that he's not a maid and a body remover and he 'doesn't want this shit to go down again.' But he should have the body out of the motel by now, and the bloodstained carpet replaced and the hole in the wall and the screwed-up plumbing fixed."

"I see," the director said bemusedly. "Now I assume with all this, that the mission has been a success?"

"Absolutely, sir," Wolfe said, tiredly. "Six for identified six." The pain was pulsing now, in his arm and shoulder and in his head. "I'm putting my partner on," Wolfe finished. He handed the phone to Carmelita and leaned back exhausted against the hangar wall, looking longingly at the Learjet that was warming up on the runway.

"Sir," Carmelita began, "we had one of our guns taken, my personal .38. We got it back from one of the bodies. You don't think there'll be a problem with anything else?"

The director laughed grimly. "Oh, not at all," he said sarcastically. "I've just got to explain why my head agent ran out on one of our people after an on-duty shooting with two dead, and isn't around out there anymore to discuss it, that's all. Not to mention that the agent on record for killing two assholes out there in Idaho was the one who was crippled by the same assholes a couple of weeks before. At least, thank God, I can step on that report from professional standards that said the guy who killed them was so suicidally nuts they had to take his guns away from him."

"Harry told me about that," Carmelita said. "Harry says they were full of shit."

"I agree," sighed the director, "and I have expressed that sentiment to our people in Idaho and Washington. The matter is taken care of. His guns will be returned tomorrow morning.

Meanwhile, we have back at least one of the weapons taken from the shooting in the forest. Our people in Spokane say that acid testing on the sawed-off shotgun used against Komeito brought up the serial numbers—the gun they tried to kill him and Harry with was one of the lot they took from the Blazer at the shooting scene."

"Uh, sir?" Carmelita hated to be a smart-ass. "Actually we have one more. The submachine gun with the drug lab silencer? We've got that back, too. We took it tonight. It's with us."

"Good." The director smiled. "How bad is Harry?"

"I want him to see a neurosurgeon," Carmelita said. "He took a hell of a blow on the head. I'm not sure the skull's not fractured. And his shoulder's all torn out. But I think he seems okay, alert, anyway."

"Good," the director said softly. "Stay with him and stay in touch. We need to talk in a week or so, when everybody comes down from all this. Your plane ready to go?"

"Ready, sir."

"Try to sleep on the plane. I'll see you in the morning, here."

THE CORONER looked out the window of his office as the chilly Idaho rain pelted his windows. It was at moments like this he wished that the state had a medical examiner system instead of a coroner, so a full-fledged M.D. would be in charge of things. He knew he was over his head. But with such a system in place, he wouldn't be coroner, would he?

What a flurry of violent death. The two at the lake, shot to pieces. Gunshot residue on both their hands, even the amputated one they'd found in the road, showed that they had fired weapons before they died.

The same day, a man had been found out in the woods with his head beaten in. Fingerprints identified him as a rather shifty gun dealer. Perhaps he'd been gunrunning and ran afoul of the wrong people. Well, no problem. That was for the cops to deal with now, not him, thank God.

And the three in the river. Tourists had noted blood splashes in the park above the Post Falls, and Kootenai County investigators had taken blood samples. It was confirmed for all three of the corpses, and a fourth blood type. Perhaps there was one the river had not yet given up.

A dope shooting, probably. Cause of death had been easy for two—gunshot wounds. The third body was the strange one. No water in the lungs of the huge man, but broken glass in his eyes and a broken wrist, and swollen testicles indicating blunt trauma there before death.

No water in the lungs meant he'd been dead before he went over the cliff into the river. But the coroner's contracted pathologists had said there was no discernible artifact in the corpse that would account for death before the plunge. They had insisted on listing death to "cause or causes unknown."

The coroner hated that. It was bad for his image, especially with the medical community yelling every year that they wanted medical examiners instead of coroners. But, he sighed, what was there to do?

Then that blessed call had come, from the Centac Northwest commander, saying an agent would be in for blood samples to take to the Washington lab. They must have flown them there by jet. In two days they had isolated the problem and given him an official report listing cause of death of the big one as an overdose of some arcane, experimental "designer drug."

It was a good thing, too, that they had come up with an answer, because there were no more blood samples left. The man had been cremated by then. The coroner breathed easier now. He'd never heard of Centac before this month, but now he thanked his lucky stars for them and for their new-generation spectrophotometry that had found what his lab could not.

It was good. The coroner hated unexplained deaths, and he knew his constituents felt the same way.

HAROLD HOWE still wouldn't let his mother come in to see him. He was on his back yelling for more painkiller when the news came on over the bedside television set. It told of yesterday's rash of killings, the Queen brothers slain in a running gun battle with drug enforcement agents, and gun dealer Walter Leonard found murdered in the woods, and the unnamed but meticulously described bodies that had washed up below the dam.

Then Harold forgot his pain. He wept silently. He remembered voices behind gauze masks, as if in some distant, long-ago time, and he sensed that somehow it was all his fault.

Harold Howe sank back in his hospital bed, wishing only to die, hoping that when the doctors were done with him his right hand at least would work sufficiently well to allow him to kill himself.

AT FIRST Leon Baldwin had been sure he was going to die. The big knife felt like a pickax through his chest. He would never figure out how that sneaky little honkie bastard had stuck him with his own knife.

His whore had spit in his face. Inside he raged. He would kill her for that!

Then, he had no more time for her. He was the one who was going to die. He tried to pray, but the words were garbled from the blood that gushed into his mouth and from his broken jaw. So he just prayed silently, in his head.

Please, God, lemme live! I never asked you for nothin' since I was a little tiny baby, but please, God, lemme live! I swear, I swear, I'll change if you let me live!

They'd made it to the hospital, and the merciful anesthesia, and the drugs and surgery that helped him breathe afterward. After many days, his chest still hurt—as much from the broken ribs as anything else—and even though his jaws had been wired shut to heal, he could communicate, sort of.

No one had come to see him. Nobody. Not his connection. None of his women. Not even his own mother.

He alternated between hate and self-pity until the little old black man with the white beard and the wise, crinkled eyes came to visit. Charles Washington was a lay preacher whose ministry was the drug rehab clinics, the detoxification centers and the violent trauma wards of Spokane. Leon had seen him with the other patients. They simply called him Padre.

At first Leon had vented his anger and his sorrow for himself. In a weak moment he had told the Padre how he'd silently cried out to God to help him, that he would change if he lived.

"And He answered you, son," the old preacher told him softly. "I talked to the docs. They said you wasn't supposed to live. The blood was all pooled up inside your chest, crushin' down your heart. But you spoke to the Lord and the Lord answered you."

The Padre smiled gently and continued, "I'm not surprised none of your street friends came to see you. The other players took your women, and your women probably took your cars, and can't nobody blame either one. Somebody treated you as shabby as you done them ladies, would *you* come to nurse 'em back to health? Or even help 'em die? An' the other pimps, they knowed you'd prey on them like a vulture on a dyin' animal, and they done unto you like you'd done unto them."

Even as he sobbed in frustration, Leon Baldwin knew it was all true. He remembered beating screaming women with bent coat hangers and holding knife blades to their nipples.

"Ain't a fuckin' thing I can do about it, Padre," he cried. "It's too late. Too late."

"Son," the old man had said, "it's never too late. I've got a book I'm leavin' you here to read, and we'll be talking some more."

When Leon got out of the hospital, it was the Padre who drove him home. Two days later Leon was baptized. A week later he began, on probation, working at a drug rehabilitation center.

It was as if the knife had cleansed him. Leon Baldwin knew now that he would never go back. That he would keep his promise.

WITHIN A YEAR of the deaths of the two agents and the crippling of the third in the national forest, the Drug Enforcement Administration reenacted the incident in a training film titled, *Forest Firefight.* The technical advisor—and, as sole survivor of the incident debriefed on screen, the star—was Special Agent Ichiro Komeito.

The film brought home training points. Two months after it was distributed to all DEA and Centac offices, agents in Machiasport, Maine, went into position for a buy-bust operation. The backup agents would say later, "That film was fresh in our minds. When we took our cover positions, we put one agent at the rear facing out to watch our own backs."

The dope gang scout team that was coming up behind the backup officers came into the sights of the rear guard's gun. When he shouted "DEA! Don't move," the attackers got off only one wild shot before the DEA rear guard's machine gun chopped the three of them into worm food. No agents were hurt or killed, and the other members of the gang surrendered at gunpoint.

THE HANDSOME YOUNG AGENT at the Spokane DEA office felt hurt that he never saw the lovely dark-eyed agent again, and doubly hurt because he never got his gun back. When he complained about the latter problem to the supervisory special agent in charge, the boss looked at the floor and muttered something about it being all taken care of, and he'd just have to wait.

A week later a pistol arrived at headquarters for the young agent. He could have sworn that it didn't have swept-back Novak sights before, and it seemed more accurate than the first time he'd qualified with it, but what the hell. He had no way of knowing that almost every part but the frame—the part with the serial number—had been replaced, and that the old parts had been turned to molten steel in a welding shop in Quantico, and that a bullet or spent casing from that gun would no longer match one that had come out of it before.

WOLFE BASKED IN THE SUN on the top deck of the director's boat as it drifted lazily down the Potomac. Debriefings on the boat had become a budding ritual, at least since the last Code Zero operation he and Carmelita had been on.

On the lounge chair next to Wolfe, the director of Centac looked down sadly at the dark roll of flab that rippled over the top of his swim trunks. He was going to have to go back to working out.

"Harry," the director said, "tell me what's strongest in your head from Operation Barbary Coast."

"It was a dumb name," Harry said lazily. "You should have called it 'Operation Assholes.'"

His boss chuckled. "Hey, they were pirates. 'Barbary Coast' seemed logical."

"Assholes," Wolfe repeated stubbornly. "All they were, was assholes. Stupid assholes."

"How do you think you two did?"

"We two? Carmelita did fine. I screwed up royally. That's how I think we did."

The director chuckled. "Would it make any difference if I told you that you and she consistently do the best Code Zeros of anybody we've got?"

Wolfe shrugged. "Skip," he said, "I don't care what the others do. I care what I do. I got so caught up in the psychological trip for a while there that I started making stupid mistakes. I failed to plan ahead. I could have gotten Carmelita killed. I thought I was running clean without a tail, and I wasn't. I never even thought to check the Queen brothers' truck for radio or cellular phone equipment before it slipped into the lake. I blew it, Skip."

The director snorted. "Like I said, you and she do the best work of any of my Code Zero people. Okay, okay, the last couple, you spoiled me. Operation Blood Penalty, my God, it was textbook. You guys made me as a power in the law-enforcement world with that one. The thing in the desert with the bikers? You did great. No loose ends to tie up, nothing.

"That last one? Hell, you ought to see what the other Code Zeros put me through. It's like trying to clean up after some death squad blows away a whole banana republic. *Easy* cleanup, all things being relative, to tell you the truth."

The director pulled himself upright in his lounge chair. "Harry," he said, "I took to heart what you told me about Ichiro, about how we had no right to throw a man away after he broke his body for us. I thought about him and how he stood up with you even after his arm was blown off. He isn't the only one. We had that gal from DEA last year, got the acid thrown in her face, still blew the guy away when she was going down even while the acid was eating her face away. Hell of a pretty girl, too. Until then."

The director looked out over the water, watching the smooth, swooping movements of the seagulls. He sighed and continued, "You were right when you told me I was an asshole for letting people like that just fall away, after they gave that much of themselves to us. I took that idea of yours upstairs, Harry. Looks like they're going to run with it. Having Ichi do that training film, and right after it came out having some lives saved, well, that didn't hurt the idea, either. Suffice to say, the people upstairs are going to extend some offers to a very small handful of select people like Ichi and that girl from DEA. People who took the worst there was, kept fighting and are ready for more. You were right. They're too valuable to throw away after they got broken."

There was a long pause. "I'm glad," Wolfe said. "Thanks, Skip."

The director said, "How's the shoulder?"

"Hey." Wolfe smiled. "Microsurgery works wonders. I can get the left arm all the way up to shoulder high now. Docs say in a couple of months it's going to be about back to where it was before."

"How about the head?"

"Clean, classic concussion," Wolfe said. "I haven't had a headache for a month."

"I don't mean just the getting hit there."

Wolfe chuckled. "It's cool, Skip. Carmelita helped straighten it out for me. So did Mickey Spillane. It all comes together. I can live with it all."

The director looked out over the water. "Harry," he said, "If you were where I am—if you ran Centac, if you did what I do—how would you run Code Zero?"

"I'd kill it," Wolfe said without hesitation. "What was it the monster said in one of the Frankenstein movies? 'We belong dead.'

"Skip, Code Zero belongs dead. I know why you made it. I know why it had to be. But what good has it done? Has it kept any agents from being murdered? They keep going down in the line of duty, we keep going out and avenging them and what good does it do?

"I'm a lawyer, Skip. I was a lawyer before I became a cop, and I was a cop before I was an agent, and I was an agent before I was Code Zero. Do you know what I've been through, Skip? Do you wonder what the other Code Zero people have been through? We became murderers. Skip, *we've become the thing we've been created to destroy!*"

The next pause was even longer, and finally the director said, "Harry, I want you to know something. If I go down—if they do to me what they did to the last director—I've put it in the contingency plan that you are the one to take command of Code Zero."

"Jesus Christ," Wolfe said softly.

"I knew you'd be thrilled," the director said dryly.

"Yeah, well, now you've got warning. I just told you, Skip, if you give it to me, I'll deactivate it. I'll kill it."

The director sat up and leaned toward Harry. "Oh, man, you don't understand! There's two reasons I put it down for you to take over.

"First one is, just exactly what you just said. You hate it, and you want to kill it. But you know what would have happened without Code Zero. There never would have been the Amytal, we never would have found out the truth and the ones who killed our people would still be out there ready to do it again. Say what you want, that capital punishment doesn't deter killers. I say, it deters them one at a time. Each dead killer stops killing, *then.* You've killed your share of people, Harry, and none of them ever came back to murder again, did they? How much grief did that save, Harry? Have you ever thought about that?"

Wolfe didn't answer. He couldn't. He knew there was no answer.

"And there's the other reason," the Director said. "Remember when Bob Montplaisir came in to back you, and he was so pissed off that there wasn't anybody left to kill? Harry, that isn't the exception for Code Zero, that's the *norm.* You said I created a monster? You were right! Can you picture Bob taking over the operations after I get run over by a truck?

"That's why I picked you to succeed me if anything took me down. This is a deadly weapon, Harry, you know that. It's power, unbelievable power, the power to literally commit murder. When you didn't argue with what I said before, you tacitly admitted that you accept the need for that—the need for something in place to kill malignant cancers before they kill again. But the power to do that can become malignant itself, and sometimes I think you're the only man I've got who actually goes out there and does it, who understands that this is really what it's all about."

Wolfe didn't say anything. There was no answer for that one, either.

The director said, "Why do you think Carmelita didn't make it here for this little boat ride?"

"Because," Harry said, "she's a better person than you or me. I'm here because I don't have any family, and I don't have any better way to spend a Sunday than to have the two of us out on a boat talking about the psychological justification for killing people. You left your wife and your kids to come out here and talk this stuff to me—and I appreciate it, Skip, I really do. But hear where I'm coming from—Carmelita is in Los Angeles with her mother and her sisters, understanding what life among the humans is all about. Dammit, she came close to going through what she went through before, the kidnap and the rest. These assholes did kidnap her! They were going to rape her!"

"God's mercy on the next ones that do," the director chuckled. "They'll need it. You know the one thing she asked me on the phone when she called me afterward? One of two things, actually. She asked me if we'd issue her a .45!"

"Hey," Wolfe said protectively, "it worked for her."

"What do you think about that?" the director asked idly. "Should we shitcan the 9 mm pistols and go to .45s? I can do that, you know, for Centac if not for DEA. I've got the flex in the budget."

"No," said Wolfe. "I've shot guys with .45s, and with 9 mm weapons and with .357 Magnums. It doesn't matter a rat's backside what you shoot them with. What matters is where you hit them. Let them carry whatever they feel confident with, whatever they can show competence with."

"My feelings exactly," the director said.

"You said," Wolfe commented, "that there was something else Carmelita asked you about. Besides the .45."

"Yes," the director said with a smile. "She asked me to take care of you. She said she was going to be in Los Angeles taking care of her sister who was in trouble, and she asked me to take care of you."

Wolfe turned toward the director. "And what's that supposed to mean?"

"I think," the black man said, "that it means she loves you."

There was a long silence.

"She does, you know. I can see it. Anyone who sees the two of you together can see it."

Wolfe didn't answer.

The director said, "When the kind of shit you did out there hits the fan, I'm your advocate. I'm her advocate, too. Let me ask you something, Harry.

"Do *you* love *her?*"

To the director's surprise, Wolfe didn't pause before he answered.

"Yes," Harry said. "Yes. I love her."

"You haven't told her, have you?"

"No," Wolfe said softly. "And I probably won't. And you won't."

"I understand," the director said.

Out on the water, a white sea bird dived down and penetrated the dark blue surface, coming back up with a fish that writhed in its beak. A cycle of life and death. It was what the world was about.

Harry Wolfe understood.

GLOSSARY

AISI—Agent Involved Shooting Investigation.

ASAC—Assistant Special Agent in Charge.

BATF—Federal Bureau of Alcohol, Tobacco and Firearms, the primary repository of gun registration lists.

bulldogging—A method for executing a felony car stop, with police cruiser pulling in front of pursued vehicle and jamming on the brakes.

Centac—Special group within the Drug Enforcement Administration, empowered to investigate major drug offenders and to bring to justice the murderers of DEA agents outside the legal system. The name originated as a contraction of "central tactical" group.

Code Zero—"License to execute," the priority code of Centac.

COPS—Community Oriented Police Services.

Crip—Member of a gang who had originally been initiated by shooting a rival gang member in the kneecap.

DEA—Drug Enforcement Administration.

DT—Defensive Tactics, police terminology for unarmed combat.

Kobans—Streetcorner mini-police stations in Japan.

OPR—DEA's Office of Profession Responsibility.

pirates—Slang for free-lance criminals who interrupt other offenders' drug transactions, stealing both money and dope and often murdering the original participants.

Pogue—Vietnam period term for behind-the-lines glory grabbers who step on the subordinates doing the dangerous work for them. Made part of police vernacular by Nam vets who became police officers.

SAC—Special Agent in Charge.

SWAT team—Special Weapons And Tactics team.

ZOG—Zionist Occupation Movement, coined by anti-Semitic white supremacist movement.

U/C—Pronounced "You-See," the term is used by both police and the underworld for undercover law-enforcement agents.

UPS—United Parcel Service.